DAWN OF A LEGEND

DAWN OF A LEGEND

Christopher Nicole

severn
House

This first world edition published 2010
in Great Britain and in the USA by
SEVERN HOUSE PUBLISHERS LTD of
9–15 High Street, Sutton, Surrey, England, SM1 1DF.
Trade paperback edition published
in Great Britain and the USA 2010 by
SEVERN HOUSE PUBLISHERS LTD

British Library Cataloguing in Publication Data

Nicole, Christopher.
   Dawn of a Legend.
   1. Digby, Jane Elizabeth, 1807–1881 – Fiction.
   2. Ellenborough, Edward Law, Earl of, 1790–1871 – Fiction
   3. Aristocracy (Social class) – England – History – 19th
   century – Fiction. 4. Biographical fiction.
   I. Title
   823.9'14–dc22

ISBN-13: 978-0-7278-6894-7   (cased)
ISBN-13: 978-1-84751-230-7   (trade paper)

All Severn House titles are printed on acid-free paper.

Severn House Publishers support The Forest Stewardship Council [FSC],
the leading international forest certification organisation. All our titles that
are printed on Greenpeace-approved FSC-certified paper carry the FSC logo.

Mixed Sources
Product group from well-managed
forests and other controlled sources
www.fsc.org Cert no. SA-COC-1565
© 1996 Forest Stewardship Council

Typeset by Palimpsest Book Production Ltd.,
Grangemouth, Stirlingshire, Scotland.
Printed and bound in Great Britain by
MPG Books Ltd., Bodmin, Cornwall.

'She walks in beauty, like the night
Of cloudless climes and starry skies;
And all that's best of dark and bright
Meet in her aspect and her eyes:
Thus mellow'd to that tender light
Which heaven to gaudy day denies.'
                                    Lord Byron

JANE DIGBY was the most beautiful woman of her time. She was also the most notorious woman of the nineteenth century, her life a long history of scandal and adventure. But all she ever sought was love.

Contents

Dreams

I do not intend this memoir to be an apology for my life. Ill-informed critics have described this as a history of lust and immorality. I cannot deny that it may appear so to that prudish majority who have never learned how to live. But all I ever sought was a man who would love me as I was prepared to love him, to the ends of the earth and back. This desire, combined with my impetuously romantic nature, has led me down some dark streets and cul-de-sacs – but I never stopped looking, and now that I have achieved my goal I can honestly look back and say I would not change a moment of it.

I fell in love for the first time when I was nine years old. His name was George Gordon Byron, and he was a member of the lesser nobility. I never met Lord Byron, for in that year of 1816 he fled England, never to return alive. But I had seen a portrait of him: he had to be the most handsome man imaginable, with strong features, a splendid little moustache, and luminous eyes. That he was rumoured to have a club foot did not seem relevant; it was not revealed in the portrait, which was of his head and shoulders only. But more than his looks, there was the undeniable attraction that he was reputed to be a very bad man. His name was on everyone's lips that summer, when all England was still basking in the reflected glory of the British and Prussian triumph over Napoleon Bonaparte at Waterloo the previous year, bringing peace to the world after twenty years of unremitting conflict.

But overshadowing his literary fame was his scandalous private life, his disastrous marriage to 'Annabella' Milbanke. She accused him of sodomizing her (the ignorant girl apparently being unaware that he was probably seeking a rear entry, the most entrancing of sexual positions), of homosexuality – well, naturally – and then of having a child by his sister.

This was too much. So off he went, never to return, in fact

to die only eight years later in Greece, at last fighting for a noble
cause. Actually he died of fever rather than with a sword in his
hand, but the intention was there. I have often thought how
splendid it would have been had he managed to survive and stay
alive until I reached those sunlit shores.

It may well be asked what a well-brought-up young lady was doing
enjoying thoughts of men and love at the age of nine, but I had
already, inadvertently, had my first experience of that side of life
which is usually hidden away from the sight of female children for
as long as possible. This no doubt helped set my feet on the path
that has led, I am told, to a life even more scandalous than that of
his lordship. But it has always been a life worth living.

   It was the early summer of 1815, that climactic year of the
great wars. For this very reason, with Bonaparte again on the
march, I was perhaps less overlooked than I should have been by
those responsible for my well-being. I happened to be staying at
the home of my grandfather, Thomas Coke, who had not yet
been elevated to the peerage (indeed for most of his life he refused
any such – to him – irrelevant social advances). For one thing,
he was a Commons man and had no wish to be lost in the Lords.
For another, he had maintained a lifelong opposition to the doings
of King Prinny and all his cronies, which effectively meant the
government. And for a third, how could a man known variously
as the King of East Anglia or the Vice-King of England ever
receive any improvement in his position?

   Holkham was an easy place in which to feel very lonely, when
all around one had other things on their minds. True I had two
brothers, but at this time Edward was only six and Kenelm four,
and although they followed my lead in most things, they were
not stimulating company. And so, neglected, I took myself to the
grounds.

   The Holkham Estate extended over 43,000 acres, a vast place
of copses and pasturage, streams and bridges. It was quite unfenced
at that time, no one in Norfolk having any doubt that it was
private property and that it belonged to the most important man
in the east of England. There were of course gamekeepers and
grooms and gardeners in abundance, but these could be avoided
by anyone in search of solitude. So there I was, on this bright

June day – in contrast to what was happening in France, where it was pouring with rain as the Duke of Wellington tried to marshal his troops – musing happily as I wandered along, about a mile from the house and outbuildings, picking wild flowers and occasionally bursting into song. I was actually forbidden to wander in the grounds unless supervised, because the previous year I had attempted to climb a tall tree, which my childish imagination chose to regard as a mast on my father's ship in the middle of a howling gale. There was no gale, but I missed a handhold and came tumbling down. I was told, probably correctly, that I was very lucky to escape with my life, instead of only a sprained ankle. Thus the restriction on my movements. But below stairs, no less than above stairs, was at this time interested only in what might be happening in Flanders, and it was a simple matter to give Nanny the slip.

My careless reverie was disturbed by a noise I had never heard before. From the amount of creaking and neighing I rapidly realized that it had to be several carts, and horses. It was also accompanied by the chatter of several voices, the barking of several dogs, and the cries of several children. Intrigued, I went through the trees, topped a slight rise, and looked down on what I now know to have been a gypsy caravan. But as I had never seen such a thing before, I merely regarded it as a most interesting accumulation of horses, covered wagons, banging pots and pans, barking dogs, bleating goats, laughing men and women, and shouting children. That none of the humans were sufficiently well dressed ever to gain admittance to the Hall (most of the children were in rags) and that nearly all the men wore beards, I merely found different and exciting. 'Halloo!' I called, running down the hill towards them. 'Halloo!'

All movement stopped, as all heads turned towards me. I may say that if I had never seen anything like them before, they had certainly never seen anything like me. Here I must admit to a sad lack of modesty. Throughout my life – and I am now getting on – I have been acclaimed, even by my many enemies, as the most beautiful woman of our time. Who am I to argue with popular opinion? Nor is it the least unlikely to be true, as my mother was once described by no less a judge than King Prinny as the handsomest woman in his kingdom, and my father was always renowned for his looks. Of course at the age of eight I was a long way from being a woman, but the foundations were already laid and plain for all to see. I already possessed the long red-gold hair, as well as the classically beautiful features and the perfect complexion, that I have retained throughout my life. Above all, I already possessed those eyes – large and deep blue (some describe them as violet) and wide set – which I have been accused of using to bewitch countless legions of men. In my pale-blue dress with its white sash, my white stockings and my black slippers, I was clearly the most entrancing sight any of the gypsies had ever beheld.

I ran into their midst, as they seemed pleased to see me, and they surrounded me, their curiosity revealing itself in the way they fingered my hair and my arms, and even my dress. I was not the least afraid. I have never been subject to physical fear for my person; and besides, how could the granddaughter of Coke of Holkham ever be afraid, of anything? At the same time, I did not wish to embarrass these good people by informing them who I was, and thus they must have supposed I had fallen into their hands from heaven. Certainly, no people could have been kinder. When one of the children, a boy not greatly older than myself, attempted to pull on my dress as if to discover what might lie beneath, he received a box on the ears from one of the men that tumbled him to the ground. I was alarmed by this, for the boy's sake, but the rest of my new hosts seemed merely amused. I was then invited to ride in one of the wagons, and as it was still not yet noon I happily accepted. It was an adventure, and I have never been able to resist an adventure.

Thus I sat between a man and a woman. They were both quite old, poorly dressed like their companions, and to tell the truth they did not smell very nice, but I gathered they were the leaders of the group – their every word was obeyed without question. I asked them where they had come from and where they were going, but I could make very little of their replies, as they spoke a language I had never heard before, interspersed with only the occasional word of English. I have always had a facility with languages, and may now claim to be fluent in nine tongues, so that I have no doubt I would have picked up the gypsies' Romany dialect quickly enough had I been given the opportunity. However, I was perfectly content as we ambled along through the sleepy afternoon, though I know now that I was being very thoughtless, both in the company I had chosen to keep and in not considering what might be happening at the Hall when I did not turn up for dinner. Sadly, such thoughtlessness, as it is considered by many, which is caused entirely by the single-mindedness with which I approach every event, has been my principal characteristic throughout my life.

I was simply enjoying the company, so different to any I had ever known, even if I could not understand what they were saying. Time meant nothing to me until we reached a bubbling stream and the wagons were halted, the horses unharnessed and turned out to graze, and a fire was lit. Clearly my new friends were intending to camp for the night. Now I did consider what might be happening at the Hall, but I did not see what I could do about the immediate situation. We were well past the dinner hour, which at the Hall was usually five in the afternoon, but as it was mid-June dusk was still some hours off. However, I had no idea where I was, or even if I was still on Grandpa's property. I had no doubt at all that it would be a very long walk back to the Hall, and I did not feel it would be a good idea to attempt it in the dark, when I might well lose my way. In any event, I was attracted by the delicious smells arising from the communal cooking pot now suspended over the fire, just as I was excited by the idea of spending a night out of doors and equally fascinated by what was happening about me. I thus determined to remain with the gypsies overnight and take my leave of them in the morning.

Of all the activities that were surrounding me as I climbed down from my seat on the wagon, the most interesting to me were those of the children and young people, who were preparing to bathe in the stream. That they should all do this together and in such a place surprised me. Bathing at the Hall was a very private exercise, supervised only by Nanny, in which nudity was kept to a minimum, and never actually accepted as existing, much less commented upon. But here, before my eyes, and the eyes of everyone else in the encampment, were children of all ages, from the very small to a boy and a girl of at least fourteen, stripping off and plunging into the water with screams of pleasure and excitement – and no one appeared to be the least put out. Intrigued, I did not demur when one of the older girls approached me and spoke to me, standing up to her knees in the water which dripped from her hair. She was also different to me in that she had breasts – something else I had never seen before and was now aware that I lacked – and hair on her body as well. I did not understand what she was saying, but could not resist asking her, 'What are those?'

She stroked herself, pleased at my interest. 'Titties,' she said. 'Them's titties.'

I still could not make head or tail of what she had said, or of anything else she proceeded to say to me, but her meaning was obvious enough: I was being invited to join them in the water. I did not hesitate for a moment, and as I was not very accustomed to taking off my clothes myself she left the water to assist me, screaming with delight when she uncovered my shift and with amusement when she got to my drawers. Having removed these, she held them up to display them to her friends, who were equally amused. They had worn nothing at all beneath their dresses. My shoes were also removed, and my stockings, so that within a few moments I was as naked as everyone else and, experiencing a tremendous feeling of freedom, entered the water beside her.

Naturally I wished to participate in their games, and soon was wrestling and splashing as vigorously as anyone, and being clutched and buffeted by eager hands. But I had not been enjoying myself for very long when we were interrupted by the leader, who I presume was also the father of several of the children and who had been watching us. Now he bellowed a series of instructions, and my friends all shrank away from me. Then he beckoned me to the bank. 'You dress,' he told me. 'Not good. You dress.' I half expected to be punished, even if I had no idea what gypsy punishment might be like. However, I was treated with such respect that I began to wonder if they did not, after all, know who I was. I enjoyed a most splendid meal, eaten with my fingers (another new experience) and washed down with a foaming mug of some drink that made my head spin, and was then put to bed in the lead wagon. The boards on which I lay were hard and the blankets that covered me had clearly not been washed for some considerable time, but as I was both tired and inebriated I very rapidly fell asleep – to awake to the most tremendous rumpus.

I sat up, for a moment unsure of where I was and astonished to discover that it was not my own bed. Then I was alarmed by the curtain at the rear of the wagon being jerked open. It was now that I became truly aware of the shouts and screams coming from all around me, and there were even one or two gunshots. I stared at the boy who was staring at me. His name was Thomas Burrows – one of my grandfather's grooms, a lad of perhaps double my age, who looked after my pony as well as my horse furniture. 'Miss Jane!' he gasped. 'Are you all right?'

Having dressed on leaving the stream, I had slept in my clothes, as did everyone else in the gypsy encampment. I have no doubt that my hair was tangled and my dress crushed, but there was no other evidence of anything having happened to me. 'Of course I'm all right,' I said. 'Why is everyone shouting?'

Thomas was replaced by Mr Carter, the head gamekeeper, who was armed with a shotgun and looked very fierce. 'Miss Jane,' he too asked me, 'are you all right?'

'Of course I'm all right,' I repeated, now beginning to feel somewhat irritated. But this was replaced by concern as I saw all of my new friends being herded into a group, surrounded by the gamekeepers, who were all as armed and fierce-looking as Carter. 'What are you doing with these people?' I demanded.

'They are under arrest. We shall take them into Norwich to be tried by the magistrate. If they are not hanged, they'll be sent to Botany Bay.' 'Australia,' he added, just in case I did not know where Botany Bay was.

'But why? What have they done?'

'Kidnapping is a capital offence, Miss Jane.'

My alarm grew. 'They did not kidnap me.'

'Aye, well,' he said sceptically, 'you'd best talk to his worship.'

A pony cart had been brought, and in this I was placed. Carter himself took the reins. I looked at my friends; there could be no doubt that they were terrified. 'Do not fear,' I told them. 'I will speak with my grandfather, and you will be set free.' They did not appear to have much confidence in my promise, and Carter looked more sceptical yet. 'How did you find me?' I asked.

'I would have found you sooner, but the alarm wasn't given until last evening. Up till then they thought you was somewhere in the house. It weren't until supper time that they began to worry. Well, as soon as I learned that a gypsy caravan had been seen on the outskirts, I knew what must have happened. But tracking in the dark is a difficult business, so it took time. Had no sleep, I didn't. None of the lads had any sleep.'

This was clearly my fault. But I had problems of my own. I now had to face La Madre – our name for Mama, given more in fear than love – and Grandpapa!

The entrance hall at Holkham was designed to overwhelm more sophisticated eyes than mine, being as splendidly adorned – from carpeting to high ceiling dripping crystal chandeliers, via suits of armour and potted plants – as any palace. Here waited Mama and Grandpa. Mama was in tears – and looking quite beautiful, as well as distraught. I may say that my mother could look beautiful in whatever circumstances. She was also, I am sorry to say, no better than any of her contemporaries when it came to snobbery. Thus although she was married to Captain Henry Digby, who had fought bravely at Trafalgar a couple of years before I was born and was soon to become an admiral and be knighted, which meant that she would be entitled to call herself Lady Digby, she preferred throughout her life to be known as Lady Andover, this being the title of her first husband, Charles Nevinson, who had been a member of the aristocracy. Lord Andover had died after only four years of marriage, leaving his widow childless. His death had also left her in a disturbed state of mind. For Mama was given to dreams; and it so happened that on the night before he died, while staying at Holkham, Mama – who, as the eldest daughter, often acted as Grandpa's hostess, since her mother had died a few years before – had dreamed that when her husband went out shooting next day he would be accidentally hit and killed. Few people take dreams of this nature seriously; but the morning was dank and foggy, and my mother was so upset that Lord Andover agreed not to shoot. But when, at noon, the weather cleared, he could resist temptation no longer and went out to join the rest of the party, only to be brought back a few hours later, dead, having been killed by the accidental discharge of a shotgun.

This catastrophe had a deep impact upon Mama, who naturally became somewhat afraid to sleep, in case she dreamed again. Grandpa's domestic arrangements were already in a turmoil, although this had little to do with his daughter's distress. As she had been required to do, my grandmother, who was also named Jane, had given birth to a boy, and thus an heir, at the first time of asking. Unfortunately, so the story goes, just about the moment of delivery a mouse got under her nightcap. This is not at all improbable, as I can say from personal experience that Holkham abounded in such creatures despite an army of cats. However, this unwelcome interruption to her labours sent Grandma into hysterics, and did the future heir no good at all – he was born dead. Following this misfortune, although Grandma duly produced, successfully, three more times, they were all girls. And then she died herself. Thus Grandpa, owing to the laws of male primogeniture, was left with only his nephew as an heir both to the estate and to his immense wealth. What made this situation all the more galling was that his second daughter, my Aunt Anne Margaret (who was a year junior to Mama) had married Thomas Anson, a grandson of the great admiral, who was to become Viscount Anson himself, and was already starting to sprog wildly – in fact she did so, successfully, eleven times in all. But her eldest son would be the Anson heir, not the Coke heir. However, Grandpa had determined that his beautiful, widowed eldest surviving child should have a new husband, and found one in the dashing Captain Henry Digby. Papa had no real claims to aristocracy, although his cousin was a baron, but he numbered quite a few equally dashing characters among his forebears, and some fairly disreputable ones too. A Digby had been one of the conspirators in the Gunpowder Plot of 1605, and as such had suffered the unbelievably horrid fate of being hung, drawn and quartered before the jeering multitude.

By one of those strange quirks that make history so interesting, Papa's ancestor had been prosecuted by Mama's chief ancestor, the then Chief Justice, Edward Coke, who founded the Coke family fortune by the judicious handling of other people's affairs. However, at a distance of two hundred years neither descendant was inclined to be bothered by bygones, and by the time he knelt before Mama and asked for her hand Papa was a relatively wealthy man. This was because, a few years before, when commanding a roving frigate, he had captured a Spanish prize of enormous value – his share of the spoils setting him up for life, although he continued his naval career. Again, fascinatingly, his success was also the result of some metaphysical manoeuvring. Papa was sailing south, in the Atlantic Ocean, when a voice came to him telling him that he should reverse course and sail north. After some consideration, and to the amazement of his crew, he obeyed this mysterious message, and next day came upon his prize. Neither of my parents ever discussed this incident with me, any more than they discussed Lord Andover's death, but I cannot help but feel that these virtually shared experiences, even if one ended in triumph and the other in tragedy, created a bond between them. And after almost exactly a year of marriage, they were blessed with their first child.

That this child was a daughter was a great disappointment to everyone. Even from my earliest memory I was aware of this; and became more aware of it when I understood the excitement, and the attention paid to them, as my brothers appeared. This was because Papa's baron cousin was childless – so were he to die in that unhappy situation, his title and estate would fall to his nearest male descendant, which would be my brother Edward. For this reason, indeed, Papa purchased a property called Forston Manor, close to the town of Dorchester, in Dorset, so as to be equally close to his cousin's estate of Minterne, and thus have his family permanently in a suitable position to succeed.

I do not think I was ever jealous of my brothers, at least not until now, when I for the first time understood how much more they possessed than I did – and I am not referring only to their possible future wealth. However, I remained very precious; my mother had given me her own names, Jane Elizabeth. Now she dropped to her knees to embrace me. 'My dearest darling,' she said, weeping into my hair. 'What did they do to you?'

'They did nothing to me, Mama.'

She pulled her head back to gaze at me, while Grandpa gave a 'Harrumph.'

'Do you suppose . . .' Mama ventured.

'The midwife is on her way here now,' he said.

I had no idea what he was talking about. 'I would not have those nice people punished,' I declared.

'Nice people?' Mama cried. 'They were *gypsies*! They abducted you.'

A word with which I was unfamiliar. 'They were very nice to me,' I insisted.

'But they would not let you come home.'

'I did not wish to come home.' I realized I would have to be careful. 'Then. We were having so much fun. I was going to come home this morning.'

'And do you suppose they would have let you?'

'Of course. They are my friends.'

Mama threw up her hands in despair, and I was removed to the nursery, where my brothers stared at me, wide-eyed. They of course had absolutely no idea what had happened, only that their acknowledged leader in all our games had done something very naughty. And soon enough the midwife arrived, and I had to lie on the bed while she examined me. I shut my eyes very tightly and so had no idea what she was doing, but I do know that I did not like it, and even less when she indulged in some incomprehensible discussions with Mama. 'She is intact, milady.'

'Oh, thank God, thank God,' Mama exclaimed. 'We got to her in time.'

'I doubt that her maidenhead was ever in immediate danger, milady. Not only because she is just a child,' – her knowledge of masculine vice was clearly limited – 'but because they undoubtedly meant to sell her at some stage, and a virgin is worth so much more than something tarnished.'

At this I could keep silent no longer, and so sat up. 'Sell me? They are my friends.'

'Sssh, my darling,' Mama said. 'You have nothing more to be afraid of.'

'I was never afraid of them,' I declared. 'They were nice to me.' Although I knew nothing of the innuendoes that were swirling about my head, my instincts warned me that it would be a mistake to confide that I had bathed naked with the gypsy children. 'Mama!' I caught her hand. 'Please promise me that they will not be punished.'

'It is a matter for your grandfather.'

'But he'll let them go if you ask him, Mama. I know he will.'

I already knew the power of my gaze when my unusually large eyes were damp with beseechment.

'Well,' she said. 'In view of His Grace's great victory, it might be possible to be generous.' Again I had no idea what she was talking about, but when I did find out I was very grateful to Bonaparte for having got himself beaten – an unusual occurrence for him.

The next day, Grandpa began fencing the estate.

Sadly, I never learned what happened to my gypsy friends, and I never saw any of them again. But I am certain they were not hanged, or surely one of the servants would have mentioned it. As to whether they were transported to the land of wombats and kangaroos I cannot say. I hope not, but I like to think that if they were, they managed to become prosperous enough to look back on their English misadventure with nostalgia rather than regret. I never did forget them, if perhaps for all the wrong reasons. For that meeting changed my whole attitude to life, in that it gave me a first indication of the glory of being utterly free of convention or restraint.

My adventure, also for the first time, aroused my interest in the male sex, as when my various cousins came to visit. The oldest of these, William Coke, was a very grand person, not only because he was fourteen years older than I was, and thus already a grown man, but because, being the eldest son of Grandpa's brother, he was the Heir. I was greatly in awe of him, for apart from his handsome looks and splendid chestnut hair, he was about the best horseman I ever saw, at least in England. He was also a man of great courage and spirit, and was famous beyond the family circle for having, while a student at Eton College, swum the River Thames with a live hare in his mouth. For all that, he was a melancholy fellow, because he dreamed of military glory but, being the Heir, was not allowed to join the army.

I was much closer to my Anson cousins, Aunt Anne Margaret's children; certainly to the three brothers who were nearest to me in age. George was the oldest of these, four years my senior; William was two years younger, and Henry was my own age. George was dark and handsome, much as I envisaged Lord Byron, although thankfully without the club foot. He also aspired to the Army, and as he was not heir to anything of importance (he had an older brother) no obstacles were put in his way. I adored him, but I suspect that at this stage in my life he regarded me as a complete nuisance, being especially resentful of my tendency to be what he called bossy and to try to take the lead in all our games. He also resented the fact that I alone out of all the children – and I suspect most of the adults (certainly all the servants), as well – was not afraid of the ghost.

Every great house has a ghost, and Holkham was no exception, although ours was a comparatively recent emanation of the spirit world. It so happened that my grandfather, great man though he had become, was not, when born, the heir to Holkham but merely a nephew of the then Earl of Leicester, who had built the Hall. He had, in fact, been in an identical situation to Cousin William.

In this instance the actual heir had been the Earl's son, Edward Coke. But this ancestor of mine drank and gambled and whored himself to death when only thirty-six, without – to Grandpa's great good fortune – fathering an heir of his own. But Edward Coke had been married at an early age to a lady named Mary. I know very little about her, and absolutely nothing about what took place in their marriage bed – save for the fact that apparently it was very little. Whether Edward managed to upset her on the first night of their wedded life – as can often happen (and who should know better than I?) – or whether she already knew something about him and where his essential manhood might have been the previous night and all the nights before then, and had thus only married him because he was a rich man and she had been commanded to it by her parents, I cannot say. But it appears that she never allowed him to breach her citadel. Edward died some forty years before I was born, and Grandpa inherited – to discover that he had also inherited the embittered widow, who continued to regard Holkham as her house, and had every intention of continuing to live in it for the rest of her life. Grandpa, being a gentleman, was not going to throw her out, but life must have become interesting when he brought home his bride, my beautiful grandmother Jane Dutton. There was never any suggestion that Grandma was going to indulge in any excessive chastity, even with mice rampaging around the marriage bed!

However, Great-Aunt Mary, as she was known, outlived Grandma and only died in 1811. I believe I remember her, a tall cadaverous woman with a waspish tongue, although what one actually remembers of events when one is four years old is of course uncertain. Mary's claim to seniority in the Coke household was, to say the least, spurious. As everyone knows, to be legal a marriage has to be consummated.

Grandpa and Mama and my aunts Anne Margaret and Wilhelmina – always, for some obscure reason, called Eliza – must have been heartily pleased finally to see the back of Great-Aunt Mary. But they were to discover that they had not seen the back of her after all. For only a few months after her funeral, one of the housemaids, unwisely proceeding at night down the long corridor that led to the turret room (Great-Aunt Mary's room, where, she was wont to claim, Grandpa had imprisoned her for the latter half of her life), encountered my deceased great-aunt coming towards her, weeping and wailing. The maid promptly dropped the clean laundry she was carrying and, doing some wailing of her own, ran for her life. Above stairs formed the opinion that she had been at the gin. Below stairs believed every word of what she had to say, and the maids would not venture into that part of the house except in pairs and, when possible, with a footman in tow. Even so, they claimed on more than one occasion to have encountered the spectre. But Great-Aunt Mary never showed herself to any member of the family (no doubt in being this stand-offish she was merely continuing the attitude she had maintained throughout her life), but as soon as I was old enough to be told and understand the story I was determined to waylay the old lady and if possible engage her in conversation. Even though any thought of death and the hereafter was an unthinkable distance in the future, I considered it would be of great interest to discover what the hereafter was actually like.

I never did succeed in meeting her, but I found that long, dark corridor and, even more, the turret room itself to be deliciously spooky – the more so as I realized that everyone else in the house was genuinely afraid of that part of the building. Even Grandpa seldom visited it. Thus I often bullied my two brothers into accompanying me, and when they were tiptoeing tremulously through the gloom would suddenly shout, 'Look!

There she is!' – which invariably caused them to shriek in terror and run as hard as they could for the safety of the nursery, while I followed and locked them in the cupboard for being afraid. I must have been a terrible child!

I hope I will not be accused of disloyalty when I admit that I far preferred Holkham Hall to our Dorset house, even though that was a sizeable mansion. Whenever Papa was at home, we lived there. But when he was away with the fleet, Mama preferred to move back up to her childhood home. By this time Aunt Eliza had taken over the running of Grandpa's household. She was, sadly, the only one of the three sisters without any claims to beauty, but as she was much younger than her siblings, having been born just before Grandmama's death (she was, in fact, closer in age to me than to my mother), she was always happy to yield to Mama's seniority. I enjoyed Forston, our Dorset house. We had a small stable and I had my own pony, and with my weakness for animals – happily shared by Mama – I also had my donkey, Turpin, my monkey, Gibraltar, and several dogs. But riding apart, there was not much else to do. At Holkham, there was always so much going on. Grandpa hunted and shot on a great scale, and during the various seasons the Hall was always filled with exciting, and excited visitors. It was at this Christmas that Grandpa made me a present of my first fowling piece. It was a child's gun, to be sure, but it fired real shot and I well remember the applause when I brought down my first bird. I was also allowed to prac-tise with Grandpa's pistols, and I became a very proficient shot.

But even when there were no guests, Holkham was a delight. My mother gave me paints and pens and paper, and I would spend hours sketching or writing poetry – pure doggerel, but still I was proud of it – while the turret was always there to be explored in the vain hope of an encounter with Great-Aunt Mary. There was also the great library – to which, as I grew older and it was realized that I did not intend to tear out the pages of the books, I was given free access. One of the best known libraries in the entire country, started some two hundred years before my birth and containing several volumes of enormous age and value, it was a wonderworld of ideas and accounts of strange places of which I had never heard, much less supposed I would ever visit.

While a splendid refuge on wet or foggy days – and there were enough of those in East Anglia – the library could of course never compare with the joy of being outdoors. Above all there were the stables, where I now had three ponies. I spent much of every day exercising these, and exercising myself as well, over the jumps in the paddock. The stable lads were my best friends, ever anxious to assist me. I liked them all, but my favourite had to be Tom Burrows, who had found me in the gypsy encampment. At sixteen he was a fine figure of a man, with bulging muscles and a ready smile. He was not very handsome, and when I suggested he grow a moustache – à la Byron – he did his best but simply could not manage it.

His admiration for me was obvious to anyone who looked twice. My future beauty was there for all to see, and in fact it was about now that Mama commissioned my portrait for the first time. It was a family study, my brothers being included, but they are hardly noticeable, even though the artist complained that I would not keep still. In the end he surrendered and painted me in action, as it were, performing a dance while Edward and Kenelm gaped. I still regard this work as one of the few good likenesses of me ever done.

But while all this was going on I was clearly leaving childhood for girlhood, which would very rapidly be overtaken by adolescence. There was also the matter of my education. As a matter of fact I was already very well educated, for a woman. Mama had herself taught me to read and write; Grandpa was always willing to take me on his knee and talk about history and politics; and there was always the library. I found this all fascinating, even if I dearly wished someone would tell me about London, and society, and great ladies. No one did, no doubt considering that there would be a more appropriate time – when I was ready to join society myself. This was something I could hardly wait to do, and I remember that one of my earliest tantrums was when Aunt Eliza, soon after her sixteenth birthday, was taken up to Town to be presented at court – and perhaps, hopefully, attract a husband – and I, being six at the time, was not allowed to accompany her, even as a spectator, although one of my Anson cousins was also being 'brought out'.

But it was obvious to Mama that I had learned all I possibly could from either her or Grandpa, if not perhaps from books. Many mothers in her position would have left it at that, reflecting that a woman's sole duty was to get married and bear children and run a household. But Mama, bless her heart, could see that I possessed an altogether unusual, not to say exceptional brain, and although she had no intention of turning me into a blue-stocking she felt it would be a sad waste not to develop my talents. Sadly, she also felt it was time for me to learn the elements of discipline. In short, she determined that I should have a governess.

Thus, taken entirely unawares, one day in the middle of the morning I was summoned to Mama's boudoir at Holkham, and there met the woman who was going to have a considerable influence on the next few years of my life – and a bane for the rest of hers.

I suppose Mama advertised the post, and interviewed several applicants before making a choice. I had observed none of this, which is not surprising because in an upper-class household such as ours I was not supposed, or required, to visit Mama more than once a day, usually just before bedtime, and we children took our meals in the nursery. So when, on my entry, Mama said, 'Jane, I would like you to meet Miss Steele,' I had no idea what it was all about.

I duly turned to face the lady, and formed the impression that she was younger than Mama, was not unattractive in a dowdy sort of way – although any pretensions to beauty were spoiled by a small and tight mouth – and that she was definitely not of our social class.

'I am pleased to meet you, Jane,' she said.

What cheek! I turned to Mama for an explanation. 'Margaret is to school you,' Mama said. 'Teach you things.' I was horrified. I much preferred to learn things on my own. 'I have had a room made over as a schoolroom,' Mama said. 'Go along now.'

I had been dismissed, into the clutches of this creature! At least she held the door for me – but when we were in the corridor she led the way, while I tried to determine what my attitude should be to this unwonted intrusion into my private world. The school-room was quite close to my bedroom, and had been fitted out with a large blackboard and several desks, and inkwells and quills and pads of blotting paper, and a good number of books. I had in fact watched these items being brought into the house, without in the least understanding that they might have anything to do with me, or being sufficiently interested to find out.

'Well,' said Margaret Steele, 'I think we shall do very well, Jane.'

'My name is Digby,' I said haughtily. 'You may address me as Miss Digby.'

'Your name is Jane, and that is what I will call you.'

I felt like stamping my foot in rage, but decided against it. 'And your name is Margaret. I shall call you Meggy.'

'You will call me Miss Steele.'

'You are a servant. I will call you whatever I choose.'

Miss Steele sat behind the large desk, which I understood was to be hers, and placed her satchel before her, opened it, and took out a leather strap. This instrument was about two feet long, with a handle. The leather was thick. which made it look all the more formidable. She laid this fearsome weapon on the desk in front of her. 'Lady Andover has placed me in charge of you and your upbringing for the foreseeable future, Jane,' she said in measured tones. 'That means I am to be your constant companion as well as your schoolmistress. Do you understand this?'

'Ha!' I commented. 'You'll be wishing to sleep with me, next.'

'My bed and my boxes are now being moved into your room.'

I ran to the door and looked into the corridor in consternation. Sure enough there were footmen carrying both bed and boxes through my door. I turned back to her. 'Mama gave you permission to do that?'

'Lady Andover has given me permission to do what I see fit in order to turn you into a proper young lady – anything. Do you understand that?' I goggled at her, wondering if I was actually in bed and having a nightmare. 'Kindly close the door,' she said. I saw no harm in obeying. 'Now,' she said. 'The first thing you have to accept is that you must be disciplined. That is, you will conform to a set of rules.'

'Who is going to set these rules?' I demanded, as imperiously as I could.

'I will make the rules, and I will enforce them.' I wanted to stick out my tongue at her but, as with stamping my foot, decided against it for the moment. 'The first rule,' Miss Steele continued, 'is that you will obey me in all things, and without hesitation.' I still could not believe my ears. 'So, the first thing I wish you to do, is pick up this ferule, carry it to the cupboard, and place it on the top shelf.' That seemed harmless enough. I picked up the strap and placed it where she wished. 'Now close the cupboard.' I obeyed. 'In future, whenever it is necessary to chastise you I will snap my fingers, and you will go to the cupboard and bring me the ferule.'

'You? Chastise me?' I cried. 'I shall tell Mama if you dare.'

'You are welcome to do so. The second rule is that you will never question any of my instructions, as you have just done.' She snapped her fingers. I stared at her. 'Failure to obey me instantly will result in your punishment being doubled.'

'You horrid hag!' I shouted.

Steele snapped her fingers a second time. All manner of possibilities and impulses flitted through my mind. The most urgent was to pick up a chair and hit her with it. But I realized that as she was much bigger than me, and undoubtedly stronger, I would merely be defeated and humiliated. The second was to make a run for the door. But for her to overtake me in the corridor and drag me back in here, when there might be servants about, would be even more humiliating. While my third option, which was to scream as loudly as I could, would achieve nothing more than a further involvement with the servants – we were too far away from my mother's apartment for her ever to hear me.

This left me with the fourth option, which was to obey her, and this offered a certain advantage – in that it would satisfy my curiosity as to whether she would actually carry out her threat. I therefore went to the cupboard, took out the strap, and laid it on her desk in front of her. 'Very good,' she said. 'I can see that you are a quick learner. Now gather your skirts to your waist and bend over the desk.'

She was actually going to do it! And for the moment I was committed to obeying her, which I did. At least she left my drawers in place, but she delivered six extremely painful blows to my unhappy backside. After the third I was bawling my heart out, but even in these extreme circumstances my brain was working. If triple punishment was six strokes, a single punishment could only be two – and I felt sure I could take two whacks at any time. I therefore embarked upon a deliberate campaign of intransigence and rudeness. I refused to learn. Then I refused to eat. This last brought me into Mama's presence. 'You really are being a very silly little girl, Jane,' she said, as severely as it was possible for so essentially unsevere a nature to be.

'I hate her,' I said. 'Hate her, hate her, hate her.'

'You will be grateful to her in the end,' Mama said, not at all convincingly.

I could tell that she was really upset, however, and the last person in the world I wanted to upset was Mama. I wrote her an apologetic letter, promising to eat my food in future (my voluntary fast had in any event made me ravenous). But it was also clear to me that she would always support Miss Steele, and that if I persisted in my overt opposition I would be, quite literally, on a hiding to nothing. I therefore needed another strategy. Reflections such as these, I may say, indicate that I did have an exceptional brain from a very early age, if only in that I was able to evaluate situations and reach immediate decisions upon what needed to be done. However, I must admit that not all of my logically clear deductions, or all of my instant decisions, have been wisely made. Not that I regret more than a few of them.

But such mistakes lay in the future. I was absolutely right in deducing that my immediate salvation lay in my own hands and that, as it did not seem possible for me to defeat the enemy, my only course was complete surrender. I counted this as dissembling rather than hypocrisy. In any event, it worked like a charm. I practised patience, as I understood that too sudden a volte-face might make her suspicious, and so waited until the next time I transgressed (which happened soon enough) and suffered an encounter with the dreaded strap. That night, after she had returned to our room following supper, which she took with the butler and housekeeper, I waited for her to change into her nightclothes, blow out the candle and get into bed. I then left my own bed, tiptoed across the room, and got in beside her. She was quite surprised. 'Whatever are you doing?' she asked.

'I am so afraid,' I said.

'Afraid of what?'

'Of disappointing you,' I said.

I have always been able to lie convincingly, and Miss Steele was entirely taken in. 'My dear child,' she said, hugging me to her bosom. 'My dear, dear child. It is not the beginning that matters, it is the end.'

I permitted myself to be hugged some more, and then allowed myself a whisper. 'I am so happy, lying here beside you.'

Another hug. 'You are the sweetest child. So beautiful, so full of energy and intelligence I wish you were my own.' I fell asleep in her arms.

Deeds

Was I not a dreadful child? From that night everything changed. I became the favourite, and it was my unhappy brothers, who were also placed in Miss Steele's care as soon as they outgrew their nannies, who suffered the strap. She let me call her Steely, instead of Miss Steele, and endeavoured to give me as much rope as her nature would accept. Which is not to say that there were not difficult times ahead, simply because of that nature. Thus she forbade me to gallop about the estate, as unseemly. As for using my fowling piece or a pistol . . .; that was going too far. Not even Mama, who held that one of a woman's great virtues was a good seat – and was proud of the fact that I was already just about the best horsewoman in the county – and that the ability to shoot was the mark of a lady, would support her in this.

It followed that my moments with Tom, innocent as they were, had to be discontinued; in Steely's world young ladies did not share intimate chats with their grooms, and grooms did nothing more than bow and hold one's bridle. As for the moment when I became a woman, I do not know who was the more distressed – myself, at supposing I had somehow haemorrhaged and was bleeding to death, or Steely at having to come into contact with such an unseemly situation, although of course it was one she had to endure herself every month.

There were, however, compensations. Even Steely could perceive that I had a real gift for sketching and painting, and it was she who suggested to Mama that this talent should be developed – an idea which Mama, with her own ability and interest in the subject, happily accepted. Steely was of course feathering her own nest, or at least that of her family, for the teacher she recommended was her own sister, who was also named Jane. As it turned out, Jane Steele had a great deal of talent and the ability to convey it to others. I thoroughly enjoyed our sessions, and can claim to have put what I learned from her to good use.

As an offshoot of this development, Mama now also employed a piano teacher, a voice teacher, and a dancing master, all intended to make me into the perfect future wife – even though I was not really interested in any man, unless Lord Byron happened to return from Italy, where he was then residing, in and out of the arms of a most fortunate young woman (married, of course), the Countess Teresa Guiccioli.

I was thirteen, and just entered upon a woman's estate, when I had my first glimpse of the outside world. Hitherto I had been confined to Holkham or Forston, and the coach ride between the two places. But in the summer of 1820 Papa, being home from the sea for a longer period than was usual, took us all off to Switzerland to look at the Alps. Like all English families, we had been barred from the Continent virtually since 1793; that we were later than most in hurrying to make up for lost time was simply because of Papa's profession. Steely came along with us, so that we could continue our lessons, but even her presence could not spoil a very enjoyable holiday, which took in France and Italy as well, and I returned home feeling very grown-up. I was now in possession of a weekly allowance of no less than two guineas. Considering that, as Steely informed me, this was equivalent to the annual income of people like the gypsies, I could regard myself as very well off indeed, but sadly I found even this insufficient once I got into the habit of buying things; and more than once I had to ask Papa for an advance. He was usually very generous about this.

But the carefree days of my youth were, in fact, already behind me by the time I celebrated my fourteenth birthday.

England at this time was in a seethe of sedition, in the main caused by the aftermath of twenty years of war, followed by the demobilization of thousands of soldiers for whom there was no employment, and by steadily rising prices, which of course affected the poor far more than the rich. The situation was made even worse by the death of our old Farmer George, which promised another political upheaval.

True, he had been demented since just after my birth, hence the Regency. But now the Prince Regent was King George IV, and this raised the matter of the Queen. Needless to say, as a life-long opponent of the Crown, Grandpa sided entirely with the Queen; and the rest of the family were required to do likewise – when they were in residence at Holkham, at least. I was now old enough to know and appreciate something of what was going on, even if Steely refused to allow the subject to be discussed. I did discover, however, that Queen Caroline was what might be described as a free spirit. There was a time when for a queen to indulge in virtually open adultery would have brought her to the block in very short order. But Caroline's peccadilloes, including such things as all-male supper parties at which, it was said, she sampled each of her guests in turn, had merely resulted in her being required to leave England.

The moment she learned she was queen, she came scurrying back, to cash in, thus plunging the country into a fresh turmoil of opposing points of view. For King Prinny would have none of it. Not only did he decree that she would not be crowned, but he also instituted proceedings for a divorce. His own position was weak because, many years before, he had undergone a marriage ceremony with a widow named Maria Fitzherbert, by whom he had several children. This marriage was entirely illegal, for a royal prince could only marry with his father's consent and this had never been given – quite apart from the fact that the lady, if she can be so-called, was a Roman Catholic, another direction in which any possible heir to the throne was, by law, forbidden to wander. But this was perhaps less important than the fact that he had always declared his love for the fair Maria and his total lack of interest in the fair Caroline, who was fat, ugly, and possessed of the most atrocious habits, of which a total absence of personal hygiene was perhaps the most repugnant to someone like the King.

No matter! The nation rallied to her cause almost with one voice – and the loudest voice of all belonged to my grandfather. How influential was his voice I cannot say, but in the end the outraged lords of England were the victors and the divorce petition was thrown out.

It was the most Pyrrhic of victories, for the Queen. She was barred from the coronation – when she tried to force her way in, there was the most unseemly brawl – and, despite all the evidence of his unpopularity in the country as a whole, the King in no way changed either his habits or his ministers. The fact is, the great British public, however quick to leap to the defence of anyone thought to be wronged, is very quickly bored with any particular subject. Now they had become bored with Queen Caroline's antics. A lampoon was circulated, which read:

Most Gracious Queen, we thee implore to go away and sin no more, but if that effort be too great, to go away at any rate.

Just a few months later she died, some said of a broken heart.

A few years before the conclusion of this unwholesome episode, the royal family had suffered a massive blow when the only offspring of this unhappy union – and the only good thing that came out of it, for Princess Charlotte was by all accounts a lovely, charming and talented young woman – died in childbirth. This event, which affected the entire nation, was to have a most notable effect on my own life, activated by another of my mother's prophetic dreams – of, as usual, a death in the house. However, the death was not of a member of the family but that of Lady Albemarle, a very good friend who was also a neighbour. She too was in childbirth – her eleventh! – when news of the Princess's death was received. She had been Charlotte's friend, and the shock was so great that she followed suit and died in the act of delivery.

These events did not have much immediate impact upon me, as I was only ten years old when they happened; and I was just coming into contact with Steely and having my life disrupted. However, Lady Albemarle's daughter, Lady Anne Keppel, was Grandpa's god-daughter, and a couple of years after her mother's death she moved into Holkham. As this took place during our European tour, it did not really register with me until after we got home, when I discovered that Lady Anne was to share the schoolroom with us Digbys, not to mention the occasional Anson. As Anne was already seventeen, this seemed to indicate that her earlier education had been neglected. As young girls will do towards their immediate elders, I formed a great attachment to my new playmate, seeking to follow her example in everything. I would not describe her as beautiful, but she had the most perfect complexion – we called her the White Lily – and a good, busty figure, and could be lots of fun. In a very brief time, I quite fell in love with her. It was all really very innocent. What she told me about sex was entirely speculation and, as I was to find out, invariably incorrect. While, in the dead of night, we shared each other's bed (I was now regarded as old enough to do without the constant presence of Steely) and hugged, kissed and fondled each other, and occasionally managed to induce the most delicious sensations, neither of us knew enough about each other's body, or even our own, to accomplish more than that.

Whether our relationship might have developed further I cannot say – for while I might have been content, Anne had a great many things on her mind. The reason she had been farmed out, as it were, was because her widowed father had designs on my aunt Charlotte Hunloke, Papa's widowed sister, an austere, stately lady in early middle age, who reputedly had very strong ideas on how a house, and the people in it, should be managed. As since her mother's death Anne had been very much her own mistress, the idea of having a martinet as a stepmother frequently caused her, if I may be indelicate, to spit.

Her second problem was that Grandpa was seeking a husband for her. His choice was William, but Anne showed not the slightest interest in my cousin. I found this inexplicable, not only because I regarded William as the most handsome man in the world – with the exception of George Anson and, of course, Lord Byron – but because the idea of refusing marriage, to anyone, was inexplicable to me. None of us, except perhaps for Aunt Eliza, were then aware that the White Lily had her eye set on the main chance. Over the preceding few years Mama had handed over her duties to her youngest sister, and Eliza – whose 'coming out' in London had achieved no tangible results, despite the sort of dowry Tom Coke's daughter would command – had settled in, as contentedly as was possible, to being the Mistress of Holkham. As this seemed to be the only position of authority she would ever hold in her life, she was not about to forego it, for anyone, without a fight. She thus regarded Anne's appearance, and apparent permanency, with some disfavour; and indeed once asked the White Lily what – or rather, who – was keeping her at the Hall? William Coke, or his uncle? To which Anne replied very shortly, 'Why, Mr Thomas, of course.'

The rest of us assumed she was joking, and even Eliza pretended to be amused. Grandpa was now pushing seventy, and as far as we children were concerned, his only interests were hunting, shooting, fishing, managing his estate, and politics. To us, the very idea that a man so old, and so long a widower, might be the least interested in matters sexual was absurd – even had any of us truly understood what matters sexual might be. How one's ideas do change with the passage of time! We did know that he appeared, at least in public or before his family, as the most morally upright, strait-laced of men. It seems likely, however, that Eliza, who had lived her entire life in close proximity to her father, knew him better than any of us; and despite Anne's offhand reply to her question, she began to push even harder for Anne to marry William. With no result. To be fair, it was not only Anne who was disinclined. William showed not the slightest interest in getting to grips with his glamorous god-cousin, even supposing she would have permitted it.

The climax to this affair was as startling as it was unexpected. Lord Albemarle duly married Aunt Charlotte at a great ceremony in London. I was over the moon. For the first time I was taken up to Town, to gape at the great crowded streets, filled with magnificent but oddly similar houses set close together, and the equally close-packed and noisy people. Along with several other young girls (I was now approaching fifteen), I was required to carry the bride's train. The street was thronged – the ceremony took place at St James's, Piccadilly – and people cheered loudly as, dressed all in white, we descended from our carriage to perform our duty. Some supposed the mob were applauding the bride, who was immediately behind us, but sad to say Aunt Charlotte had long lost her beauty (I am not certain that she ever had any) and I prefer to assume that the applause was directed at me – for Steely had taken the greatest care over my appearance, and in my white gown and sash and gloves, with my yellow-red hair floating out from my headdress and down my back, I felt I could compare with anyone.

The reception that followed was a riotous affair. But I saw less of it than I would have liked, because I had several glasses of champagne and had to be put to bed early, and therefore missed the departure of the bride and groom. When I went down to breakfast next morning, I discovered that the house was as subdued and gloomy as are most houses the day after a big party, not to mention a wedding. Anne was toying with her porridge, as were my brothers, while Grandpa sat at the top of the table, as always, clearly with a hangover. Papa was away, but Mama and Aunt Eliza sat with him. The Ansons had already left for their town house, and we Digbys were due to begin our journey back to Dorset later that morning (this generally occupied at least two days). Eliza and Anne were planning to remain in town for another week, shopping. Thus, when he had finished his meal, Grandpa – who was going back to Norfolk – came round the table to give the boys a pat on the head, and bestow kisses on myself and Anne. 'I shall see you again soon,' he said, and left the room.

His boxes had already been carried down, and in five minutes he would be away. For some reason I looked at Anne, and she looked at me. Her cheeks were crimson. Well, I had noticed that Grandpa's chaste kiss on her cheek had been accompanied by a somewhat unchaste squeeze of the side of her bodice, and I supposed this to be the reason for her embarrassment. So my astonishment, and that of my mother, can be imagined when, without a word, she suddenly leapt to her feet and ran from the room. As she was clearly heading down rather than up, we went to the window to look out – and, just as Grandpa's carriage was about to move off, saw Anne leave the house and run across the pavement, drag the carriage door open, and scramble in beside him. 'Good lord!' Mama remarked. 'Whatever can the girl be doing?'

I have no doubt at all that Mama knew exactly what the girl was doing, or intending to do, or intended to have done. But even she did not suspect the outcome. For whatever Grandpa, that strait-laced old gentleman, and Lady Anne did in the coach on the long ride out to Holkham, he liked it so much that within very short order we were celebrating another marriage and on Boxing Day 1822 the bride was brought to her bed, with far greater success than my first grandmother. Mice were conspicuous by their absence, and Grandpa had the son he had always wanted.

Most of the family attempted to take this disconcerting event in their stride, though there was a great deal of ribaldry concerning the ability of a sixty-eight-year-old man to get it up and the fifty-year gap between bride and groom continued to be a source of gossip for a long time. But however it might be regarded, the marriage of Grandpa to Lady Anne changed all of our lives, for ever. Hitherto we had lived in a most ordered world, where everyone had their place in the pecking order, allotted from birth, and never expected to change. Mama, for instance, had always had pride of place amongst the Holkham ladies, both because she was the surviving first-born and because of her upward-moving first marriage. Now, with drastic suddenness, she had been replaced by a vigorous stepmother who was less than half her age! While I, still only fifteen when the marriage took place, had an eighteen-year-old grandmother!

Mama was always able, as they say, to roll with the punches. But Aunt Eliza lacked the security that can be provided by a husband and children and a separate establishment. Now she had been reduced to the most junior member of the household, for Anne took over the running of Holkham herself, and would brook no argument. In fact, she turned out to be quite as severe a martinet as her own new stepmother. I don't know how genuinely religious she was, but she determined that a public display of piety was a good thing, and so instituted the practice of after-dinner prayers. As, in Grandpa's adoring eyes, she could do no wrong, there was no escaping this ordeal. Evan Mama had to get down on her knees following the meal. She did not find this a great hardship, except perhaps for her dignity, but some of our guests had an unhappy time. These were mostly ladies and gentlemen friends of Grandpapa's, and therefore of an age with him, which meant they had a comparable girth. Getting down was one thing. But getting up again was another thing altogether, and the footmen were kept busy hurrying round the room to re-erect various dowagers and peers of the realm. We children found this vastly amusing.

Poor William suffered most of all, and not on account of the after-dinner prayers. Whether or not he had been interested in Grandpa's god-daughter (and in his happy position he had no doubt not felt it necessary to dissemble), up to Christmas 1822 he was the Heir, with all the promise of untold wealth coming his way in the very near future. Twenty-four hours later he was nothing.

Oddly enough, despite her initial chagrin, the one person who positively benefited from the changed situation at Holkham – apart from Grandpa and Anne – was Aunt Eliza. Finding life at Holkham intolerable, she finally stirred her stumps and actually got married herself, to a gentleman named Spencer Stanhope, who was neither handsome, witty nor wealthy, although this last was not a problem to a Coke heiress. However, the event caused me to wonder whether Aunt Eliza's earlier attempts to find a husband had foundered because she had set her sights too high?

The effect this remarkable event had on me was probably greater than on anyone else, even if their changed positions were more obvious. My position wasn't, visibly, changed at all, except that when I was at Holkham I was left in no doubt that while I was still a child my old playmate was now a great lady. I did not resent this. I have always been in favour of people getting on as fast and as well as they can. But I had to realize that Anne had got on so fast and so well through her determination to take her fate into her own hands, no matter what else she might have had to grasp. I thus determined to follow her lead. At fifteen I was just about full grown, with an unusual height (I could match Grandpa eye to eye), a splendidly mature if still somewhat slender body, utterly magnificent hair which now reached my thighs, features which it was said might have been carved by a god, the best seat in the county (when I rode to hounds, crowds gathered to watch me), as well as the reputation of being the best female shot in the county, and in addition to all this, thanks to Steely, I was just about the best educated young woman in all the land. I already spoke French like a native, High German well, and had no problem with Latin. I had read all the classics, and thanks to Grandpa I was completely *au fait* with politics. On top of all this, my arithmetical talents were prodigious, as was my memory, while Mama had bequeathed, apart from her looks, a talent and taste for sketching and painting, brought to fruition by Jane Steele, and for poetry. Add in my great desire to share my beauty in the most physical of ways, and I think I can fairly ask 'Could any man have wished a better wife?'

I have no doubt that Mama's mind was drifting in the same direction. But I had observed that among the upper classes marriages are too often a business of horse-trading, of the 'I have a pretty little daughter and you have a passable young son. I have twenty thousand a year and you have thirty thousand acres. Would it not be a splendid match?' variety. The question of whether or not the young couple had ever seen each other, much less liked each other, was considered irrelevant. I did not wish anything like that to happen to me. In fact, I now know that Mama would never have forced a marriage on me, but at fifteen I did not know that, and I determined that my best, my only, course was to find a husband as soon as possible, and present the family with a *fait accompli*.

Once I had reached this decision, I would not have been human had my initial thoughts not drifted to cousin George, newly commissioned in the Army and so dashing in his scarlet tunic. But he was my first cousin and, whatever the antics of royalty, I knew that such a liaison would be unacceptable to the family. Worse, George, perhaps for the same reason, showed absolutely no sexual interest in me. As I could think of no one else of my class I had any desire to marry, I became extremely depressed.

Although I was unaware of it, my prolonged mood was not lost on either Mama or Steely; and, again unknown to me, they began to make plans with some urgency. But the penny did not drop until the following summer when, after a thoroughly disagreeable winter, we were again in residence at Holkham and Step-grandma Anne one day remarked, 'So, your Papa is to take a town house for next season. I will be able to come and visit you.'

I was delighted with this news, and approached Mama on the subject. To my surprise, she looked positively embarrassed, an unusual state of affairs with my mother. 'We thought it might be interesting,' was all she would tell me.

Well, I was not so thick that I could not add two and two. Next summer I would be seventeen years old; and would be required to 'come out', with the objective of finding me a husband. In the abstract, I was all in favour of this; it was the form the concrete might take that concerned me. My alarm was increased by the fact that I was now old enough to be included in formal dinner parties, and during the rest of the summer there were quite a few of these – at all of which I was seated next to some gentleman or other who, before the soup dishes were removed, invariably informed me that he was either a bachelor or a widower. I did not like any of them. They all tried very hard to be gracious and complimentary, but without exception they were all so old. Unlike Step-grandma Anne, the idea of sharing a bed with a man old enough to be my father or grandfather did not attract me in the least – and their bad habits were inexhaustible. They all either openly smoked or stank of stale tobacco; they all either drank too much or stank of stale alcohol; none of them could shoot straight and very few of them had any idea how to manage a horse, much less have a good seat. But worst of all was that they sweated profusely and unpleasantly, and that they liked to touch. I am well aware that all human beings, male and female, need to sweat – although, of course, we females, if ladies, only perspire – but being aware of this fact, it is necessary to change at least one's linen as often as possible, something of which these gentlemen appeared unaware. As for touching, well, I have never been averse to being touched, but it has to be done by the right man in the right place at the right time, and *always* with clean hands. Having my hand clutched by buttery fingers, or gravy stains deposited on my skirt, filled me with distaste.

I complained to Mama, but she merely remarked that 'Men will be men. What would we do without them?' I later learned that dear Papa was against these proceedings, on the grounds that I was too young; nor, having now retired, did he take kindly to the idea of wasting a summer in London, when he could have been spending his time much more usefully, and enjoyably, in the country – quite apart from the expense of the whole exercise. But Papa, however bold and famous as a naval warrior, was always the junior partner when on land. Obviously this had something to do with Mama's superior birth and antecedents, and the wealth and power of her family, but I also like to feel it was because he was genuinely in love with her throughout their joint lives.

I therefore spent that summer thoroughly out of sorts, compounded by the looming disaster I considered about to overtake me. And to make matters worse, I was back to first principles with Steely, who seemed to feel that my ill humour was a reflection upon her, and that my sometimes snapped and often negative responses to her strictures were insubordinate. Apart from being both taller and stronger than Miss Steele, I was now far too old to suffer the strap, but she still indulged in the most petty points of discipline.

However, I was not the only member of the family capable of making a mistake. Mama's birth and upbringing, no less than her innate snobbery, did not allow her to conceive of a situation where a lady could possibly look more than a single step beneath her. As my only real pleasure was riding, I spent as much time in the saddle as possible, while also hopefully seeking congenial company. It was therefore natural for me to choose Tom Burrows as my usual companion. In the eight years since my gypsy adventure I had seen him nearly every day when I was at Holkham; and as is often the case when one is in constant contact with someone, such things as growth and development, that happen gradually over a period of time, may go unnoticed, certainly with regards to an inferior. I had also, over the past four or five years, not taken even much notice of him, because I had had so many other things to occupy my mind.

Now, as we galloped together over the meadows and between the trees, I realized what a strong and handsome young man he had become. Eight years older than me, he was already legally a man, and looked it, too – tall and broad-shouldered, and sporting a luxuriant moustache, in strong contrast to his earlier efforts. When on one of our rides together I congratulated him on it, he blushed, and replied 'It is yours, Miss Jane.'

'Mine?' I was so surprised that I drew in the reins.

'You commanded me to grow one, oh, five years ago.'

I had entirely forgotten! 'Then I am most flattered,' I said. I was still too innocent, and, like my mother, too aware of the differences in our stations, to regard the exchange as anything more than a pleasantry. But over the next few weeks, as we rode and talked, I discovered that he could read and write; and although his reading had consisted mainly of the Bible, he had concentrated on the Old Testament, which is considerably more meaty than the New. So there came the day when I mused aloud as we walked our horses, 'There are so many things I wish I knew, or could understand.'

'You, Miss Jane? The servants say you know everything.'

'I know a great deal of idle rubbish, you mean. Nothing of importance – *amo, amas, amat . . .*'

'Miss Jane?'

'That is Latin. Do you not speak Latin?'

'Well, no, ma'am. There is no call for it in the stables.'

'Do you know what the words mean?'

'No, ma'am.'

'I love, you love, he loves . . . Have you ever loved, Tom?' He did not reply, but urged his horse into a canter. I kicked Wonder and rapidly caught him up. 'You are supposed to ride beside me, not in front of me,' I pointed out. 'Why is your face so red? You are not about to have a seizure, I hope?'

'Would you care if I did, ma'am?' I looked at him with my mouth open, quite unused to being addressed like that by a servant. 'I apologize, ma'am. You asked me a question which I dared not answer.'

His eyes roamed over me, and the penny dropped with a resounding clang. 'Tom!' I said. 'Oh, you dear, dear boy!' – and without thinking I leaned across and squeezed his hand. I am not sure what happened next. I know I found myself standing on the ground and in his arms, but whether I actually dismounted or was dragged from the saddle I cannot be certain. He was kissing me so savagely that I tasted blood and my hat fell off; and his hands were roaming over my habit, sliding down my back to squeeze my buttocks and pulling up my skirts to do so, before coming back up to caress my breasts. No man had ever touched me there before; and no woman either, save for Anne during our illicit cuddles – and this was a far superior sensation.

Now the sensation threatened to overwhelm my mind, and before I could control myself my hands were similarly busy, roaming over and inside his shirt (it was a warm September day and he wore no jacket) and then sliding down to his breeches to feel his crotch, and feel too what was rising within the cloth, so that I began to fumble at his belt. He paused in his own minis-trations to assist me, and then laid me on the ground – with a bit of a thump to be sure – so that I found myself looking up at Wonder, who was giving me a very critical look. While I was thus temporarily winded I felt a coolness on my legs, and under-stood that he was lifting my skirts. This was something else no one had ever done to me, and I wondered if I should stop him – for, whereas his touch on my breast had had to penetrate three layers of cloth, this was a matter of thin stockings and then bare flesh.

I felt this was going a bit far, and attempted to sit up, but he gently pushed me flat again, while releasing the ties of my drawers. So I lay still and allowed him to remove the cumbersome garment, while gazing at his manhood, his pants and drawers having descended past his knees. 'Oh, Jane,' he said. 'Oh, Jane. Can I?'

'Can you what?' I asked.

My ignorance did not immediately register. 'I want to have you,' he said, beginning to breathe very heavily.

'You have me,' I said. 'At least for this afternoon.'

'You mean I can?'

Kneeling between my legs he was very close to accomplishing his object, even if I did not yet suspect what it was. But I was curious to discover what he had in mind. He came down on me, and I felt him touch my flesh, and wanted to scream with anticipated joy, only to have him roll away from me with some violence, and lie himself on his back, staring at the sky. I rose on my elbow and turned to him. 'What is troubling you?'

'It would be wrong, so wrong.' He turned his head to look at me. 'We would be fornicators.'

He clearly remembered a good deal of the Old Testament. Fornication was a word I also remembered, without ever having understood what it meant. 'By playing with each other?'

'No, no. If I put him into you.' He sat up. 'Don't you know how babies are made?'

I sat up also. 'Babies are made when a man and a woman get married.'

'That is how it should be. But babies are made when a man puts his prick into a woman, whether they are married or not.'

I stared at him in utter consternation. 'But . . .' I looked down at myself. With my skirts around my waist I was totally exposed, virtually between knee and navel. The idea that such a vision could also be put to a practical use was overwhelming.

'All babies,' he insisted. 'Even you.' My imagination simply could not cope with the concept of Papa pushing his 'prick' into Mama. Or Grandpapa and Anne indulging in such a fantasy.

Anne, possibly, even probably – but Grandpa? 'When it happens in marriage,' Tom went on, 'it is called intercourse and the child is legitimate. When it happens outside marriage, it is called fornication, and it is a sin and a crime, and the baby is called a bastard.' So many words, which I had heard from time to time, without having any idea what they meant. 'That is why a woman must be a virgin on her wedding night,' he explained. 'To prove that she has not sinned before marriage.'

However simplistic that explanation was, at that moment it seemed very logical to me. But the fact that he was explaining it to me, instead of just taking advantage of the situation, when he must have known I would not resist him, was even more important. Here was a real man, as opposed to the fops I had been seated next to at dinner parties, and a real gentleman, too, whatever his lack of breeding. But the moment had passed. His prick (I really had to find out exactly what that meant) was going to be pushed nowhere in its present dwindling state, except back into his pants – unless I again took the lead. 'Then we should get married,' I said.

Looking back, I am astounded at my total inability to consider anything more than the present, my determination to let the future take care of itself. Sadly, I have never lost this weakness, even with all the experience I have gathered over the years. I knew that there would be the most tremendous to-do; but I was in the mood to throw the family into a tizzy, and I did not see what they could do about it if I presented them with a *fait accompli*.

Although clearly delighted at my suggestion, Tom was far more practical. 'Marry? You and me? You are a lady, and I am . . .'

'A gentleman. You have proved that by the way you have conducted yourself.'

'I would not harm you for all the world, Miss Jane.'

This form of address was a retrograde step, from my future husband. 'I never supposed that you would. As for being recognized as a gentleman, I shall see to that.'

'I have no money.'

'You shall have money. Old Carter is soon to retire, you will be head groom.'

'But there are several of the lads senior to me.'

'Unlike them, you will be married to me. I will see to it.' I leaned towards him, and we spent several minutes kissing and cuddling. I was able to indulge myself to my heart's content, and was amazed and delighted by the constantly changing character of my new plaything, even if I was alarmed when it suddenly seemed to explode, leaving my hands covered in a slippery white liquid. 'I have hurt you,' I cried, fearing that the discharge was some kind of vital fluid. Well of course it was, though its loss was not vital to him.

'No, no,' he assured me, indulging in some very heavy breathing. 'You have made me the happiest man in the world.' But it was off again, retreating into its comatose condition. I may say that while I was indulging myself, he was also at work, stroking my bottom and my thighs, opening my blouse to play with my now growing breasts, and bringing me to a state close to explosion, while having only the faintest memory (the circumstances were so different to those with Anne) of how it would feel. However, I knew it was there, and was thus the more disappointed when again he suddenly fell away from me. 'Your mother would never permit it.'

'Then we shan't tell her, until it is done.'

'That is not possible. We cannot get married without posting the banns. We cannot post the banns without going to the parson. And he would never agree to it without referring to your mother.'

I considered, and remembered, other snatches of conversation I had overheard from my elders and my gentlemen dinner companions. 'Then we must go somewhere I am not known.'

'There are still the banns. We would have to be residents, wherever we went, for at least three weeks. And if we left Holkham, your mother and the squire would have the whole country out looking for us. As they did when you were kidnapped by the gypsies.'

'I was not kidnapped by the gypsies,' I reminded him. 'I went with them because I liked them. And there is no problem which cannot be solved.' Ah, the confidence of youth! 'Have you ever heard of a place called Gretna Green?'

'Is it in Suffolk?'

'It is in Scotland.'

'Scotland!' I might have mentioned the far side of the moon.

'A place where weddings are performed, on the instant, without banns or questions.'

'Scotland,' he muttered. 'That is a long way away. They will still send after us.'

'No doubt they will. But they can travel no faster than we can, and we will have a head start. But let us get to Gretna, and we will be married, and there will be nothing they can do about it.' It will be noted that I was neglecting a great deal of perhaps tiresome detail in my exposition, but it was looming in my mind as a tremendously exciting adventure and I was prepared to let the details fall into place as they cropped up. Now was the time for plans, and here I was quite prepared for practicalities. 'I reckon it will take us about four days to reach Gretna,' I said. 'Have you any money?'

'I have seventeen shillings worth of savings.'

That didn't sound very much. 'I have five sovereigns,' I said. 'That should be enough to get us there.'

'And back?'

'Well . . . we shall obtain employment, for a day or two, before returning. You can chop wood, and I . . . I will be a waitress. Oh, what fun it is going to be.'

My idea was that we should go for our morning ride perhaps an hour earlier than usual. No one would really know or care that I had not returned until dinner time; and thus if, instead of aimlessly cantering about the estate, we left the grounds and headed north-west we should have a start of several hours and perhaps thirty miles on any pursuers, while I also felt confident that those would in the first instance confine themselves to scouring the estate – a matter of another several hours – before realizing that I had left its confines, which should give us another thirty-odd miles. With such a start, we could not possibly be caught.

Of course various emotional difficulties appeared almost immediately. The first was when I joined the family for dinner that afternoon. Everyone was in the best of humours, even if tinged with regret, for we were to leave for Dorset in two days' time. Papa was already there. I did not care to consider what his reaction would be when he discovered that I was married, and had a slight twinge of apprehension. Not having spent enough time in my father's company, I was more than a little afraid of him. But that went for all of them, in my projected circumstances. As I looked around the table, I became quite disturbed. 'Are you all right, Jane?' Mama asked.

'Just a little tired, Mama.' But her loving solicitude added to the knowledge that I was deceiving her, and brought back the tears. Not that my awareness of guilt deflected me from my purpose. I had no doubt at all that I could make it up to her, just as I was sure she would grow to love Tom. One of my happiest traits has been an incurable optimism.

There were also more practical matters to be considered. I was leaving home, whether Holkham or Forston, for at least a week, probably longer. Therefore I would need some changes of linen. I had never had to pack for myself before – this always having been done either by my nannies or, more recently, by Steely – and so contented myself with a couple of pairs of drawers and stockings, and a reserve shift. In fact packing even these few items in a reticule without allowing Steely to suspect anything was one of the most difficult parts of the exercise.

I was also miserable at leaving my pets – most particularly Gibraltar, who, unlike my ponies, who were permanently based either at Holkham or in Dorset, had always accompanied me to and fro in my biannual perambulations. But, as I stroked him and kissed him before leaving the house in the morning, I reflected that I would be back in a little while, and I knew that he would be well looked after in my absence.

Leaving Holkham for the first time under what might now be called my own steam (this was some ten years before the appearance of the famous *Rocket*) was another exciting experience, but soon we were urging our mounts towards the high road running from London to Chester – the old Roman Watling Street. We felt sure that somewhere along this route we would pick up the road for the border and Gretna. Which in fact we did. However, by sticking to main and therefore easier thoroughfares we undoubtedly left a very visible trail. At the hostelries where we spent the various nights on our journey, eyebrows were inevitably raised. We of course travelled as man and wife. I wore a reversed gold signet ring on my wedding finger, and kept my gloves on whenever possible so that it could not be closely inspected. But there can be no doubt that I was recognized as somewhat young for such a role – just as my beauty and clearly expensive clothes, in some contrast to those of my 'husband', must have been a source of speculation once we had gone to bed and no doubt caused us to be remembered after we had left. Equally, our inquiries as to the quickest way to Gretna must have aroused some interest, as that destination would hardly have been of importance to us had we actually been married.

On the other hand, no one attempted to interfere with our journey; and as we had no knowledge of what might be happening behind us, we were perfectly happy. Even deliriously so – at least up to a point. Despite my efforts to progress – as I felt further procrastination was pointless when we were within a couple of days of truly being man and wife – Tom refused to consummate our relationship in advance of the ceremony. For this I now know I should have been profoundly grateful, but at the time I found it frustrating. At the same time, I found great pleasure in hugging and kissing, in fondling and being fondled, and even in 'wanking' him – a term I had never heard before, and did not really care for but which I felt I must get used to if I was going to spend the rest of my life at his side. It may be supposed that this elementary but essential lesson in pleasing the male sex should have been invaluable to me – and indeed it was, in later years. In the short term, however, it tended to be catastrophic, owing to the vast difference in class, and thus in expectation, of the man who was soon to take Tom's place.

And so we finally crossed the border and rode into the little village, exhausted but triumphant; and upon inquiring and revealing our purpose, were told that the man we wanted was Mr Mackenzie, the blacksmith. To the smithy we therefore repaired, to encounter a heavy beetle-browed man with red hair – who, disappointingly, was not wearing the kilt. 'Aye, well,' this worthy remarked, 'it will be a pleasure.' He studied me. 'Ye're a lucky man, Mr Burrows, if I say so meself. Come along to the hoose.'

This, a small but comfortable cottage, was situated close to the smithy, and possessed a stable where we unsaddled our horses and made them comfortable; both Wonder and Tom's stallion were exhausted by their four days' hard riding. Then we were escorted into the house and greeted by a no less formidable looking woman, who turned out to be Mrs Mackenzie. 'Ye'll take tea?' she inquired.

It was now about four in the afternoon, and we had eaten sparingly over the past four days in order to conserve our limited funds. 'That would be very nice, thank you,' I said. 'But when are we to be married?'

'Hoots, child, that canna be before the morrow.'

'Tomorrow?' I had assumed that once we set foot in the village we were home and dry.

'Tomorrow,' she said, firmly. ''Tis the law. Now come along, and I'll show ye to your rooms.' We followed her up the stairs. 'Ye've nae luggage,' she said over her shoulder. It was neither a question nor a comment, merely an ascertaining of the facts.

'In our satchels,' I said, as Tom was clearly intending to leave all the talking to me.

'Aye, well, 'tis best to travel light. Ye'll be in here, Miss . . .?'

I had been going to call myself Smith, but that had been before I had realized that we were going to be placing ourselves in the hands of a real smith, while Jones was out of the question because I could not assume a Welsh accent. So I opted for Brown. The room itself was small and neat and clean, like everything else in the house, but it contained only a small, single bed. 'Where does Mr Burrows sleep?' I asked.

'Along the corridor,' she said. 'We've two rooms. Ye canna sleep together until ye're wed.' She frowned at me. 'Ye're chaste?'

Having no idea what she meant, I looked at Tom. 'Oh, yes,' he said. 'She is pure.'

'Aye,' Mrs Mackenzie said. 'I'll have nae sluts in ma hoose.' I didn't know what to make of that, either; and so, while she removed Tom, I took off my bonnet and sat on the bed, for the first time really feeling nervous about the whole thing. When my door opened again, I jumped. 'Ye're a bonny lass,' Mrs Mackenzie remarked, entering.

'Thank you.'

'And ye've a fine-looking man there. Known each other long, have ye?'

'All of our lives,' I said, with perfect truthfulness.

'Aye, 'tis the best. I'm nae here to pry, ye understand, but . . . ye're certain this is what ye wish?'

I bridled. 'Why should it not be?'

'There's the difference in station.' She touched the sleeve of my habit. 'Expensive. Anyone can see ye're a lady.'

'Well, of course I am. And Tom . . .'

'Is nae gentleman.' She held up her finger as I would have spoken. 'Hear me oot. 'Tis nae ma business to interfere. But 'tis ma duty to make one thing clear to ye. Once ye're wed, ye're wed. Remember the Good Book: whom God has put together, let nae man put asunder. Being married is for life. What I am saying is, now is your very last chance to reflect and be sure. Once ye stand before ma husband tomorrow morning, ye'll nae be able to change your mind. So, if ye've the least doot . . .'

Well, after a speech like that, how could I avoid having doubts? But I was certainly not going to let her know that. 'I have no doubts, thank you.'

'Aye, well, ye know your own mind, nae doot. That'll be ten shillings.'

'Ten shillings?'

''Tis five shillings each, for the rooms. I'm nae running a lodging house. 'Tis ma own home ye're sleeping in. I asked your man for the money, but he said ye'd pay it.' Simply because we had already spent all of his money, and had not thought to share mine. I was annoyed, because that oversight had undoubtedly raised Mrs Mackenzie's suspicions and brought on the homily. But I opened my purse and gave her the money. She put it in her pocket. 'Ye're a good girl. Tea's waiting.'

It would have been churlish, and self-defeating, to take offence; the poor woman was only doing what she had described as her duty. So I brushed my hair, replaced my hat, and joined the family at the very well laden table in the parlour. Here was everything from scones to lamb chops, with home-made cakes and tarts in between, washed down with all the tea we could drink. I was seated next to Tom, but although we could look at each other there was no opportunity for a private discussion, and following my chat with Mrs Mackenzie I was sorely in need of at least a reassuring kiss and cuddle.

I reflected that this time tomorrow we would be an old married couple setting out on our joint journey through life, and re-covered some of my spirits – even managing to smile at Tom and allow him a surreptitious squeeze of my hand. This went a long way to improving my mood, and for the first time since Mrs Mackenzie's homily I felt everything was going to be all right. But we had not finished our meal when there was a great deal of noise outside, followed by a thumping on the door. Mr Mackenzie went to open it, and was brushed aside, and I found myself staring at Grandpa.

The Bride

'Oh, Jane,' Mama said. I stood in front of her, feeling at once contrite and both frustrated and angry. Grandpa had hardly addressed a word to me during our three-day journey home from Gretna. Nor had he said much at Gretna itself. He had merely instructed me to get up, fetch my things, and get into his carriage; Wonder was secured to the back to trot behind us. The Mackenzies had made no objection, Grandpa being accompanied by six men led by Mr Carter and exuding wealth and power, while a single glance from his face to mine sufficed to convince them that he was an outraged relative.

I did not speak either. I merely wished the floor would open up and permit me a speedy descent to the nether regions. I could not believe that such a thing had happened, and was struck so dumb that I could not even say farewell to Tom. In fact I im-agined I would shortly see him again when the whole business would have to be sorted out – but I did not, nor did I ever see him again in my life. I know he was returned to Holkham, but only to be held in custody until it was thought best to release him and dismiss him, after it was determined that I had not been penetrated. What became of him after that, I have no idea. I suppose, if we count the gypsies, he must be regarded as the second severe stain on my moral record. At the time, I could not even weep for him; I was too concerned with my own situation. Grandpa and I rode in the same carriage, and indeed sat oppos-ite one another; but he spent his time looking out of the window, and when I endeavoured to address him, with the intention of presenting some kind of case for the defence, as it were, he ignored me. We sat together at table when we stopped for the night, but as there were always several other people present there was no way I could approach him then, while after dinner I was confined to my room, with one of the gamekeepers seated outside my locked door all night.

I was so miserable that I would have welcomed it had Grandpa taken off his belt and laid into me like the most profound Turk, if at the end of it he would stroke my head and say the matter was now forgotten. But sixteen-year-old girls are not flogged, at least not by their grandfathers. Their lot is to suffer, far more seriously, by being excluded, however temporarily, from family love; and all the time I knew that a far greater ordeal was awaiting me when I got home.

And now that moment had arrived. 'Oh, Jane,' Mama said again. 'How could you do such a thing?' At least I had been taken straight into her presence and, although the route had been lined by Steely, my brothers and numerous servants, no one had been given the opportunity to speak to me – save for Step-grandma Anne, who was of course a law to herself in her own house, and who remarked 'Well, really, little Jane, what a silly thing to do.'

I have no doubt that her sensibilities were all the more outraged by my being the cause of her elderly husband having to ride the length of the kingdom to regain me, but like everyone else she assumed that I had yielded my virginity to a stable boy. As did Mama. 'You realize that you have ruined your life,' she said.

She seemed more sorry for me than angry at me. 'I fell in love,' I said. This was the only defence I possessed, even if I now know it was quite untrue. I was in love, but not with Tom. I was in love with love, and with the concept of man. Tom had been the first of his sex to give me what I wanted. Well, almost.

Which, was not something that La Madre could understand. 'With a *groom*?'

'He is a man, Mama. He is handsome, and gentle, and kind, and . . .'

'Was he gentle when he raped you?'

'He did not rape me.'

'I suppose you accepted it without a murmur.'

'He did not enter me,' I said, vehemently.

She frowned at me. 'You spent four nights together . . . In separate rooms?'

'He would not . . . interfere with me.' At least in the sense she meant. 'He is an honourable man.'

'If only I could believe that . . . You will, I hope, not refuse to have the truth ascertained.'

I accepted the inevitable. 'If that is what you wish, Mama. But Tom . . .'

'If what you claim is true, it would be best for you not to see him again.'

'You mean if we had fornicated, you would let us marry?'

Mama fanned herself vigorously. 'That is not a word one expects to hear from a young girl of gentle breeding,' she pointed out. 'I mean that if you are still chaste, it may be possible to retrieve the situation. But not with Burrows about.'

'You intend to punish him.'

'Well, obviously he cannot remain here. Your grandfather is very angry. However, if he did indeed behave like a gentleman, I shall intercede for him.'

'Thank you, Mama. And me?'

'First, let us see what Mrs Ogilvie has to say.'

Mrs Ogilvie had been the midwife who examined me after my escapade with the gypsies. I had actually seen her again quite recently, as she had been in attendance on Step-grandma Anne, but we had exchanged no more than a greeting. Now I had to go through the whole embarrassing business of lying on my back with my skirts about my face and my legs spread while her fingers went where I had only ever wanted Tom's to touch. But the outcome was entirely satisfactory. 'Miss Jane is intact,' she informed Mama, sounding more surprised than anyone.

'Oh, Jane,' Mama said, and actually embraced and kissed me. Not that my forgiveness was complete. My life might not, after all, have been irretrievably ruined – but in view of the fact that she had no idea what I might do next, it seemed essential to Mama that I be removed from temptation just as rapidly as possible and, as this was now not possible until the following year, that I should spend the interim months in the most severe purdah. Thus a few days after my session with Mrs Ogilvie, the Digby family left Holkham and returned to Forston, where we remained over the entire winter.

This entailed, of course, a confrontation with Papa, which I anticipated with a good deal of apprehension, fathers possessing many more powers than grandfathers. In the event I was relieved, I suspect for two reasons. One was that Mama had a chat with him before I was called into the presence, and with her gentle but dominating demeanour had convinced him that I had been punished, or at least humiliated, enough. The other was that my father was always more than a little afraid of the strangely wayward beauty he had sired, and was more than happy to leave the whole affair in Mama's capable hands. Not that I was the most popular person at Forston that winter. This was the first Christmas we had not spent at Holkham, and Edward and Kenelm were thoroughly fed up. Of course Jenny – as they called me (a detestable nickname!) – was to blame, and this was a universally held opinion.

Mama obviously confided to those who she considered mattered – Grandpa and Step-grandma, Papa and Steely – that my physical condition at least was not disastrous, but this happy fact in no way assuaged their displeasure. Grandpa, in fact, continued to refuse to speak to me, which I felt was a bit much after his behaviour with Anne. But, of course, his adventure had been with someone of his own class, tainted only by the extreme age difference and the suggestion of moral incest. Anne was unfailingly polite, although she clearly felt that I had stolen her thunder, even if in a most backward manner. As an American cousin might have said, she hadn't seen anything yet! And Steely viewed me with a mixture of apprehension and disapproval, clearly uncertain where and when and what and with whom would be the next scandal I visited on the family.

But, thanks to Mama's careful handling of the business, there was no scandal. Only rumour. Poor Tom was sent off before he could be subjected to inquisition by his fellows; and all the servants were warned not to discuss the business or spread it abroad, on threat of instant dismissal. Even Aunt Anne Margaret was kept in the dark, which was a great relief to me.

My brothers had no idea what had happened, only that I had apparently run away from home, taking a groom along for my protection (they were even more ignorant of sexual matters than I had been at their ages), and that my escapade had spoiled everyone's Christmas. While the Forston servants had no idea that anything had happened at all, they were equally disgruntled – in their case, at having the family home for Christmas instead of having the house to themselves.

And what of the eye of the storm? My anger, my resentment, even my humiliation, bubbled for a while, but then was overtaken by practicalities. I reflected that I had had a great adventure (all the greater because it had been so illicit); that I had got together with a man for the first time and most thoroughly enjoyed myself; and that I had been saved in the nick of time from an undoubtedly unpromising fate – as the wife of a groom, even if I had managed to have him made head groom. I was young, beautiful, talented, educated, and now, in addition, regarded myself as sufficiently sophisticated to make any man happy. All that was now needed was the right man.

It was at this juncture, just as I was regaining my confidence, that I received a crushing blow. News arrived of the death of Lord Byron. As I have mentioned, he had left England eight years before, while I was still a child. I am sure that mine was not the only potential broken heart he left behind. But we still received news of him, and for several years following his departure he continued to titillate the world with his various amours, mainly in Italy, while, as he continued to be a prolific writer, every year a new work was published in England, more often than not to sell out its entire first edition on the morning it became available.

Needless to say, he was not well regarded by my family. Grandpa would not have his name mentioned at Holkham, and Mama did not much care for him either. As for his poems, I was unable to get hold of any of these, except when Anne, before she became my step-grandma, brought home an edition of *The Corsair* which the two of us devoured in private with a great deal of giggling. Byron's exploits sufficed to keep his name before the public, and his image firmly lodged in my mind. Thus I was delighted when suddenly he threw away the trappings of a rake and became a profound patriot, if not for his own people. At this time I of course had no idea that I would ever become perhaps even more closely involved with Greek culture and politics than his lordship, but from my readings of the classics I was already wholly fascinated (as was nearly all educated England) by that most ancient and splendid of civilizations. I had read my Homer from cover to cover more than once and – as I suspect was the case with many people far older and more experienced than myself – had no idea that modern Greek men, after nearly four centuries of Turkish rule and oppression and intermarriage, could be any different to Achilles or Ulysses in either character or appearance, or their women any less beautiful and compelling than Helen or Penelope.

It will therefore be understood that I, again in common with so many of my compatriots, supported with all my heart the Greek fight for independence from their Turkish masters, and was overjoyed to learn that my hero had taken up arms in defence of the cause; at fifteen, the understanding that people who fight in wars do from time to time get killed was always once removed, as it were. And when a portrait was published of Byron in Grecian costume, looking more handsome than ever, I fell in love all over again. It will be noted that this sublime passion did not prevent me from also falling in love with Tom. I have always been a realist, and the possibility of Lord Byron ever returning to England, meeting me, falling in love, and sweeping me off my feet was so remote as firmly to confine it to the realm of dreams. Although it was, in fact, not so remote as all that. Had Byron survived, and come home a national hero, he would have done so just about the time I was coming out. We would certainly have met, and if I was truly the most beautiful debutante in London that summer, and given that I was nicknamed Aurora ('Light of the Dawn'), after one of the central characters in his newly published *Don Juan*, we would certainly have had a liaison; he was, after all, roughly the same age as the man I was soon to marry.

And now he was dead. I felt quite shattered – but I had little time for moping.

Looked at from the perspective of more than fifty years and a great deal of real experience and adventure, 'coming out' is a dreadful business. But at the time, I thought it was terribly exciting. We moved up to town as soon after Christmas as the roads were passable, taking up residence in the house Papa had rented, and soon purchased, spurred on no doubt by Mama. It was situated in Harley Street, a prosperous neighbourhood, and we were there in time to celebrate my seventeenth birthday. It was a very nice house, and throughout the winter had been thoroughly renovated, repainted where necessary, recarpeted and redraped, and in certain aspects was quite splendid, though I am afraid I did not pay the décor much attention. The idea of being able to explore the metropolis filled me with exhilaration, but despite all the time we apparently had in hand before the start of the season, there was very little available for seeing the sights: I needed to be fitted out.

I have no idea of, and I shudder to consider, the cost of all this to dear Papa, but for me it was a sojourn in heaven. I had never paid a great deal of attention to my appearance, resting secure in my natural beauty. Although I did enjoy wearing nice things, all of my things were nice; and that I did not have a very extensive wardrobe had never bothered me. Now I was made to realize that to be seen twice in the same dress in the entire season would be a considerable social gaffe. Thus for several hours in every day I found myself in the hands of a variety of seamstresses and haberdashers, always with both Mama and Steely in close attendance.

I found this business tedious in the extreme, but heavenly in the outcome, as I saw my wardrobe grow beyond my wildest expectations and learned how even my looks could be enhanced by skilful decoration. I should mention here that, because of the French Revolution, women's fashions had undergone as great an upheaval as any accomplished politically by that unfortunate affair. For a generation the old corset had been entirely discarded, as had all but the scantiest underclothing, while the gowns themselves, made of thin and revealing materials and with the waist situated immediately beneath the breasts, were designed to display every asset any woman possessed. Sadly, by the time I began to leave adolescence behind, what many considered a becoming modesty had started to return. Thus I made my first acquaintance with the corset or, as it was popularly known, stays, so that a large part of getting dressed consisted of having this lamentable garment strapped round me and hanging on to the bedposts while Steely and various maidservants tugged and strained to reduce my girth to as small a measurement as possible. The whole thing was an absurdity in my case, as I was naturally slender and there was very little difference in measurement between me in the nude and me strapped up. When I pointed this out, however, I was informed that no gentlewoman would dare be seen in public without her stays, even if they remained invisible.

To be honest, the obnoxious garment, when in place, was not uncomfortable, and if it could do little for my waist, it was of great assistance in pushing up my breasts – which, though steadily growing, had not yet achieved their fullest dimensions – and thus in making me appear more voluptuous than I actually was. Our outer garments had also in a measure returned to a previous decorous appearance. Gone were the indecent shifts of the Empress Josephine's court; waists were back in their proper place, often belted or sashed, and thicker and more concealing materials were now in vogue. There were, however, some compensating factors, principally the disappearance of the long train, which had prohibited the wearing of the same garment twice because of the dirt swept up from the floor. In its place, we wore elaborately decorated hems.

The actual presentation of the female figure was still in a state of flux. The revolutionary period had seen the first revealing of the leg, among civilized people, since the Dark Ages, albeit glimpsed only through a diaphanous covering. Now our legs were again firmly consigned to anonymity outside of the bedroom. The breasts were a different matter. All of us had seen pictures of the beauties of the Stuart courts, where the only point at issue had seemed to be whether the nipple should be utterly exposed or just glimpsed as its owner moved. The Empire had been more decorous in this direction, though a good deal of cleavage had been considered permissible, the problem being that without sufficient underpinning to jack the globes up only those naturally well-endowed stood out, although the sheerness of the material in use again made it a simple matter for the eager connoisseur to discern that dark pimple and aureole so beloved of men and babies. In our generation, the deep décolletage was on its way back, at least for evening wear.

However, the greatest difference between our gowns and those of Josephine's disciples lay in colour. The French romantics had believed in white, or at least pastel shades. Pastel shades were still popular in my youth, certainly for day wear, but more and more colour was creeping in after dark. In this regard, when I became mistress of my own wardrobe, I rather went overboard, not to everyone's approval. But then, I have spent my life going overboard, in one direction or another, and always to a chorus of disapproval.

Beneath all of this finery we were required to wear three starched petticoats, as decorated as if they were outer garments, which were designed to set up a fascinating rustle as we walked, enhanced by the material of our gowns, which was as often as not taffeta or organdie, and beneath the whole a plain chemise to protect our skin from the worst ravages of the corset. We were not, at this pre-Victorian stage of British culture, required to wear anything more than this, and certainly not the ghastly waist-to-ankle monstrosities which I understand are now considered essential. I have never worn anything like that myself.

Nor did I much indulge in the cosmetics which were considered enhancers of a woman's beauty. Indeed, I put down the perfection of my complexion – which has stood the strain of seventy years, often exposed to the ravages of wind and storm, and even flying sand, without losing an iota of its smoothness – to my careful use of only cream and powder. Jewellery was another matter. I have never met a woman who did not feel her appearance improved by a few diamonds or rubies scattered about, and I was no exception to that rule. Then there were gloves of every conceivable material, and slippers for every conceivable occasion; and scores of reticules, for each bag had to be matched to the style and colour of our gowns. And of course, fans. These were regarded as almost the most important part of any ensemble, because of the code of signals a fan provided. I found it fascinating to discover how a wide-spread fan could indicate, without a word, that one found one's companion of the moment interesting; a flutter, accompanied perhaps by drooping eyelashes, could suggest that a closer acquaintance would be acceptable. And various other movements conveyed other messages, all apparently understood by any gentleman, culminating if necessary in the click of this potent weapon being sharply closed, to indicate displeasure and that the conversation should end and not be resumed.

But our crowning glory, and the article of apparel in which we were allowed the most individuality, was our hats. The scope and variety of these was as splendid as it was sometimes outrageous.

When Aunt Eliza and her niece were presented at court, the roof of their carriage had to be cut away to make room for their towering headdresses. If not intending to go so far, one could still indulge in a gamut ranging from wide-brimmed straw bonnets decorated with fluttering ribbons to more close-fitting versions (popularly known as poke bonnets, but described by the unkind as upturned coal-scuttles) with or without a crown, all the way to smaller and prettier silk versions, passing on the way such things as turbans.

In the house, we usually wore mob caps to protect our elaborate coiffures. For all of these arrangements were designed to show off our hair, such as it was. This was the only aspect of becoming a woman that I truly disliked. My red-gold hair had always been my crowning glory, and was to be again when given the chance, softly enveloping my features. Now I had to allow those superb locks to be trimmed and then collected in a vast bun at the back of my head, while a few selected strands were combed and twiddled to make them conform to the passion for surrounding the face with tight ringlets – not in themselves unattractive, but leaving the features woefully exposed. In fact I suffered less than most of my acquaintances by this misfortune, my face and complexion being entirely able to stand on their own. Not everyone was so fortunate.

Clothes, while the essential foundation of a society beauty, were only the foundation. One had to walk or, rather, glide with becoming grace, an ability achieved by parading, in private, with a book balanced on one's head; sit gracefully, a slow descent to one side followed by holding the body rigidly upright; and rise with equal dignity (a much more difficult task). And one had to learn to dance. The carefree expressions of one's youth had to be forgotten, their place being taken by the stately movements of the quadrille and the abandoned misbehaviour of the waltz. Even the most stuffy old spinster could not take exception to the delicate bowing and finger-touching of the quadrille, which – being, as its name indicates, a business of two couples together – precluded any private conversation, much less a flirtation other than with the eyes. But the waltz – where one is obliged to place oneself in the arms of a man one might only have met that same evening and allow him to place his hand on the centre of one's back (which would, if one's décolletage extended to the rear as well as the front, mean that he was actually clutching one's naked flesh, admittedly with gloved fingers, while one whirled about the floor in an ecstasy of rhythm) – was sufficient to send the strait-laced into a swoon. I could hardly wait to practise it with someone more attractive than my dancing master.

There remained one final step before I could be thrust into society: my mother had the Countess of Oxford to tea. I was becoming quite confused by the names of the great ladies who dominated the social scene, none of whom I had ever seen, much less met, but I did understand that Lady Oxford had been one of the great beauties of her time, that time being some twenty years before mine. I was fascinated when Mama confided, in just about the first woman-to-woman talk we had ever had, that our guest had been among the more profligate of the Regency *grandes dames*. 'Do you know,' Mama remarked, 'that each of her seven children was by a different father? They call them the Harleian Miscellany. Her name is Jane Harley, you see.'

'You mean she is still married?' I did not see how this could be.

'Things were different during the Regency. In those days a man valued his wife more by the status of her lovers than for her ability as a mother. Why, do you know, Lady Oxford was the mistress, for a while, of that poor boy Byron?'

Now that really roused my interest. I could hardly wait to meet a woman who had been so fortunate, even if I could not fathom why my mother, who was about the most moral woman I had ever met, should wish to introduce me to such an erratic character, however noble. In fact Lady Oxford was still a beautiful woman, with classical features, a full figure and lustrous dark hair. She was also one of the most powerful hostesses in London; this was what had attracted Mama, with my future in mind. I had no idea what this meant, but behaved as instructed, curtsying to her and then sitting beside her as she seemed to wish. 'Entrancing,' she remarked, and then switched to French, at which I was able to hold my own. She appeared pleased, and patted my hand. 'You have a treasure, Lady Andover,' she remarked. 'I trust you will allow her to join our circle.'

To my surprise, and I must confess my dismay, as I had never witnessed such a thing before, Mama positively simpered. 'It will be my great pleasure, Lady Oxford.'

'After she has been presented, of course,' Lady Oxford reminded her.

Shortly afterwards she left. I was by then quite put out, although I continued to be politeness itself. I had never expected to see my mother accepting a position of inferiority to anyone. 'Is her circle so important?' I inquired.

'My dear girl,' Mama said. 'You have just been invited to Almack's.' She considered for a few moments. 'After your marriage, or course.'

It was now time for the presentation. I was accompanied by Mama and Papa, both of us ladies decked out in our finest attire, our ensembles topped by white ostrich feathers, which at that time were considered essential appendages. In my ignorance I had supposed that this would be a private affair, and was taken aback to discover that our carriage was only one of several dozen large equipages that blocked Piccadilly all the way to St James's Palace, where each of them came to a halt virtually against the one in front. It was as if we were in the middle of a battle, with the horses whinnying and stamping, and some even rearing and kicking; the liveried grooms (we had six with us), all of them wearing huge bouquets that did nothing for their freedom of movement, rushing about opening doors and lowering steps, as well as trying to control their errant animals; the formidable array of overdressed matrons, all shouting greetings at one another and fussing about their charges, while their husbands (many, like Papa, in uniform, to give a flavouring of scarlet and blue to the scene) looked embarrassed and greeted each other stiffly, and their charges, most of whom appeared to be in a state of abject fright (one girl actually fainted and had to be revived with smelling salts) were brought out of the carriages. In the midst of this pandemonium, a throng of knee-breeched courtiers struggled to keep order. And above all, I was conscious of the immense effluvia of a crowd of people closely gathered together in a state of high excitement.

Happily, I am not the fainting sort, although I might have been excused for collapsing from sheer fatigue as we entered the palace and joined the long line of those awaiting the King's pleasure. By this time I was as excited as anyone, though unsure what to expect. I had never seen the King, or indeed any king, but my preformed impression that a king must always be majestic, if not handsome, had been infiltrated by Grandpa's often repeated opinion that our present monarch was not fit to rule anything, even a chamber pot. Thus, when we finally reached the reception chamber and found ourselves standing before the man himself, I was utterly confounded by the huge, repellent mountain of flesh with which I was confronted, the cheeks rouged and the entire face layered with cosmetics in a vain attempt to conceal the ravages of his dissipated life, not to mention the clammy quality of his flesh when he held my hand, and the limbs swollen with gout. I was of course wearing gloves, but to my disgust he slid his fingers up the kid to stroke the bare flesh above my elbow. Although I was horrified, he was plainly delighted. 'What a beauty!' he said. 'What a beauty! Why, my dear Lady Andover, were I only twenty years younger I would beg your permission to call.' All those within earshot apparently found this delicious, and broke into polite applause. In those few seconds I was projected to the forefront of society.

I had been presented, and acclaimed. But in the King's absence – for which I thanked God – it was now necessary for someone else to come calling. To ensure that this would happen, my parents began to entertain on the most lavish scale. No. 78 Harley Street became the cynosure of all eyes. Of course all of the other mamas and papas we had encountered at the palace were doing the same thing, but none of them could boast a Jane Digby, a lack which did not make me any the more popular in their circles. But the men were fascinated.

As was I, as supper party followed dinner party, at every one of which I was the guest of honour although they all took place in my own house. I was always seated next to the man Mama currently thought most eligible. Dancing was a different matter, because there were strict rules. Laid down by Lady Cowper, another of the *grandes dames* who dominated London society, they decreed that at every dance there had to be three men invited for every woman – one to dance, one to eat, and one to stare – and that no one was ever to dance with the same man twice in the same evening. This had both advantages and disadvantages. It was delightful to have access to such variety and to waltz in a stranger's arms, but at the same time I more than once encountered a most pleasant partner, in whose arms I would happily have spent the rest of the night, only to have him return me to my seat when the music stopped, bow to Mama, and disappear into the throng, presumably to eat or to stare or, worst of fates, dance with someone else.

There was no question about the staring. It was after a couple of dances that someone began calling me Aurora, the Light of the Dawn, and the name caught on. I thought it splendid, even if every time it was used it made me think, sadly, of poor Byron.

Unfortunately, the compliments, vast revelries and even vaster expense did not appear to be bearing any positive fruit. There were men a-plenty, fawning over my hand, but . . . After every dinner party Mama, Papa, and I would sit down with Mama's lists and talk − and delete. Anyone with less than five thousand a year had to go for a start. This was particularly distressing for me, for it turned out that the only guests I actually found attractive − the younger ones − were nearly all below the permitted figure. Of the rest, the few that were eligible on the grounds of finance had other insuperable drawbacks, principally my revulsion to them. Matters were growing desperate as July went into August, with the end of the season only a couple of weeks away. Indeed, most of the hunting and shooting set were already packing up. Mama and Papa thus determined to risk all: we would have a ball.

Now we really got down to the lists, seeking at once a bevy of comely young women, none of whom would outshine me, and, of course, the necessary proportion of men to women. Thus any refusals were a serious matter. 'And *he* can't come,' said Mama with as much vehemence as she ever expressed, striking out another name on her list. 'Bother! Now we are a man short.'

Papa gave a gentle cough, and she glared at him. 'I was thinking of young Law.'

'Oh, really, Henry. You can't be serious. He has already been married.'

'Well, he's a widower, my dear. That means he at least knows how to share a house with a woman. And he is healthy, and has a place in the government . . .'

Mama snorted. She shared her father's views on the government. 'And Miss Harriette Wilson?' she inquired.

Papa went red in the face and cast me an anxious glance. 'Well, really, my dear, I don't think you can hold that against him, in view of, well . . .'

'You mean that every gentleman in London has called upon her,' Mama said, and patted his hand. 'Except you, I am sure, my dear.'

At which Papa went redder yet, while I was intrigued: who could this person be? But Papa had hidden weapons. 'I happen to know he has ten thousand a year.'

'Hm,' Mama commented. 'But still, the man is . . .'

Papa gave another cough, this one a warning, and they both glanced at me. But my interest was thoroughly aroused. 'Surely,' I said, 'if I am to marry this man, I should know something about him?'

'There is not the slightest chance of your ever marrying Ellenborough,' Mama declared, thus informing me that he was a titled gentleman.

'He is looking for a new wife,' Papa pointed out.

'That is exactly it. He has made this very plain, and has indulged in heaven knows how many flirtations, and worse, over the past few years.'

Could he possibly be a rake? Oh, seventh heaven! But . . . 'Did you say *new* wife?' I inquired.

'As your father has explained, Lord Ellenborough is a widower,' Mama said, acidly. Having been a widow herself, she felt hers was the proper order of things.

'His first wife was Octavia Stewart,' Papa said. 'Poor Castlereagh's sister.'

Now I had heard of Castlereagh, if not of his sister. He had been Foreign Secretary for several years, becoming prominent during the Congress of Vienna, following the defeat of Bonaparte. In this role he had found himself opposed to most of the crowned heads of Europe, as he had endeavoured to prevent them from using the excuse of lurking republicanism to interfere in the affairs of other nations, and had equally refused British support, in the

form of either men, ships, money or words, for such interven-
tion when it did take place. In my opinion this was all very
honourable, but sadly Lord Castlereagh had not only made enemies
at home but nursed dark secrets of which his enemies were quick
to take advantage, and when he was faced with allegations of
homosexuality he had, only two years before, cut his own throat.
That Edward Law, Lord Ellenborough, had been his brother-in-
law, interested me less than the suggestion that he was both
well-endowed, at least financially, and had a way with women.
That, like Byron, he was double my age no longer seemed as important as it had done a year or two previously. He was undeniably
handsome, and his somewhat cold and aloof air gave him a suggestion of concealed force – which I, at least, found attractive, although
many others held the opinion that he was an ambitious, arrogant
and utterly self-centred rogue. But in the beginning I could see
no evidence of this and, although I did not fall in love with him
at first sight, I definitely found him attractive. I cannot possibly
say that he fell in love with *me* at first sight either – I do not
think he ever loved me at all – but he definitely determined, at
first sight, that I was the bride he was looking for. Just what he
was looking for I of course had no idea, but I am sure I cannot
be criticized for assuming that he sought beauty, intelligence,
intellect, vigour and, above all, passion, as these were the assets
displayed by my every movement, my every word. Nor did I have
any immediate reason to think otherwise. Within a week of our
first meeting we were riding together in the park, smiling at each
other at parties and, above all, exchanging poetry, written with
some warmth, which made me more than ever certain that he
was a true romantic. I did attempt to convey to him that I was
on the rebound from another romance – meaning Byron, rather
than poor Tom – but this he chose to ignore. Within another
week he was asking Papa for my hand.

I had no hesitation in convincing myself that this was to be
the love of my life. Papa did not disagree. Mama did. She could
not cavil at either Edward's income or his prospects for advancement (some were even speaking of him as a future prime minister),
save for the fact that such advancement would necessarily be under
the aegis of the Tory administration. But on the debit side was the
fact that however he might have been taken up as a protégé by

Castlereagh (in his prime just about the most important man in the government, if we except the Great Duke himself), he was still a 'new' man, which is something the British aristocracy have always found difficult to accept – notwithstanding the obvious point that every family in the land had at one time been 'new'. The charge against Edward was that down to the previous generation no one had ever heard of the Laws. But then they had suddenly blossomed. More than one of his uncles was a prominent churchman, another had made a fortune in India (but then blotted his copybook by emigrating to America, where he married George Washington's step-granddaughter), while his father had outdone the lot by rising, from being a humble lawyer, to become Lord Chief Justice of England, a triumph that had not only brought him a peerage but also considerable wealth – both of which had been inherited by his eldest son. But of course a man whose grandfather had occupied a very humble station in life could not really be acceptable to a Coke of Norfolk.

The absurdity of this point of view was that only two hundred years ago the Cokes had themselves risen from obscurity by means of an ancestor who became Lord Chief Justice and before that happy event my mother's family had been unknown – whereas when Edward's family tree was investigated it was discovered that he was actually descended from a daughter of King Edward III! Even this did not persuade Mama that it was going to be a good match. There remained the impediment of his age – which was thirty-four – and the several years he had been a widower, during which he had openly been looking for a new wife without success. Whether this indicated that he was a difficult man to please, or that previous prospective brides had found some evidence to put them off, no one could be sure.

Pitted against all this was my enthusiasm for the match. Thankfully, it never did come to a contest of wills between Mama and myself, at least on this issue. For Edward, always the consummate politician, now enlisted the assistance of his erstwhile mother-in-law, the Dowager Countess of Londonderry, who wrote Mama to say how pleased she was that her darling boy had found himself so delightful a prospective bride. As mothers-in-law who actually approve of their sons-in-law are usually difficult to find – especially when the said son-in-law is still living in perfect health when the daughter of the house has been buried, and as no one could possibly quibble at the antecedents of the Stewarts – Mama surrendered and announced my betrothal, and I looked forward to a long and exciting engagement. We were thus both considerably taken aback when Edward approached Papa with the proposal that we do away with such tedious niceties as banns and engagement balls, and instead obtain a special licence and have the business done with immediately.

This put Mama into a tizzy all over again. A mother needs a considerable time both to get used to the idea that she is losing a daughter and to prepare the daughter for the event; a trousseau is not created overnight. But Edward was insistent, Papa was not against – having already spent a fortune upon launching me, he was no doubt relieved not to have to fund a huge wedding – and I thought it was a splendidly romantic idea. Thus Mama was outgunned and laid down her arms, the precious licence was obtained, and on 15 September 1824 I became Lady Ellenborough. I was not quite seventeen-and-a-half years old.

The ceremony took place at our Harley Street house, the service being conducted by Edward's uncle, the Bishop of Bath and Wells. It was a small, private affair, but there were certain people who had to be invited, mainly members of our far-flung family, some of whom I had never even heard of before. However, I had very little time for any of these comparative strangers; I could hardly wait for the congratulations and the wedding breakfast to be completed, so that I could change my gown and take my place beside my husband in our carriage for the drive to Brighton, where we were to honeymoon. This was to be a journey of several hours, over roads that were not in the best repair, but it was no more uncomfortable, and considerably shorter, than travelling from Holkham to Dorchester, and I was tumultuously excited at the idea of spending that length of time entirely alone with a man who was also my husband, and therefore permitted by law to do anything he liked to me – just as I assumed that I could do anything I liked to him. My maid, a London girl named Lucy, only recently taken into our employ, was required to ride on top with Edward's man.

The journey began uncertainly. We were accompanied by several bottles of champagne, and as soon as we were away from Westminster Edward opened one of these and filled two glasses, handing one to me. This operation, in a moving and bouncing coach, is inevitably fraught with danger, and sure enough some of the sparkling liquid leapt out of the glass and deposited itself on my cleavage, most on the bodice but sufficient reaching my flesh. 'Oh!' I gave a little shriek.

'Oh, good Lord!' he said. 'I am most terribly sorry.'

'Please do not be,' I assured him.

We gazed at each other, and I allowed my tongue to come out and circle my lips, as my fan was on the seat beside me. I do not believe there could have been a more open invitation for him at least to touch me, if not to kiss away the liquid, and I did not imagine I could be considered lewd in extending such an invitation to my husband. But he did not accept it, and after a brief hesitation produced a handkerchief which, instead of using himself he gave to me. 'You had better dry yourself,' he suggested.

This I did, after taking a drink of the offending liquid. I refused to be discouraged, nor did I consider that I had any reason to be, for while I was patting myself dry, he suddenly leaned forward and kissed my forehead. 'Did I ever tell you how beautiful you are?' he asked.

Well, now, this was more what I had anticipated, and wanted. I dropped the handkerchief in favour of wrapping my arms round his neck to kiss him. As we were both holding glasses this involved some more spillage, on him as well as me. 'Oh,' I cried, and gave a girlish giggle. 'I am a goose.'

He disengaged himself. 'We have several hours ahead of us,' he remarked, his expression indicating that he was regarding the situation from a point of view of spending that much time with champagne spilt on him, rather than in my arms. 'And you must remember that we are virtually in public.'

I did not agree with him, as the servants were on the roof and the coach was travelling fast enough to protect us from any inquisitorial gaze, but it is not a wife's business to contradict her husband – at least not on the first day of their marriage. 'I am sorry,' I said. 'I have a tempestuous nature, and I was so flattered by what you said.'

'It was not intended as flattery,' he pointed out. 'It was a simple statement of fact.' I reminded myself that he was by training a lawyer. 'As for your nature,' he said, 'you must remember that you are now a grown woman, as well as the wife of a peer of the realm, and must at all times conduct yourself with dignity.'

I could have been sharing the carriage with Steely, on whom I hoped, optimistically, to have turned my back for ever. But my husband was entitled to have me behave as he wished. 'I shall endeavour to do so,' I promised.

'Of course you will,' he said, with alarming confidence. 'Would you like another glass?'

'Do you think I should?'

'I see no reason why not, providing you promise not to spill it.'

I clutched the glass in both hands while sitting bolt upright, and tried desperately to think of something to say. 'Tell me about Roehampton,' I suggested. This was the village, not far from London, where Edward's house was situated. I had never been there, but I would be returning there after the honeymoon, as mistress.

'You'll like it,' he said.

This was hardly a description. 'You said I could bring my pets,' I reminded him.

'Certainly. You do not have a cat, I hope?'

'No, no,' I said.

'Good. I cannot abide cats.'

'I have three dogs, a donkey, and a monkey. Apart from my mare.'

'Did you say *a monkey*?'

'He's a lovely little fellow, you'll adore him. His name is Gibraltar.'

'Have you been to Gibraltar?'

'No, no. But that is where monkeys come from, isn't it?'

'Those are apes. You mean this creature is an ape?'

'No, no. He's a monkey. I just called him that because I associated monkeys with Gibraltar.'

'Ah,' he said, and we had another silence.

'Tell me about your pets,' I suggested.

'I have no pets. That is, I did not have any pets, till now.'

'You're sure you won't mind?'

'Not at all. As long as they do not become a nuisance.'

There was no adequate reply to that, as there is no such thing as a pet who is not from time to time a nuisance. I was thoroughly glad to reach Brighton, having slept, or pretended to sleep, as much of the way as possible.

I awoke in a much better frame of mind. After all, my relationship with Tom had had a slow start, but once we had got down to business our only problem had been the criminality of what we were doing. As that did not apply in this instance, I had no doubts about the coming hours. My confidence was enhanced when Edward remarked, 'You are lovely when you sleep.'

'Thank you. I trust I didn't snore?'

'Only very softly, and very prettily. You talked a bit.'

'Talked!' I was horrified. No one, not even Steely, had ever accused me of that before. And suppose I had mentioned Tom?! 'Whatever did I say?'

'I have no idea. I could not understand a word of it.' That was a relief. I hastily looked out of the window, at Brighton. I had not been there before and was agog to see the famous Pavilion, which was regarded as either grotesque or fantastic, depending on one's point of view. I longed to see the interior, but it was in the process of being dismantled, at least of its paintings and ornaments, most of its treasures being carted up to London to decorate the King's new residence – named Buckingham House, after the somewhat disreputable royal favourite who built it a couple of centuries ago.

It was already quite late when we arrived at the Norfolk Hotel, where we were warmly greeted by the manager and all the under-managers, and shown up to the bridal suite, magnificently decorated with flowers, where our supper was served with a great deal of fuss. Needless to say there was some more champagne, together with a couple of bottles of wine. It was all much more than I was used to, and I had to concentrate very hard to prevent myself from falling asleep, which I presumed would be a disaster. I would have liked a bath before going to bed, as it had been a long and arduous day, but as Edward was obviously not going to indulge I had to forego the pleasure. But he had been in the best of humours during the meal, and my confidence grew.

He left me to join his valet in the dressing room as soon as the meal was cleared (it was now nearly midnight), and Lucy

and I got to work. Despite my confidence, I will admit I was
quite in a twitter. I seemed to have waited all my life for this
moment – though my expectations were to some measure clouded
by my memory of what I had already experienced, with wondering
if he would be anything like Tom and what it would feel like
(from which it may be gathered that Mama had still not considered it necessary to inform me of the facts of life). However, my
undressing was finally completed, my hair released and uncurled,
I was enveloped in a new white satin nightgown, which I was
resolved to be rid of just as soon as possible, and I was tucked
into bed, sitting up, my red-gold locks arranged around my shoulders. 'Do I look all right?' I asked Lucy.

'You look enchanting, Miss Jane.'

As I have mentioned, Lucy had not been in my employ for
very long; and apart from the fact that she had produced very
good references, I knew nothing about her. On the other hand,
she was a couple of years older than me, and we all know what
the working classes are supposed to be like . . .

'Have you ever been with a man, Lucy?' I asked.

She blushed. 'Oh, Miss Jane.'

'I shan't tell anyone, really. But I need to know . . . well, what
it's like. I mean, when he . . . when my husband . . .'

'Oh, it's good, Miss Jane. After the first couple of times.'

I didn't like the sound of that. 'But I am about to, well . . .
have it for the first time.'

'It hurts, Miss Jane. Something terrible. But then, oooh . . .'

'Hurts?'

'Well, you see, Miss Jane . . .'

But at that moment, perhaps fortunately, there was a knock
on the door.

'May I come in?' Edward asked.

I had not anticipated such formality. 'Oh, yes,' I said. 'Please.'
He was wearing a silk nightshirt and a tasselled cap; I had decided
against a cap this night, as I was sure it would very rapidly be
dislodged. As this was the first time I had seen a man in a nightshirt (Tom had not possessed one), I was a little taken aback.
'Thank you, Lucy,' I said.

'Yes, Miss Jane. Goodnight, Miss Jane.' She curtsied to Edward.
'Goodnight, my lord.' She closed the door behind her.

Edward advanced to stand beside the bed. 'That girl is too familiar. She must call you either milady or ma'am.'

'Oh,' I said. 'Yes. I will speak to her in the morning.'

He sat on the bed, his thigh against mine, and to my delight stroked my hair. 'I feel as if I have come into possession of the most precious piece of porcelain in the world.'

I decided to be facetious. 'I assure you, sir, that if you drop me I shall not break.'

His response was straight out of heaven, for he thrust his hands into my armpits, having to touch my breasts, even if inadvertently, to do so, raised me from the pillows, and kissed me most passionately. This was more than I had hoped for. Even when we had been pronounced man and wife and he had been instructed by his uncle to kiss me, he had merely brushed my lips with his own; otherwise, hitherto he had only ever kissed my cheek. But here he was, parting my lips with his tongue to allow it inside, while his hands continued on their journey round my back to hold me closer yet. As he was inside my arms, they were entirely free. I hugged him in turn, as tightly as I could, and then allowed my hand to slide down his arm to his side. I was so anxious to let him know that I could respond to anything he might wish to do to me, that I would please him in every possible way, thus I continued with my caress, now across his thigh. As I did so I felt his body stiffen, but I assumed this was a sign of pleasure, and so sought and found my goal, even if it was still protected by the silk of his shirt, and even if I had to reject a slight sense of disappointment that it did not appear to be either as large or as anxious as Tom's had been.

I was then utterly consternated – for as I sought to hold my prize, he threw me on my back on the bed and leapt away from me, chest heaving and cheeks suffused. For a moment, I was breathless. I was also afraid, for he was not looking the least happy. 'Edward?' I asked.

He was standing up. 'What are you?' he demanded. 'Some kind of slut?' I clutched the sheet to my throat. I had no idea how to reply. And he realized that he might have gone too far. 'I am sorry,' he said. 'I did not mean to insult you. But . . . to touch me there . . .'

My bewilderment was increasing. True, Tom had seemed

surprised by my wishing to touch him, but then surprise had very rapidly changed to delight. 'I am sorry, too,' I said. 'I did not mean to upset you.'

'Upset me! My dear girl, ladies do not touch gentlemen in their private parts.'

'But . . .' I tried to choose my words with care. 'Will you not touch me?'

'Good heavens, no! I would not presume.'

'But . . . do we not have to . . . well . . .'

'It happens,' he said, 'when it will. When we lie together. When . . . well . . .'

I sat up again and held out my arms, surely the most enticing sight in the world. 'Then lie with me, Edward, dear Edward, and let it happen.'

Half a loaf is always better than none; and besides, once I had got him into my arms . . . But again to my consternation, only this time it was something close to horror, he shook his head and retreated. 'It will not happen tonight. It could not. I am too . . . Damme!' He turned and left the room.

The Light of the Dawn

I was absolutely shattered. I was equally bewildered – and, being me, somewhat miffed. I threw myself across the bed, on my face, in a paroxysm of outraged disappointment, which was soon replaced by apprehension. My marriage had not been consummated! Did it, then, not exist? Shades of Great-Aunt Mary! In retrospect, I must be grateful to the amount of wine I had consumed, as despite my misery I rapidly fell asleep. But when I awoke, I was alone in the bed; Lucy, who was pottering around, nearly jumped out of her skin when I stirred.

We gazed at each other. 'Good morning, Miss Jane,' she said.

'Ma'am,' I said, absently. 'You must call me ma'am. Or milady.' And then reflected as to whether or not I yet had any right to call myself that.

'Yes, Miss . . . ma'am. Will you breakfast?'

'I would rather have a bath, first.' I would dearly have liked to inquire after the whereabouts of my husband, but I felt that would be too great an admission of defeat.

Lucy looked embarrassed. 'The tub will have to be brought in here.'

'That will not do at all. Why cannot it be placed in the dressing room?'

'Well, you see, Miss . . . ma'am . . . well . . .'

The penny dropped. Things were actually better than I had dared hope; I had been apprehensive that Edward might have left the hotel. 'Ah,' I said. 'Then bring me my undressing robe, and have the tub brought in here.'

She hurried to fetch my robe, and I got out of bed to put it on. But now my curiosity got the better of my discretion. I had never actually been into the dressing room. 'Is there a bed in there?'

'There is a cot, ma'am.'

Poor Edward. 'Go and order my bath,' I said. She left the room, and I followed her into the lobby and opened the dressing-room door. It was certainly a narrow cot, with only a few coverings. These were very tousled, suggesting that Edward had spent a restless night; and indeed, he was fairly tousled himself. He awoke at my entry, and sat up, violently, clutching the sheet against himself like any blushing maiden. Had I not known he had been married, and was reputed to have had several affairs – quite apart from the mysterious Miss Wilson – I might have supposed him every bit as much of a virgin as myself. 'I did not mean to disturb you,' I said. 'I was concerned that you might have had an uncomfortable night.'

At this he looked more embarrassed yet. I took his mood to indicate that he was ashamed of his behaviour – as indeed he was, though not in the direction that immediately concerned me. 'This is not the most comfortable bed,' he conceded.

'Then why not come to mine? Ours,' I hastily added. He scratched his head. I determined to make my case while he was in an apparently receptive mood. 'I am deeply sorry if I upset you last night. If I knew what I did wrong, I would do everything in my power to set it right. My sole desire is to be a good wife to you, dear Edward.'

He held my hands and, to my great gratification, drew me forward for a kiss – although when I attempted to touch his tongue with my own, he again jerked away from me. 'Edward!' I begged.

'We have a lot to discuss,' he said. 'I suppose it is your upbringing.'

My instincts were to bridle at this implied criticism of Mama, but I did not wish to cause a fresh crisis, so I dissembled instead. 'If you would tell me what is lacking . . . I have always been told I was somewhat accomplished.'

'I am sure you are,' he agreed. 'But perhaps not in the essentials of a successful marriage.' I could not really take offence at this, however much I felt like doing so, as in that direction I had received no education at all. At least he continued to hold my hands. 'Above all else,' he said, 'a marriage, to be successful, must be based upon mutual respect.' I would have said, mutual understanding – I did not feel up to contemplating mutual love, at that moment – but I was prepared to learn. 'As you swore yesterday,' he went on, 'you are to honour and obey me, as I am to bestow upon you all my worldly goods.' He held up his finger, as I would have spoken. 'The respect engendered by those words, that oath, is implicit. But it depends upon you at all times behaving like a lady, and me behaving at all times as a gentleman. Now, as I am sure you know, a gentleman would never intrude upon a lady, much less his wife, in matters of a private or, ah, carnal nature. That is, it is not my province ever to watch you dressing or undressing, or to inquire either what you wear beneath your gown or into your, ah, bodily functions Any more than it is your province to inquire into mine. As for, ah, touching one another's private parts, the idea is quite unacceptable.'

My growing confusion was trembling on the brink of anger and, instead of attempting to reply, I posed a question of my own. 'Are we not then to consummate our union?'

'The words you use. You do not have to tell me where you got them, and your most peculiar ideas.' I stared at him, open-mouthed. I could not believe that he had somehow learned of Tom. 'It is that despicable woman, is it not?' If my mouth now closed, it was in consternation. He could not possibly be referring to Steely! 'I really feel that your dear mother deserves a measure of censure for exposing you to her vulgarity so often and for so long. Still, that is behind you now. I shall not hold it against you, because I know it is not your fault. But I would take it very kindly if you were to desist from visiting Holkham in the future, except in my company.'

And that was never likely to happen, certainly in view of the contempt in which he was held by Grandpa. My initial reaction to his homily was again one of anger, as I finally realized of whom he was speaking: for all her recent airs, I still counted my step-grandmother as my closest female friend. At the same time, and entirely to my discredit, my ability immediately to assess a situation had me realizing that here was a quick and easy way out of the dilemma in which I had inadvertently placed myself; and I could assuage my conscience by reminding myself that Anne herself had not cared who she offended, and had not even confided her plans to me when she seduced Grandpa into marrying her. So I contented myself with saying, 'I am sure she meant well.'

'I doubt that,' he remarked. 'It is my experience that older women who debauch the minds of young girls invariably do so for an ulterior motive, or for their own amusement.'

I could have reminded him that far from being an 'older' woman, Anne was only three years my senior. But I did not. At that moment I conceived it to be my sole duty to rescue my marriage by agreeing with my husband in all things, even if I was beginning to realize that he was a pompous prig. The idea that I was now committed to spending the rest of my life at his side should have appalled me, but I have always been one for putting first things first; and in this regard I was now reassured, as he said, 'As for the consummation, why that should take place as soon as possible. Whenever you are in a proper frame of mind.'

'Oh, I am now,' I said eagerly. 'I promise not to offend you again.'

He ruffled my hair. 'I know you shall not. But the urge is not upon me at this time. Never fear, it shall be done.'

Looking back, I am astonished that I did not leave his bed and board there and then. But I did not even consider it. Quite apart from the scandal that would have ensued, and which I did not then feel I could inflict upon Mama and Papa, I had, although Edward might consider that I had been exposed to bad influences as a girl, in fact been very strictly brought up in the things that mattered most. A woman's duty was to marry and bear her husband children, and to remain at his side through thick and thin. A simplistic view, to be sure, but all of our views are formed by example and experience. Apart from Mrs McKenzie's lecture, I had the example of my own parents as the ultimate in wedded bliss. I had never doubted that I would be similarly blessed; and if my own marriage had got off to a shaky start, I equally never doubted that it could be put right, even if to do so would mean suppressing a most urgent part of my nature. Whether I should have been so meekly subservient had I then known the truth of my wedding night, I cannot say. For I later learned that while Edward's mores could not accept that his wife might have carnal thoughts and that she might ever seek to turn such thoughts into deeds, he had nevertheless been aroused by my beauty and my ardour. Feeling that he could not at that moment indulge his passion with me, he had, after leaving me, gone downstairs and assailed a parlour maid. Presumably the mere fact that he was a lord made her accept her rape without demur, but it had been that exhausting encounter that had left him unable to do his duty as a husband the following morning.

No doubt fortunately, I did not discover this fact for some considerable time, not that there was a great deal I could have done about it – a husband's peccadilloes being entirely acceptable to society, whereas a wife's are regarded as outrageous. In any event, by the time I learned of that unsavoury incident our marriage was already over.

But first, the consummation. This was at once painful and embarrassing, for me. The pain was inescapable, but my embarrassment was caused by his. Being resolved to do only what he required, I had simply to lie on my back and keep as still as possible. Once I was thus arranged, and after he had kissed me once or twice, entirely chastely, he moved down the bed and folded my nightgown across my waist. I could not believe that he could look upon so much beauty and not at least wish to touch it, but he revealed no desire to do so, apart from spreading my legs, very slowly and carefully and hesitantly, while I endeavoured not to precede him. Then he was inside me in a great plunge. Naturally, in view of the total absence of any precoital sexual stimulation, not even a passionate kiss, I was quite unprepared for this operation and let out a piercing scream. Hence my embarrassment – firstly because I felt it would put him off, and secondly because I had no doubt that my inadvertent protest must have been heard throughout the hotel, and possibly throughout Brighton as well.

My first apprehension was entirely unfounded. Far from being deterred, my husband continued ramming away with the greatest energy, emitting quite animal-like grunts. Well, I was making various noises myself, though they were all of discomfort. Edward, however, when he had climaxed – it seemed to take a very long time – rolled off me and lay on his back with every aspect of pleasure and indeed victory. He even kissed me again, on the cheek, to be sure, but nonetheless a gesture of affection. My second apprehension was certainly realized, at least as far as the hotel was concerned, but in a totally different manner to my expectation. When I finally ventured from our bedroom, I was greeted with smiles and even congratulations on every side. Lucy summed up the whole affair by saying, 'Well, it all turned out all right, then, Miss . . . ma'am.'

Had I been the sort of woman Edward intended that I should be, I would now have been vouchsafed a very pleasant existence. My husband was a wealthy man; and being a profoundly honest one, when he had reminded me that he had sworn to bestow upon me all his worldly goods he had meant just that. I found myself with virtually inexhaustible credit at my disposal, mistress of a fine house, admittedly only a fraction the size of Holkham, and indeed even smaller than Forston, but amply large enough and beautifully appointed. Nor did I have to lift a finger in its operation. Edward had a most efficient housekeeper, Mrs Blundell, who – far from resenting the arrival of a new mistress, as we are told is so often the case – seemed delighted with me and every-thing about me. Moreover, she allowed me full rein, when I was in the mood, to do or go or command or require whatever, whenever and wherever I wished, quietly and discreetly resuming control when I lost interest – and when need be reversing my more outrageous inclinations, always with such good-humoured deference that I could never take offence, and indeed usually accepted that she was right.

Mrs Blundell's province was within the house. Outside it I was even more my own mistress; and this, after what appeared in retrospect to have been a lifetime of Steely, was bliss. Given my bottomless purse and, though it makes me blush to confess it, my tendency to extravagance, my days were spent moving from emporium to emporium, being fitted for dresses here and boots or slippers there, trying on hats and purchasing half a dozen at a time . . . Well, there was not much else to do. True I had my pets, but riding Wonder or playing with Gibraltar or feeding Turpin or walking the dogs could not possibly occupy the entire day; and the time I spent practising with my pistols was the only one of my pastimes that brought direct criticism from my husband. 'Are you anticipating having to fight a duel?' he inquired.

More importantly, he never criticized my dress sense, such as it was, and when I went shopping I was able to indulge my taste for colour and what our French cousins might have called *avant-garde* costumes. As long as I remained at Roehampton, there was no one to criticize my taste. Even Mama, when she came to visit shortly after we returned from honeymoon, dared do no more than raise her eyebrows. I doubt that Edward ever actually noticed what I was wearing sufficiently to form an opinion, and he never questioned any of my accounts.

Mama, of course, wise in the ways of the world, immediately discerned that I was not as happy as I had clearly expected to be, but I assured her that I was. And she accepted this, adding her wish to be informed the moment I became pregnant, this being regarded as the ultimate test of the success of a marriage. Well, chance would have been a fine thing. Edward had worked out a pattern for his sex life, as he did for everything else; and having, in his eyes, overindulged on our honeymoon, when we had copulated on no fewer than six occasions over the fortnight, he now visited my body once in every ten days. I assume he made the required notations in his diary, so as to ensure he did not miss a date. Mad, passionate love! Moreover, I was well aware that even these sacrifices were governed entirely by his desire for an heir. Well, I certainly wanted to become pregnant as rapidly as possible, if only to alleviate the tedium of my existence, but with such limited encounters a positive outcome seemed unlikely. I had to remember that my predecessor had never conceived, either.

It would have been insipid of me not to seek an answer to my problem, and reflection could lead me in only one of two directions. To all intents and purposes I was the perfect wife. I did not upset the existing household arrangements; I got on well with the servants; I occupied my time without impinging on my husband's; that I was extravagant was only to be expected in a woman (without ever actually putting his finances under any strain); and when we were in bed together I behaved exactly as he wished, performing like a well-stuffed dummy. Yet he clearly did not love me. The reason for this had to be either that – as had been alleged of his brother-in-law – he was a homosexual who had taken a wife simply for convention's sake, or that he was still in love with his first wife.

The first of these two possibilities I refused to accept, I am sure correctly: not even the worst of Edward's many enemies ever brought that charge against him. The second I soon deduced to be the case. No doubt this realization should have served as a cue to model my dress and behaviour on the fair Octavia. But sadly, it had quite the reverse effect: I found myself hating the woman, not only for cluttering up my prospects but because, judging by her portraits which remained scattered about the house, she had not been half as handsome as I; thus for our joint husband to prefer her memory to my reality I found insulting.

However, during this first winter of my married life I no more considered the possibility of committing adultery than I considered the possibility of flying to the moon. Had I wished, the opportunities were already there. Having returned from Brighton in time for the opening of Parliament, my husband plunged into his real pleasures, the joys of political debate and the temptations of political advancement; his great desire, in the first place, was to be made Foreign Secretary, the position filled so famously by his unhappy brother-in-law. Thus I rarely saw him during the day, and often enough was left alone far into the night as well. But even had I been inclined to put these empty hours to positive use, I lacked, shall I say, the wherewithal. When we entertained, which was not very often, it was always fellow politicians and their wives. I did my best to play the gracious hostess, and there can be no doubt that the men found me very easy on the eye, but they and their wives, being Edward's friends, and thus all considerably older than me, were inclined to regard me as a child (which I suppose I was) and to consider my attempts at bright conversation – confined principally to the doings of my pets and liberally larded with perhaps gooey nicknames (a weakness of mine) – as frivolous. As for going out, when Edward could spare the time from the House, we moved in the same limited circle. Our visits to the theatre were rare, as Edward found it boring; and when we did go, although no doubt I attracted many an admiring gaze, I was more interested in the play than the audience and found the constant conversation in our box – as often as not on the subject of politics – an irritant, and thus constantly irritated our guests in turn by requiring them to 'Sssh!'. The general opinion seemed to be that my demeanour would improve with age.

I repeat, I had absolutely no ambition at that time other than to be a good and loyal wife and, if possible, mother; but once the initial pleasure of being free of restraint and able to indulge my passion for shopping wore off, I realized that I was confronting a very wearisome existence. This was brought home to me most forcibly at Christmas, when we attended Lady Londonderry for an entirely sober and vastly over-religious holiday, during which I was taken aside by my mother-in-law once removed, as it were, for a private conversation in the course of which she informed me that the nickname I had devised for my husband – 'Ouzey' – was *quite* unseemly. The only cheerful note in the whole proceedings was provided by the new Marquess of Londonderry – like Castlereagh, named Robert Stewart – a man not greatly older than myself, and a fund of fun and laughter. When I reflected on the festivities that would be going on at Holkham, I wept. But Christmas became a memory as we endured winter, and looked forward to spring, with no very positive expectation as far as I was concerned – until at the beginning of June I received a letter from Lady Oxford.

I opened it with no great interest, as since Mama's revelations I was not at all sure of my feelings towards a woman who had so happily ventured where I had dreamed of going, nor was I greatly concerned by its contents, even if they were flattering enough:

> *My dear Lady Ellenborough, you do us no good by remaining locked away in that dismal place. London needs you! Why do you not join us on Wednesday, at Almack's? There will be dancing. Any time after eight will do. Yours ever, Jane Harley.*

I was flattered more by the intimate form of address than by the invitation, and I had an immediate reflection that getting more closely acquainted with her might gain me some insight into what Byron, who remained the outstanding romantic attachment of my life to that point, had actually been like. But I could not imagine Edward, a lifetime Tory, being likely to want me to cultivate a friendship with a Whig hostess. Nevertheless, I showed him the invitation – and was utterly surprised. 'I never knew you had an acquaintance with Lady Oxford,' he remarked.

'She is a friend of my mother's,' I explained.

'Of course. Yes, that would be it. Well, I am sure you will enjoy yourself.'

I gaped at him. 'You mean we will accept?'

'No, no. *You* will accept, my dear.'

'I don't understand.'

'Almack's,' he explained, 'is probably the most frivolous place in London, if not the country. It is where people who have nothing better to do, meet, and converse, and drink, and dance, to be sure.'

'Well,' I said, 'if you so disapprove . . .'

'It is also the apogee of London society, and the apogee of Almack's society is the Wednesday-night ball. It is a place for you to be seen.'

I could not believe my ears. 'And you do not object?'

'Not at all.'

'But . . . alone?'

'You will not be alone. I shall drop you at the door, the carriage will return for you, and when you are inside you will be looked after by Lady Oxford and, I am sure, by dear Mama.'

I knew this was how he referred to his ex-mother-in-law, and was more astonished yet. 'You mean that Lady Londonderry attends these balls?'

'My dear girl, Mama runs the place. I think the outing will be good for you.'

And for your ambition, no doubt, I thought. The beautiful Lady Ellenborough out on the town, even if as the protégé of a Whig hostess. Or, perhaps, *because* I would be the protégé of a Whig hostess. Edward was well aware that his failure, as he saw it, to travel as fast and climb as high as quickly as he wished was in a large part due to the dislike held for him by many of his parliamentary colleagues, and by everyone on the opposition benches. This was his opportunity to show the world that however vehement his Tory principles might appear while in the House, he could be as broad-minded as any man in his private life. But I was in no mood to consider that, nor to consider whether or not Lady Oxford might have an ulterior motive in taking up the wife of a Tory minister (Edward had recently been made President of the Board of Trade) or wonder why the invitation had come from her, and not from Lady Londonderry. I was being set free, if only for one evening, and intended to make the most of it. And so, if I may borrow a phrase from Julius Caesar, I went, I was seen, and I conquered.

My first appearance at Almack's was a nerve-racking experience. I had only recently turned eighteen; and though I was a wife of more than six months, my married state had not done a great deal for my confidence – rather the reverse. Throughout my admittedly short life to that point, I had relied on my beauty and my passionate approach to living to see me through all crises and carry me over all obstacles; but Edward had demonstrated that those two supreme natural gifts were unwanted, and indeed to be rejected or at least disguised in his company. In addition, I now found myself adrift in a world of innuendo and double meaning. My fears that the new friends I was about to meet would all be prigs proved groundless, but Almack's was the home of something far worse – hypocrisy.

Unaware of all of this, and wishing that I could make my entry on Edward's arm, I was not reassured by his parting words as I left our carriage (he was of course on his way to a political meeting): 'Enjoy yourself, my dear. Carpenter will return for you at midnight.' As if I were indeed a child, or at least Cinderella. Thus I entered the lower portals alone, and encountered a veritable army of footmen and major-domos, who regarded me with some suspicion. I presented my card. 'Kindly convey that to the Countess of Oxford, if you please,' I said in my most haughty tone.

There was a brief exchange of glances, a nod, and one of the footmen took the card and hurried off, the chief flunkey – having looked at the card himself before handing it on – unbending so far as to say, 'If I may take your coat, milady.'

I divested myself of my coat, and felt even more exposed, for other people were arriving, some of whose faces were familiar from last summer's parties, but who seemed uncertain whether to greet me or not. I was seriously considering abandoning the whole venture and seeking a cab to take me home, when I was accosted by a hearty 'Aurora, by all that's holy!' – and turned to face my cousin George.

I'm afraid I goggled at him, not only in surprise at seeing him at all in such a place but equally at seeing him in such a dress – for he wore knee breeches and silk stockings, like any of the footmen. 'George,' I inquired, 'whatever are *you* doing here?'

'I am attending the ball,' he replied somewhat stiffly. And – as he could not help but notice the way I looked at his garb – added, 'I'm dressed as required by Lady Jersey.'

I goggled at him some more, as although I knew that the Countess of Jersey had once been a mistress of King Prinny, that had been a long time ago, and I had never heard of even a royal mistress instructing an officer in the Army on how to dress. George, I should explain, had recently been promoted to colonel, the early age at which he attained such a rank being due to his father's money and influence. But further conversation was prevented by the return of my footman, who bowed most obsequiously and said, 'The Countess of Oxford begs you to join her, milady.'

This left George speechless, and all the other onlookers within earshot, who included several of the waiting new arrivals. I smiled at them all and followed the footman up the huge, wide staircase, aware of the approaching sounds of both music and much movement and conversation. Arriving at the top, I beheld a huge room crowded with men and women, all the ladies dressed in the height of fashion and all the men wearing the apparently obligatory knee breeches. I now found myself standing beside a most superior major-domo, who held both my card and a staff. The staff he banged on the floor, while holding up the card to shout in stentorian tones, 'Milady Jane Elizabeth Law, Lady Ellenborough.'

The music stopped, heads turned, I suspect with indifference at first, and then there was actually a moment of total silence while the throng took me in. I was wearing one of my newest purchases, a gown of red and dark-blue silk – very military colours – with a décolletage deep enough to expose as much of my now very well-developed bosom as was respectable. A pearl choker surrounded my throat, and I wore several rings. I knew I made a striking figure, but I could not help but feel very much like a Christian about to be hurled to the lions, and again had a strong impulse to turn and flee. But at that moment I saw Lady Oxford approaching me, as elegantly beautiful as always, and with a most

welcoming smile on her face. 'My dear Lady Ellenborough,' she
said. 'Jane, how good of you to drop by!' – as if I had indeed
done just that, on the spur of the moment, while on my way to
some much grander entertainment.

An immediate confirmation of my acceptance was supplied by
the major-domo, who pressed a dance card into my hand.

Such a greeting, from such a woman, naturally made my
evening, but there were still ordeals to be endured. Before I could
join the dancing I had to be presented to the five other ladies
who, one might say, managed the Wednesday-night balls, although
they preferred to be regarded as patronesses. Lady Londonderry
I already knew, and Lady Sefton did not make a great impression on me. Formidable females as they were, they were nothing
compared with the Countess of Jersey, a woman whose amorous
past had long vanished with, presumably, the beauty that had
inspired it, but whose word was absolute law in London society.
It was she who once had the temerity to turn the Duke of
Wellington away from one of the balls because he was wearing
trousers instead of breeches. I may say that such a snub, which
would have ruined a lesser man, had had no effect whatsoever
on either the morale or the social standing of the victor of
Waterloo, who had fought so many successful battles, both on
the field and in the bedroom; but it had certainly enhanced Lady
Jersey's reputation.

Second to her was Lady Cowper, who everyone knew was a
one-man woman. Unfortunately the man was not her husband,
but an up-and-coming politician named Henry Temple, who had
succeeded his father as Lord Palmerston at the early age of
eighteen and who, unlike Edward, was to achieve all his ambitions and become both Foreign Minister and then Prime Minister.
Moreover, he even eventually married his lady love (both Lord
Cowper and Lady Palmerston having by then died), a fine example
of constancy – I cannot say faithfulness, for it was well known
that he went through countless other women while continuing
his liaison with Lady Cowper. I flatter myself that I would have
been as faithful as Lady Cowper, had I been able to find the right
man in England. But I would never have been able to accept
Palmerston's peccadilloes.

Then there was Princess Esterhazy, wife of the Austrian

ambassador, another fading beauty but one who was still in full practice, one might say (it was reputed that throughout every day her lovers arrived, in strict succession, at her door on the hour). The sextet – an appropriate word – was completed by Countess Lieven, wife of the Russian ambassador, the youngest and most attractive of the lot, if we except Lady Oxford. She was also the most arrogant, and is reputed to have once declared, 'It is not fashionable, where I am not.'

All of these *grandes dames* greeted me with affection and compliments, so far as I could judge. I was still too young and innocent to understand the *double entendres* and hidden meanings with which their conversation was larded. Thus when Princess Esterhazy gushed, 'My dear, you are so beautiful. And that dress, oh, it so takes the eye! What colours!', I did not realize that what she was actually saying was, 'Well, here's a pert little floozie, and that dress, with its garish colours, is more suited to the stews than a ballroom.' However, Lady Oxford seemed well enough pleased with my reception, and I was turned loose to dance; and thereupon put every female nose in the place quite out of joint, as men converged on me from every quarter of the room to fill my card. I was quite overwhelmed, and more important, inebriated with the attention and compliments, and with being constantly passed from one pair of arms to another, something I had not enjoyed since before my marriage. But I was no longer a seventeen-year-old virgin and, excited as I was, found my thoughts wandering far beyond the pleasures of a man's arms. It was at this juncture George finally got his hands on me: he had been slow to join the throng, and there was only one premidnight dance left when he did so. But now at last he held me in his arms. 'Who's the belle of the ball, then?' he asked as we waltzed. 'But then, you have always been the belle of every ball you ever attended.'

'Do I denote a touch of envy, sir?' I asked.

'Never of you, my dearest cousin. Only of those louts who preceded me.'

At that moment, the music stopped and we were forced to release each other. Also, the clock struck twelve. 'I must go,' I said.

'Are you about to turn into a pumpkin?'

'My carriage is waiting, sent by Edward.'

'Ah. When will I see you again? Will you be here next week?'

'I cannot say. But . . .' He was so handsome, and an old friend as well as a cousin. And I was so lonely. Might he not be the friend, the intimate, I so desperately wanted and needed? I drew a deep breath, still uncertain what I really had in mind, and apprehensive of his response. 'You may call, if you wish.'

'On you at home?'

'Why not?' I was gaining in confidence. 'You are my cousin. I am sure there are family matters that need to be discussed.'

'With your husband, as well as with you, no doubt?'

'Edward is never there during the day,' I said. 'Can you not spare the time from your military duties?'

I awoke the next morning in a considerable tizzy. This was partly caused by the amount of champagne I had consumed the previous night, and partly by the excitement of that night, the people I had met, the swathe I had cut. But my seething mind was mostly concerned with my invitation to George. Of course I had done nothing, yet. But I had set in motion a possible train of events that could only have one outcome. Did I dare? Would I be damned for ever? From which it may be gathered that I was, indeed, still a child. But last night had given me a glimpse of a life beyond that of the humdrum housewife, and I did not wish to let it go. I was also able to reassure myself that if I was ever going to have an affair with anyone, George had to be the safest man in the world. I knew I could utterly rely on his discretion.

But did I want to have an affair? What of my marriage? And Edward? I was suddenly stricken by pangs of conscience. When I considered my marriage dispassionately, I could see it was a vast mistake, at least from my point of view. But I had no idea whether loveless, or sexless, marriages were the norm rather than the exception. As Mama had never discussed the subject with me, I did not even know if her own relationship with Papa had been sexually warm. True they had had three children, and true they seemed very fond of each other. But might this not have been mere familiarity? I would dearly have loved to have been able to have a heart-to-heart talk with Stepgrandma, but that was not practical unless I visited Holkham – to which I did not suppose Edward would readily agree.

And in any event I did not really trust sharing confidences with Anne, who was an inveterate gossip.

What did seem clear was that I was taking a considerable risk, and that in possibly bringing Edward's name and reputation into disrepute I would be committing at least a social crime of the first order. These feelings were accentuated at breakfast – when he was in the best of humours, expressed the hope that I had had an enjoyable time (although he showed no interest in what I had actually done or who I had met), and then kissed me quite tenderly before departing for Westminster. There could be no doubt that by his own lights he was being the perfect husband, while I was considering being the less than perfect wife. I sat at my desk straightaway to write to George and withdraw my invitation, and was brooding on the wording when the post arrived. There was a letter for me, and I snatched at it, at once hoping and fearing that it might be from him, making the decision for me. Instead it was from Lady Oxford, congratulating me on my triumph and extending an open invitation to all Wednesday-night balls in the future. I was overwhelmed with guilt, as I had to suppose she would not have been so generous had she had the slightest idea of what I was contemplating. Had been contemplating, I told myself, again reaching for my pen – when I heard the sound of hooves, and a moment later the doorbell rang.

I sat absolutely still, unable to move, until there was a rap on my door and Mowlem, our butler, announced 'A gentleman caller, milady.'

It had not crossed my mind that George would respond so promptly to my invitation. I managed to pull myself together, and stood up. Mowlem opened the door. He was a somewhat cadaverous-looking individual at the best of times; now he looked positively sepulchral as he presented his silver salver. I picked up the card. 'Why, it is my cousin, Colonel Anson. Oh, Heaven forbid there has been some family disaster! I must see him.' Why, it may be asked, had my parents not placed me on the stage?

I hurried downstairs, congratulating myself on my stroke of genius which would explain my agitation, all thoughts of guilt forgotten in the excitement of the moment. George was in uniform and looked handsome and dashing – and suitably agitated. 'My dear cousin,' he said. 'I had to come down. My sister . . .'

I held my finger to my lips, which was reasonable enough, as I surely would not wish to discuss a domestic matter in front of the servants. 'Come into the library,' I said. 'And Mowlem, I would be obliged if my cousin and I were not disturbed.'

'Of course, milady.' He took George's shako and cloak and stood to attention as I gestured towards the library door, which I closed as soon as we were inside.

'Is it safe?' he asked.

'My people will obey me,' I assured him, and was in his arms.

Apart from what might be termed the accident of my first embrace with Edward, this was the first passionate kiss I had enjoyed since Tom. Not only was it all the more enjoyable for that, but it kicked my last resolution, and feelings of guilt, right out of the window. We kissed, and kissed, and kissed. And while we did so, his hands roamed over my shoulders and back, and down to caress and squeeze my bottom, before returning to attend to my breasts. As I had not been going out and, up till a few minutes before, had not intended to receive, either, I was not wearing stays, and was thus the easier of access, but while he was exploring me I was unbuckling his sword belt and unbuttoning his tunic. A few minutes of frantic wrestling had me down to my shift and George to his drawers, and a few seconds later my shift was about my shoulders and his drawers were about his ankles.

Now we really could indulge each other to our hearts' content, although I was disappointed by his haste as he laid me on the settee, one leg draped over the back and the other trailing on the floor, while he knelt between. This gave me only a few further seconds of holding him, feeling the growth between my hands, before it was clear that he urgently needed to be allowed to enter. This he did with no great impetus, but with most satisfying certainty. I may say that our wrestling, brief as it had been, had left me fully ready to receive him, a pleasure I had never known during Edward's tumultuous assaults. If I was disappointed at his climax – which left me feeling that I was on the edge of something tumultuous of my own, without being at all sure if such a goal was there to be achieved, or just a figment of my overwrought imagination – I was nonetheless more satisfied than I had ever been in my life before.

Then we lay together for some moments, stroking and nibbling at each other. 'Oh. Jane, Jane, Jane,' he said. 'I adore you. What a tragedy it is that we should be cousins!'

'I think it is probably a good thing,' I argued. 'If we were married, you would soon tire of me.'

'I could never tire of you,' he said. 'No man could ever tire of you.'

'You don't know my husband very well,' I suggested. 'I think he tired of me before we had consummated our marriage. But there is no need for you to tire of me.'

He sat up. 'You mean we can meet again?'

'I sincerely hope so.'

'Here?'

'I do not think that would be wise. There is a limit to how many family crises you could possibly need to discuss with me. Do you not have rooms in town?'

'Yes.'

'Excellent. I come up to town most days.'

'But I am not often there during the day. I have my military duties.'

'Well, you will have to forego your duties, for at least one afternoon a week.'

He kissed me. 'And there are always Wednesday nights.'

'Only for dancing,' I reminded him.

Thus I committed adultery, after less than a year of marriage, and became a fallen woman. My sin was compounded into a crime almost immediately, as I disguised it with a lie. This was neces- sary, as of course all the servants knew of my visitor; and Lucy had only to examine my discarded clothes to deduce what had happened, though as she was entirely in my camp I had no fear of betrayal from that quarter. 'You will never guess what happened today,' I remarked to Edward when he returned that evening.

'Well?' he replied, with his customary lack of interest in my doings.

'My cousin called.'

'Indeed? That was very civil of her. Which one was it?'

'It was not her. It was Colonel Anson. My cousin George.'

'Ah, the soldier.' Thoroughly putting my back up by his faint intonation of contempt. 'I understand that he may be being sent to India. Did he come to say goodbye?'

'No, he did not. He said nothing about being sent to India.' India? Just as I had found him! I felt quite faint. 'He wished to discuss the situation with regard to his sister Anne. Do you know of it?'

'I have heard about it. Something do with a gambling habit, is it not? I do not think it would be in your best interest to become involved.'

'The family is very concerned.'

'I'm sure. However, as far as I am aware, your cousin has a husband, a father and a mother, and, as you point out, several siblings. Should these feel it necessary to go further afield, there are also two aunts, including your own mother, and a grandfather, who appears to be in full possession of at least some of his faculties. I would have supposed that you would be the last person they would turn to. Unless . . .' he actually looked at me. 'You have not been to the tables yourself, I hope?'

I was furious at both his comments and his derogatory reference to Grandpa, but I kept my temper. 'I have no interest in gambling,' I said. At least not with cards, I thought. It was more exciting to gamble with lives – including my own.

My discussion with Edward, confirming as it did my opinion that he was a self-centred bore, quite assuaged my conscience, and I plunged into my affair with George with all the passionate intensity that was my nature. We met at his rooms once a week, while every Wednesday night, at Almack's, we broke the rules by dancing with each other more than once, and whenever we found ourselves at a mutual picnic we usually also managed to find ourselves together, and more often than not, alone. We also managed to ride together in Hyde Park often enough. This was a heady period for me, as apart from my illicit romance, my emergence into the public eye, whether at Almack's or on Rotten Row, attracted a great deal of attention; and when I went shopping I actually, on occasion, found myself looking at portraits of myself in the windows, done by uncommissioned artists and therefore from a distance, but quite good, and always flattering, likenesses nonetheless. When I remarked that I could not understand anyone wishing to purchase a portrait of me, I was assured that they sold like hot cakes.

I was concerned that Edward might find this offensive; but on the contrary he seemed delighted, just as he seemed delighted at the way I had suddenly sprung to life, as it were. It never occurred to him that there could be any other reason for my metamorphosis than my acceptance of married life; and it suited him very well to have as his wife the most talked about beauty in London – and, so far as he knew, for no reason other than her extreme beauty. However, others were not so unobservant, and as the summer drew to an end I received an invitation to take tea with Lady Oxford.

The Mother

Although I always attended the balls as Jane's guest, we had never done more than exchange greetings and mutual admiration. Now I considered this invitation as merely an end-of-season get together. But I was a little taken aback, if decidedly flattered, to discover that we were tête-à-tête. 'Two Janes,' she remarked, realizing my surprise. 'Should we not be the closest of friends? Tell me, my dear, have you had an enjoyable summer?'

'It has been the best summer of my life,' I declared. 'I am so grateful to you.'

'Think nothing of it. I was young once, and even beautiful.'

'You still are,' I insisted.

'That is sweet of you. I meant that I also had to make my way, as a young bride, in a world of which I knew very little, and married to a man who, shall I say, did not entirely appreciate my points of view.' She studied me as she spoke. I drank tea, uncertain how to respond; and realizing that she was not immediately going to obtain a confidence, she went on. 'And what are your plans for the winter? Will you visit Holkham? Or go down to Dorset?'

'Neither, I'm afraid. Edward does not indulge in hunting, or shooting. His heart is in Westminster, and he prefers to be in attendance.'

'That must be very tiresome for you. And perhaps a pity.' She delicately conveyed a piece of cake to her mouth, chewed daintily, swallowed imperceptibly and then laid down the fork. 'One of my most pleasant memories of this summer is of you dancing with your cousin. Colonel Anson,' she added, just in case I had any doubt as to whom she was referring.

'He dances very well,' I agreed, my mind still at ease.

'As do you. And the pair of you – why, there can be no more handsome couple in the kingdom.'

'You are flattering me.'

'Indeed not. That is impossible. I am, perhaps, warning you, if you will not take offence.'

For the first time, I felt all was not well. 'About George? We have known each other all our lives.'

'And that he is as fond of you as you of him is obvious to all. That is my point.' She rested her hand on mine. 'There are too many people with too little to do except to allow their imaginations to speculate on matters which neither concern them nor should interest them. Gossip is like the Hydra of fable, and every time it touches the ground it grows another head. Thus, you see, if Lady Ellenborough dances several times a night, night after night, with Colonel Anson, it follows that they must be having an affair. Please forgive me, I have only your well-being at heart.'

I met her gaze. 'People are saying that I am having an affair with my cousin?'

'They are speculating that it may be so. And, speculation soon turns to gossip, and gossip mysteriously hardens into accepted fact.'

As always, I adopted attack as my best means of defence. 'I assume this gossip originated at Almack's?'

'I'm afraid so.'

'Put about by women who themselves all have lovers. With respect, milady.'

'Please do not take offence,' Jane said again. 'Yes, they all have lovers. Some of them even have several lovers at the same time.'

'And are these affairs not widely known, even by their husbands?'

'Of course. In this day and age it is quite impossible to keep a secret.'

'Then I do not see how anything I might do, whether the rumour is true or not,' I hastened to add, 'can be of the least consequence.'

'The consequence lies in the great difference that exists between you and them.'

I bridled. 'What do you mean? Is there a better family in the land than the Cokes of Holkham?'

'Indeed not. The difference of which I speak is a personal one. They are all mothers, you are not.' I stared at her with my mouth open. 'You see,' she said, 'any society, however corrupt, still needs to live by certain rules. Otherwise all is chaos.' She was starting to sound like Edward. 'Every man, every gentleman, certainly, needs an heir. To inherit his fortune; or in the case of the nobility, his title.'

'I understand that. And I look forward to becoming a mother, believe me.'

'I know you do. The point is, that the first child – certainly the first son – that emerges from your womb, must be without question your husband's. Once a wife has performed that duty, why, then she is welcome to have as many lovers and as many children by those lovers as she chooses.' Her mouth twisted, as she no doubt considered her own situation.

But I was distracted, as a terrible thought crossed my mind. 'What if the wife produces only girls?'

'Then she is a most unfortunate creature. Daughters are sublime, but sons are a necessity. Now, my dear girl, we will drop the subject. I only brought it up to warn you, to beg you, to do nothing rash until after your first, and hopefully happy, confinement. Carry out that one duty successfully, and the world is your oyster.'

She was being so sweet that I almost confessed that she was several weeks too late in outlining the facts of life, or at least the rules of society. I held back, as I could not imagine what her reaction might be. Instead, I again counter-attacked. 'Was that how you found it?'

'Very much so. Sadly, another inescapable rule of society, and indeed of life, is that we all grow old.'

'But you lived life to the full.'

'I was fortunate enough to be able to do so.'

'And Lord Byron? I do so admire his poetry.' I dared not say more than that.

Her mouth twisted again. 'Dear George. Yes, he spent some time with me.'

'At your home?'

'At my country home, yes. The children, as they then were, adored him.'

'And your husband allowed this?' I could not imagine what Edward's reaction might be were George to move into Roehampton, no matter how many previous male children I might have borne him.

'Oh, yes. By then we had reached a very comfortable arrangement. I ran his various homes, hosted his various parties, allowed him the use of my body whenever he wished it and could spare the time – which was not often enough to be a nuisance – and the rest of the time was my own.'

'Was Byron as passionate a man as he appears in his poems?'

'I would say more so. He was perhaps the most passionate man I ever met. He gave me greater pleasure than any other man.' She glanced at me. 'You do understand me?'

'Of course.'

She gazed at me for some moments. 'I don't believe you do.'

My brain was reeling. I sought to stick to essentials. 'Was Lord Byron in love with you?'

She made a moue. 'I do not think so. Love is a word that is far too freely bandied about. He was in love with my body, and perhaps my reputation.'

'Were you in love with him?'

'Certainly not. I was old enough to be his mother. Besides, I knew he only sought me out because he was trying to end his affair with Caro Lamb. Do you know about that?'

'A little.'

'Well, she imagined herself to be in love with him, to the point of hysteria. So her husband, poor Willy Lamb, packed her off to Ireland to get over it. That didn't work, so Byron decided to demonstrate that they had run their course.'

'Did he succeed in putting her off?'

'I would say no. When she learned he was living with me, she sent him a letter in which was a clipping of her pubic hair, and asked for one of his in return.' She laughed. 'We sent her a clipping of mine.'

I was fascinated. This woman had lived on a scale which, not possessing the gift of foresight, I could not imagine myself ever achieving. But now she looked at the clock, somewhat pointedly. 'Good Heavens,' I said. 'I had no idea of the time. I must go. But . . . may I ask one more question?'

'Of course, my dear.'

'Have you ever heard of a woman named Harriette Wilson?'

It was Lady Oxford's turn to stare in consternation. 'How on earth did you come by that name?'

'I heard it mentioned. Do you mean that it is not a real one?'

'Oh, she is real enough. My dear, Harriette Wilson is at present London's most famous courtesan.'

'Oh,' I said. According to Mama, Edward had been known to visit her. But how had Mama learned that?

'You do know what a courtesan is?' Jane asked.

'A woman who offers herself to men for money.'

'That is true. They give themselves airs, charge exorbitant prices, and claim only to sleep with men they choose, and from the top drawer. But they are only one degree above your common prostitute.'

'Oh,' I said again. 'I see. But . . . is not their relationship with their . . . clients, confidential?'

'It should be. But this Wilson is an arrogant bitch. Realizing that her beauty was fading, a couple of years ago she wrote her autobiography. And do you know what she did to enhance the possible sales? She devoted a chapter to each of her more famous or wealthy clients, sent them a copy, and invited them to purchase it for an exorbitant sum, to prevent it being published, of course – thereby revealing their vices to the world.' She laughed. 'She even sent a relevant chapter to the Duke of Wellington. Do you know what he replied? Publish and be damned. One has to admire the man, even if he is a Tory.' I was speechless. Did that mean that Miss Wilson had sent a chapter to Edward, and that he, following the example of his mentor, had snubbed her? But that had to mean that Mama had read the book, or had certainly had a detailed account of it.

I rose, and Jane escorted me to the door. 'Again, I must ask you, dear Jane, not to take offence at anything I have said. I wish you only happiness and success.'

'Thank you. May I . . . ask one last question?'

She smiled. 'One.'

'Have you ever been in love? I mean, the sort of love for which you give up everything, regardless of the consequences.'

Another twist of the lips. 'I have never been that fortunate.'

'And if you had been?'

'As you say, for that sort of love one would give up everything. I would have certainly. But Jane, little Jane . . .' – though I was taller than she! – 'you must be sure, and so must he. Otherwise the consequences could be unthinkable.'

I count that conversation as one of the most important in my life. It entirely changed my earlier estimation of her. Now I considered Jane Harley to be the most successful woman I had ever met – the most successful at being a woman and whether I intended to take her advice or not, I knew I would never forget it. Equally did I increasingly regret not having had the courage to tell her that I had already broken the rules by which she, and all polite society, lived. Much as I adored her, I understood that she had reached an age where, as personal experience was perhaps no longer available to her, interference in the lives of others – especially of a protégé, as she certainly considered me – was the next best thing, and therefore remained apprehensive of the consequences of such a revelation. And I was even more apprehensive that I might damn myself in her estimation.

But what she had suggested left me in a state of considerable agitation. Just as her warning had me in a state of some apprehension. Obviously, common sense told me I should give up George, at least until after I had borne a child for Edward. But I had no idea how long it might be before that occurred – and if I gave up George I might never get him back, just when I had had a Pandora's Box of pleasures opened before my eyes. In his arms I had had inklings of ecstasy. Give him up? That I could never do, whatever the risks. Besides, it was not in my nature.

However, as is often said, man – or in my case, woman – proposes and God disposes. Or perhaps, more accurately, our plans are always at the mercy of other people's, of which, all too often, we are quite unaware. I saw very little of George that winter, which he largely spent away from London, either at various house parties or engaged in military manoeuvres; nor was he available very often throughout the next year. Indeed, his appearances at Almack's became so rare that I began to wonder if Aunt Anne Margaret had been lecturing him, just as Jane Harley had lectured me.

In fact, this was about the most boring summer of my life, as conversation was concerned entirely with the apparently vital question of whether Parliament should be reformed – either by enlarging the franchise or redistributing the seats to give more representation to growing cities like Manchester and Birmingham, at the expense of the so-called rotten boroughs, which might, through emigration and natural wastage, have shrunk to an electorate of a dozen men. Needless to say, Edward's Tory friends were against any change in the system that had kept them in power for so long, but they were aware that there was a rising tide of public opinion of which they would, eventually, have to take heed.

As I, being a woman, did not have a vote, and was not going to have one no matter what reforms might eventually be implemented, I was more concerned with my own problems – as by the end of the summer it was clear that George was avoiding me and, lacking information, it seemed to me obvious that he must have moved his affections elsewhere. I went through agonies of uncertainty, compounded by jealousy and frustration. Now that Pandora's Box had been opened, I desperately needed someone to fill it.

The great ladies of Almack's were not the only people exchanging points of view regarding me, and what I might or might not be doing. I later learned that Edward was approached by more than one of his friends with the suggestion that he pay a little more attention to his wife. These approaches were always rebuffed. Continuing to regard me as a child, Edward was certain that my overenthusiasm – as he saw it – on my wedding night had been a result of suggestions made by Step-grandma Anne, who he continued to regard as a debauched woman. Thus I was left to mope, and my discontent was augmented when, at the end of the summer, I received a visit from my cousin Henry Anson. Henry was altogether different to his brother. For whereas George was all dash and ambition, Henry was much quieter. And yet he was also all for doing the unusual, as he now confided to me.

He was accompanied by his friend John Fox-Strangeways, the Earl of Ilchester's son, and they were both in a state of high excitement. 'Papa has at last given us permission,' Henry announced, 'and we are off to see the world – Palestine, Syria, the desert . . .'

I nearly exploded with envy.

'Petra!' he continued. 'The Rose-Red City. It is supposed to be the eighth Wonder of the World.'

'But . . .' Fox-Strangeways put in. 'Can you keep a secret, Jane?'

'Certainly. If I am required to do so.'

'We are actually bound for Mecca,' Henry said.

'Mecca?!' I cried.

'Sssh.' As if all our servants were Arabs!

'You can't go to Mecca,' I said in a lower tone. 'You're not Muslims.'

'We shall be adequately disguised.'

'But if you're found out . . .'

He grinned. 'You mean they'll cut off our prospects?'

'Here, I say,' Fox-Strangeways protested. He did not know me very well.

'That's what they do, don't they?' I asked.

'We'd be eunuchs,' Henry agreed. 'But we are not going to be found out. It's all been very carefully planned. But you see why it has to be a secret? Until we get back home, at least.'

'Then we'll tell everybody, and be famous,' Fox-Strangeways added.

'Does your father know of this?' I asked Henry. 'Or Aunt Anne Margaret?'

'No, no. That's another reason for keeping it secret.'

'They'd forbid you to do anything so crazy. What about George?'

'Oh, never stuffy old George!' They were obviously not *au fait* with current London gossip. 'But we wanted you to know, dear Jane, because if you were a man we're sure you'd be coming with us.'

'Oh, yes,' I said. 'Oh, yes!'

'Then will you wish us good fortune?'

I kissed them both. 'I wish you all the fortune in the world,' I said. 'Do come back safely.'

But the event left me more depressed than ever. They were no older than me, and they were off on a great adventure. If I was aghast at the risks they intended to take, I was totally admiring of their courage and determination, of the way they were intending to broaden their minds, not by the usual aimless grand tour of Europe but by venturing where no Englishman had ever gone before and returned alive. Why, I asked myself, did one have to be a man to adventure? True, women had undertaken such voyages of discovery before – perhaps the most famous being Pitt's niece, Lady Hester Stanhope, who a few years previously had ventured into the wilds of Syria and liked it so much she had remained there, to the astonishment of her compatriots. But Lady Hester had been widely known as an eccentric long before her departure; she was closely connected to the most powerful man in the land; and, most important of all, she had not possessed a husband. My situation was different, on all three counts.

Even Edward could see that I was not my usual ebullient self, and my mood of depression grew after another dismal Christmas at Lady Londonderry's. Thus it was that when early in the new year Step-grandma wrote to inform me that she had just given birth to her third child and that there were great celebrations going on at Holkham, it was Edward who suggested that I might like to revisit my childhood home for a couple of weeks.

I was happy to take advantage of the offer, principally to be able to see Grandpa again, for the first time in three years. But equally I could not help but wonder if George might be there. Needless to say, he was not. In fact, none of the Ansons were there when I arrived. But although all the Digbys were there, I rapidly became aware that a gulf had opened between myself and my family, even between myself and Mama. To make matters worse, Steely – now apparently regarded as one of the family – was also present, as disapproving as ever.

Grandpa, it seemed, was not yet prepared to forgive me – perhaps for my misadventure with Tom Burrows but more, I think, for having married a Tory. And Step-grandma, who certainly seemed pleased to see me, was too full of her newborn to be much company. There was some relief to be found in the other guests, for these positively fawned on me. But they were mostly strangers, friends of Step-grandma's, and I did not find any of them very attractive. I was thus coming to the conclusion that the visit had been a mistake, reflecting sadly that one can never recreate the past, when one morning, a few days after my arrival, I wandered into the library, where I had spent so many pleasant hours as a girl.

★　　★　　★

For a moment I was too surprised to take in more than my immediate surroundings, for the large room was a mass of books. Well, of course, a library is supposed to be a mass of books, but usually neatly arranged on shelves. Today the shelves were mostly empty, and the books were in piles on the floor and all the available tables. It was only after I had stood there for several minutes, staring at the mess, that I discovered I was not alone. From behind one of the piles of books – he had been seated at the table on which they were accumulated – a man stood up and addressed me somewhat censoriously, as he had, apparently, been disturbed by my entry. 'May I ask . . .?' Then he began to take me in. 'I'm afraid we have not met,' he finished.

'My name is Jane Law,' I told him.

'Lady Ellenborough?'

'That too.'

He hurried round the table and threaded his way through the books. 'Milady! Do forgive me!'

'It is for you to forgive me, for interrupting your work. You *are* working?'

'Oh, yes, milady. I am cataloguing the library.'

'You mean you are in my grandfather's employ?' I always like to get my facts straight. 'And have you a name?'

'Madden, milady. Frederick Madden. My friends call me Fred.'

I studied him. He was by no means handsome, but had a very pleasant countenance. Tall and strongly built, he looked more like an athlete than a bibliophile. I liked what I saw. 'I am pleased to make your acquaintance, Frederick.' I extended my hand, and he bent over it. I was not wearing gloves, and his lips actually brushed my flesh. However, I chose not to reprove him. Instead I waited for him to release me, which he seemed somewhat reluctant to do, and then I strolled around the room. 'I imagine this is something that has long needed doing,' I remarked. 'It must be an immense task.'

He was following me. 'It is not the first large library I have been required to put in order.'

I turned to face him. 'This is your profession?'

'I am employed by the British Museum.'

'Ah! And Grandpa obtained you from there?'

'Actually, it was Mrs Coke.'

So Step-grandma was not above a few peccadilloes of her own, although I could not believe that she would ever risk adultery. 'Well, I have interrupted you for long enough. Would you believe that when I used to live here I spent many hours in this room?'

'I would believe it,' he declared. 'I wish I had been here then.' He flushed. 'To assist you.'

I regarded him for some more moments. 'I'm sure you would have been bored.'

'That could never be, in your company . . . milady.'

'You must get on with your work,' I told him, and left him to it.

I had found him pleasant enough, but dismissed him from my thoughts until the next day, when, thoroughly fed up with the company I was being forced to keep, I took myself to the music room and played some of my favourite pieces, from time to time breaking into song, as I was wont to do. And then I became aware that I was not alone. The music room was quite close to the library. 'Oh, dear,' I said. 'I have again interrupted your work, Mr Madden. I do apologize.'

'Your voice is the sweetest I have ever heard,' he said. 'And you play divinely.'

As this was the most fulsome praise, it suggested that we might be approaching a critical stage – and so soon after our first meeting! I ceased playing, and we sat together and talked for a while. I was totally uncertain about how I wished things to go, because such a situation was outside my ken. Even if I had cuckolded my husband, I reflected, it had been with a man I had known all my life, who, throughout that life, had been my favourite male. It could almost be classed as 'unfinished business'. Thus I had never truly regarded it as a sin. Moreover, I had always been certain that there was absolutely no risk of George ever betraying me; and over the months I had lost my fear of pregnancy, as I had always taken the precaution, recommended by Lucy, of thoroughly douching myself every time we shared our bodies.

In contrast, this apparently adoring young man was a complete stranger. To allow him access to my favours would definitely make a mockery of my marriage vows. But I was frustrated, both sexually and emotionally, by my apparent abandonment by George and by my desire to adventure – even if it was only as far as a strange man's body. Besides, it turned out that we were not such strangers after all, or certainly I was not to him. For he had been at Holkham some weeks before my arrival and had heard all about me from the servants, who remembered me, and about those of my escapades of which they were aware.

Before we parted, I promised to lend Frederick Madden my sketching books, and to walk with him in the garden the following day. The books I faithfully delivered, and equally faithfully I presented myself for the walk. But this did not go according to plan, for as we were setting off we were joined by one of the house guests, a Captain Greville, who made himself a perfect nuisance, giving himself airs to establish himself as my equal, while reminding poor Frederick of his humble station.

Perhaps this incident helped to harden my resolve, but it was still a week before I could make up my mind. Partly this was because the house party suddenly became expanded by the arrival, for a brief visit, of most of the Anson tribe – although happily, perhaps, George did not accompany them. However, they wished to spend a good deal of time in my company; and I was happy to be with them, as they had letters from Henry, who seemed to be having the time of his life. Of course, he did not refer to the intended climax of his expedition, but I had no doubt he was going to accomplish his objective.

In addition, any development of my relationship with Frederick was hindered by the antics of Step-grandma, who, whether she had designs on Frederick herself or not, certainly did not wish to see him taken over by her, dare I say it, more glamorous grand-daughter. She had become aware that I had taken up spending some time every day in the library, and that when I repaired to the music room to play every afternoon before dinner I was invari-ably joined. She thus suddenly took a great interest in our young librarian, had him make sketches of herself, myself and various Ansons, and invited him to join us most nights for our after-supper round of cards. Her machinations amused me, as I guessed that her purpose was to embarrass him by playing for stakes he could not possibly afford – intending, no doubt, to graciously refund his losses later on. However, he revealed himself to be a perfect genius, whether it be at écarté or whist. Every time he played, he won.

Nor were her attempts to fill our time any more successful, for we steadily inclined towards each other, finding that we had much in common, at that stage purely intellectually – until the day came when I was bending over his shoulder as he was showing me an illustration in some book or other, and he suddenly turned his head. My head was very close to his, and before we knew it our lips were touching. A moment later, he had turned me round to sit on his lap and was kissing me quite desperately, while his hand roamed over the bodice of my gown – before suddenly withdrawing, to stare at me with startled eyes. 'Milady,' he gasped. 'What have I done?'

'Enough to warrant calling me Jane,' I suggested. 'At least in private. But this is not.' I disengaged myself and stood up, although my knees were quite weak. But Step-grandma had developed a disconcerting habit of suddenly appearing, and to lock the library door would have been a dead giveaway.

'You are angry with me,' he said.

'Not at all,' I assured him, straightening my dress.

'Well, then . . .' He rose also, and came towards me.

I shook my head. 'I have said, this is not sufficiently private.'

'But where is?'

'We shall have to see,' I said.

His kiss had been even sweeter than George's, and I felt quite sure the rest of him would measure up. I understood that with a comparative stranger I really could not look for ecstasy, but I am always the optimist. Thus I set the stage, choosing Saturday night, when I knew that it was Anne's habit to stay up later than usual, so that invariably most of the other guests had gone to bed before she retired. I told Lucy not to wait up for me, as I would undress myself – it is, of course, impossible to have secrets from one's personal maid. Lucy had now been with me for more than two years, my entire married life, in fact; and if she did not know who I had visited in the afternoons during my frequent trips to London two years previously, she certainly knew that I had been visiting someone masculine and that it had not been for the purpose of discussing the state of the nation (sexual relations invariably scatter evidence about). She thus received my instructions with some concern. I do not think she was morally high-minded; but she understood that every time I kicked over the traces the risk to my marriage was great, and she was concerned that if a scandal were to develop she might lose her position.

Everything went according to plan – which was not surprising, as only I knew that there was a plan – and Frederick, as usual, was invited to the card table after supper. I was a little disconcerted when I realized our fourth was to be Mama, but she played for only a couple of hours before retiring, her place being taken by the ubiquitous Greville. At last, at midnight, Anne called a halt, kissed me goodnight, and left the room, as did Greville. I knew that my step-grandmother would be waiting for me at the stairs, so I quickly said, in a low tone, 'Come in half an hour. There will be no one about.' Then I followed behind her. I did not look back to observe Frederick's reaction: I had established the situation, and if he lacked the courage to take advantage of it, he was very unlikely to prove a satisfying companion in bed. Yet as it was too long since I had held a man in my arms (sexual encounters with Edward did not include hugs of affection), I was quite stirred up.

Anne was waiting at the foot of the stairs. We mounted together. 'What did you have to say to our Frederick?' she asked.

'I told him I wished I had his skill at cards.'

'Ah.' We had reached the top. 'Well, I will wish you goodnight, my dear.'

I realized that she no more considered me capable of adultery than I had considered her capable of seduction, and allowed myself a contented smile. She might have taken a gamble beyond the imagination of most girls and scored a great triumph, but I had no doubt who was getting more out of life. I undressed and got into bed, leaving my door unlocked. About ten minutes later the handle was tried, and then opened. I had doused the candles, but there was a good fire in the grate, and the room was an exciting mixture of dark corners and sudden flares of bright light. Frederick came towards the bed, hesitantly, and then discovered that I was sitting up, the sheet folded across my waist, and thus that I was naked. Despite the fire there was a chill in the room, and I have no doubt that I looked most inviting. He sat on the bed beside me. 'Oh, milady,' he said. 'Jane!'

I was in his arms, while his hands roamed in a promising manner. 'I also have my rights,' I reminded him. He released me to undress, while I slid down the bed beneath the covers. His body did not disappoint me and he was most attractively ready for the fray, but once again I was confronted by the masculine curse of haste. Thus after the most cursory caress of my breasts and an even quicker stroke of my buttocks, giving me no time at all to find the object of my desire, he was inside me – and only a few moments later was spent. At least he managed one passionate kiss while doing so. Then he was lying on his back, panting.

I was also panting, but it was more from his weight than any excess of passion. As had happened so often before, I could feel my passion waiting to be released. But not by Frederick, it seemed. And yet . . . he raised himself on his elbow. 'Oh, milady,' he said. 'Jane! I adore you.'

I kissed him. 'Well, then . . .'

'When can we, well . . . do it again? Tomorrow night?'

Presumably he meant tonight, as it was nearly one o'clock. But I was too distracted to be pedantic. 'Why not now?'

'Now? I could not manage it again, now.'

'I know that. But surely in half an hour . . .'

'I must leave.' He was already getting out of bed.

I reached for his hand to bring him back to me, then changed my mind. 'Where are you going?'

'To bed.'

'You are in bed,' I pointed out.

'I meant, my own.'

'Is it a better bed than this?'

'Well, of course it is not, milady. But . . . well, someone may come by.'

Ardour, satisfied, was being overtaken by conscience and apprehension. I knew that to retain him would be useless. 'At least kiss me goodnight,' I suggested.

So, back to the drawing board or, certainly, my own devices. This was most necessary, as my ardour was not in the least satisfied; I had taken a considerable risk, for no gain whatsoever. I slept badly, and awoke in a thoroughly ill temper, so much so that I did not visit the library that morning, nor did I play the piano that afternoon. When Frederick came up to me like a puppy anxious for a stroke, I snubbed him; and I declined to play cards after supper. He was clearly upset, so much so that on the night before I was due to leave Holkham I relented, and allowed him back into my bed. This was at least partly because I feared that if not requited, his passion might lead him into an indiscretion, either by word or deed. Again he reached a seventh heaven in a very rapid space of time, leaving me far behind. He then went through the adoration routine, while again making preparation for a speedy departure. 'You are leaving tomorrow,' he reminded me. 'Will we be able to meet again?'

I nearly asked, whatever for? But I did not wish to hurt his feelings. 'It may be possible. Will you boast of your conquest?'

'Heaven forbid. It is our secret. Will you return to Holkham?'

His assurance was a great relief, if it could be believed. But the best way to make sure of his discretion was a promise of the future. 'I doubt it. At least not this year. When will you complete your work here?'

'I would hope by the summer.'

'And then?'

'I shall return to the museum.'

'Well, perhaps I will visit the museum this summer.' That seemed to satisfy him; and when I made this half-promise I was of a mind to do so, if only for the necessity of keeping our liaison a secret. But circumstances conspired to make sure we never saw each other again.

I had not been back at Roehampton more than a few weeks (I could discover no evidence that Edward had even been aware that I had been away) and summer was still only on the horizon when I, and all the family, were stricken by news of a catastrophe. The news arrived in England in the form of dispatches from the English consulate in Baghdad. Edward told me one day, on returning from Whitehall, 'Oh, by the way, your cousin has got himself killed.' I stared at him in horror, my thoughts naturally first turning to George, although as far as I knew he was still in England. But even in England, constantly engaged in activities such as manoeuvres, soldiers are more prone to accidents than other people. I felt quite faint. Edward, who was busily flicking through the day's domestic post, did not notice and went on speaking. 'You will not credit this, but he and some friend of his, travelling in Arabia, attempted to get into Mecca to view the Kaaba, the shrine containing the sacred black stone.' He raised his head. 'That is the Muslim holy of holies, you may know, and is forbidden to non-believers.'

'Henry!' I said. 'Oh, my God, Henry!'

'That's right. It seems that they had taken the trouble to disguise themselves as Arabs – but incredibly, when they wished to enter a mosque, they neglected to remove their shoes. To enter a mosque with one's shoes on is blasphemy. The people around them took offence and seized them, whereupon their disguise was penetrated, and, well, it all became very unpleasant, if our consul is to be believed.'

'They will have cut off . . .'

'Please,' he protested. 'How do you know about such things?' I burst into tears. 'My dear!' There was actually concern in his voice, and he sat beside me and put his arm round my shoulders.

'My cousin,' I moaned. 'My favourite cousin!' Obviously that was not strictly true, but at that moment I felt it was.

'Oh, my dear, dear girl,' Edward said, actually hugging me, while I sniffled into his coat. Then he stood up, lifting me with him, put his other arm under my knees, and carried me up the stairs and into my bedroom, something I had felt he should have done on our wedding night. I then realized that he intended to remain with me, for when Lucy hurried in he sent her off with a wave of his hand. I have never been able to determine what sparked this sudden show of real affection. Was it the sight of beauty in distress? In which case, I should have gone in for tears long before. Whatever the reason (and even though he did not concern himself with such niceties as undressing – merely removing such garments as were necessary), he gave me the best five minutes of my life to that moment. Indeed, when he had finished and left me, looking somewhat embarrassed, I felt thoroughly ashamed of my behaviour at Holkham, and resolved to make a success of my marriage.

Those five minutes had a further, unexpected, result. Three months later it became evident that I was pregnant.

Sadly, for our marriage to have been the success I sought, one of my cousins would have had to have been brutally mutilated or murdered at least once a month, and there were not enough to go round. Edward was naturally delighted to discover that he was at last going to be a father (it did not seem to occur to him that the responsibility for this not having happened earlier was entirely his) – but, the fact of my pregnancy being established, he moved out of my room and never entered it again with amatory intent.

In justice to him, I am bound to confess that almost immediately after our set-to he became greatly distracted, as the Prime Minister, Lord Liverpool, died. True, Lord Liverpool had never been very important, most of the governing of the country being left in the capable hands of the Duke of Wellington. Still, the death of a prime minister meant at least a cabinet reshuffle, and in this instance the crisis was aggravated by dispute concerning the choice of his successor. Was he to be replaced by the Duke (the obvious choice, so far as the right wing of the Party was concerned) or by George Canning, the darling of the left, a man Edward detested, who had once fought a duel with Castlereagh. The matter was settled by Wellington's decision not to stand, and thus Canning became Prime Minister – to the great distress of Edward, who felt that his future was in doubt. However, his gloomy prognostications did not prevent him from triumphantly informing everyone he could reach of the coming happy event – news which naturally brought Mama hurrying to Roehampton, accompanied by Steely, who seemed determined to resume complete control of my life. Anxious as I was to have nothing go wrong with my pregnancy, I was actually grateful for her company.

Quite apart from his political problems, the presence of various female members of my family of course precluded any intimacy between Edward and myself; and as regards sex, I was quite prepared, such is the uncertainty of the medical profession on the subject, to accept that total abstinence would probably be a good thing during the term of my pregnancy. Thus I spent another very quiet and subdued year, unable to attend Almack's or any of the summer parties, even though I did not really begin to show until the autumn. Clearly, a visit to the British Museum could not be contemplated, even had I had any desire to make it. I knew that Frederick would learn of my condition quickly enough, and put my faith in his obvious good breeding to keep him from attempting to see me or contact me. Nor was my trust misplaced: I never heard from him again.

I did not lack for visitors, who arrived in a steady stream. Lady Londonderry was a regular, as if it was her own grandson hovering on the horizon. I may say that no one gave a thought to the possibility that I might give birth to a girl. Jane Harley also called regularly, hugging and kissing me, and whispering in my ear, 'I am so happy for you!' – her congratulations bearing the veiled suggestion that she had been responsible. Even George came, with his mother, she clad all in black and he wearing a black armband and looking as embarrassed as it was possible to be. With them was John Fox-Strangeways.

He brought with him the truth about what had happened in Arabia – which, if not perhaps so titillating as I had first supposed, was possibly even more horrible. The two boys, for they were hardly more than that, were confined, as were all malefactors in those parts, in conditions of apparently indescribable filth and squalor, fed barely a subsistence diet, and forced to drink water in which a variety of living organisms could readily be discerned. Fox-Strangeways had managed to survive this ordeal, although when finally returned to what we might consider civilization (my personal views on this have changed considerably over the years) he was both ill and weak. Poor Henry had not done so well, and had been so unfortunate as to contract the plague.

The visit of Aunt Anne Margaret and George sent me into a depression all over again, not only because my lively imagination could picture poor Henry lying there in his own filth, certainly dreaming of the happy, carefree and, above all, healthy life he had enjoyed at home, and perhaps even seeing my smiling face before him as he died. I could also see how terribly they were affected by Henry's death. In comparison my own problems seemed very minor, and my spirits were entirely uplifted when, shortly before Christmas, the news arrived of the Battle of Navarino. The Greek War of Independence had now been going on for several years, watched with suspicion by the Great Powers – Britain, Russia and France being no less suspicious of each other than they were of the Turks. The Greeks had got on quite well, until the Sultan called to his aid his nominal vassal, Mohammed Ali, ruler of

Egypt. Ali possessed a first-class army, commanded by his son Ibrahim, one of the leading soldiers of the day. He also possessed a large fleet, which, when combined with the Turkish navy, would undoubtedly be capable of blockading the entire Greek coast. On learning of these developments, which appeared to indicate that the rebellion would be finally crushed, the Powers determined to act together, and the British commander in the Mediterranean, Sir Edward Codrington, was required to 'dissuade' the Turkish-Egyptian fleet from taking action. Codrington had only a small squadron, and although the French and Russian squadrons that joined him were even smaller (I do not believe there were more than thirty ships in all), he entered Navarino Bay on the south-west side of the Morean Peninsular, where the Turkish-Egyptian fleet was anchored. This numbered something over fifty vessels of all sizes, a formidable array. Negotiations were begun, and then a shot was fired; no one seems certain by whom, but within a few minutes every ship was engaged. The Muslims, for all their immense superiority in numbers, were no match for the gunnery of the Allies; and after no more than an hour their entire fleet was annihilated.

Hailed in England as another Trafalgar, this perhaps unnecessary demonstration of Western superiority in weapons and technique put everyone into a fine humour – enhanced in our family when, without the least difficulty, on 15 February 1828 I was delivered of a boy.

By then the political scene had undergone another convulsion. For Canning, who even Edward agreed was a brilliant man and would probably have made a brilliant prime minister, was dead. He had felt duty bound to attend Liverpool's funeral, although this took place in the pouring rain and he was suffering from a streaming cold. The effects of this got to his lungs, and he died in August, after only four months in office. The Duke still being unwilling visibly to take the helm, Canning had been replaced by a nonentity, Lord Goderich, who in turn departed in January, removed from office by request rather than by death, and so at last the Duke had accepted the inevitable and taken over the country. My successful delivery seemed the icing on the cake. Everyone was delighted, and Edward was over the moon. Well, I was quite pleased myself, the more so at the ease with which the often harrowing business had been accomplished. We called him Arthur Dudley after various members of Edward's family. I was assured that I would have the choice of names for our first girl.

I would have liked to feed Arthur myself, but I was told this was unfashionable and could well ruin my figure – so after the babe had been permitted a few tentative sucks, he was removed into the care of a wet nurse, and then into the supervision of two nannies. He was presented to me for a hug and a kiss every evening at six, immediately before he was bathed and put to bed. Again, these were not ceremonies at which I was expected to attend. But I did not really find anything strange about this; I had been brought up in the same way, and I knew this applied to every other upper-class household in the land. Parents brought their children into the world, provided them with the best education in the best surroundings they could afford, and which they considered appropriate according to their lights, whether inspired by religion or politics or both, and expected their sons to grow up to be leaders of the nation, or the Army, or the Church. Praise was never offered or expected; tenderness was regarded as weakness, and once children were out of the cradle parental love was considered debilitating to the spirit. Those who reached the top of their respective trees, or close enough, were respected. Those who fell by the wayside were mourned, but not excessively; those who fell from grace morally were expelled from the family circle and thereafter shunned.

Girls were treated only a shade less harshly. They were not allowed to interfere in the governing of the country – or the Church – just as it was unthinkable that they should ever risk stopping a bullet in its defence. But their social code was just as strict. Their duty was to achieve just sufficient education to manage a household, host a dinner party, and bear their husbands children, or certainly an heir – but as infant mortality was a considerable problem, it was generally regarded as safer to have a clutch. That there were quite a few women of wealth and position who, as Jane Harley had explained to me, indulged in extramarital activities of a most scandalous nature was known by everyone but admitted by no one – at least not publicly, and thus there was no scandal.

It was my misfortune, as my critics would have it, but my great triumph, as I would have it, to cut through this fog of hypocrisy and whispered gossip as a soldier might cleave his enemy to the bone, to break every one of the rules of traditional behaviour, to be cast out by the society into which I had been born, doomed – as they saw it – to a life of darkened rooms and scurrilous gossip . . . and to triumph!

The Prince

But I must not let myself get carried away. Whatever I was going to achieve, I had no knowledge of it when I celebrated my twenty-first birthday on 3 April 1828. At that moment, filled with domesticity and an anticipation of a rejuvenation of my marriage, I wished only to be a successful wife and mother, and to put the follies of the past few years, as far as possible, behind me.

In honour of the occasion, Edward threw a dinner party. As always, the guests were mainly from the Tory establishment, but as I was to be the guest of honour he was kind enough to allow me to invite some guests of my own. My first thoughts inclined towards my parents and brothers, but when Mama discovered that they would be sitting down with a clutch of Tories and their wives she declined (the reform debate was growing very hot and some of the exchanges positively vituperative), while expressing the hope that I would be able to join the family for a private celebration at a future date. Thus abandoned, as it were, I sent an invitation to Jane Harley. I knew she was a profound Whig, but I also knew she was not the woman to be put off by other people's opinions, however strongly expressed. As I had hoped, she graciously accepted.

The occasion was a great success, even if I had little to do with it save look beautiful and smile at everyone, as Mrs Blundell saw to all the details. But I know I filled my role to perfection, with diamonds in my hair and round my neck, a low-cut gown offering a glimpse of my now considerable bust, accentuated as it was by the presence of so much unwanted milk, which had to be squeezed out every day. I had no doubt that all our guests felt that Edward was the most fortunate man in the kingdom, though subsequent events lead me to doubt whether he shared the common view.

However, Jane Harley perceived the true character of our

marriage. 'He is a cold fish, isn't he?' she remarked when after dinner we were at last able to share a tête-à-tête.

'Well,' I said. 'It is his manner.' I could hardly take umbrage at such an accurate statement.

'Absolutely, I have seen him in the House. Still, he must be a proud man, even if he chooses not to reveal it. Now tell me, my dear, when are we again going to see you at Almack's? It has been so long.'

'Well,' I said again. 'I doubt I shall attend for a while. There is so much to be done here . . .' I paused, because she was gazing at me with a half-quizzical, half-amused expression.

'My dear,' she said, 'I had no idea. You have no housekeeper?'

'Well, of course I have a housekeeper,' I protested.

'But she is incompetent? Or do you suspect her of dishonesty?'

'Good lord, no. Mrs Blundell is a paragon.'

'I see.' She tapped her teeth with her fan, as if confused. 'Ah! You have no nurse for little Arthur?'

'I have two nurses for Arthur.'

'I see. Well . . . you are pregnant again?'

'For Heaven's sake! It is only two months since my delivery.'

'That is not a total defence. But I agree, you could hardly know as yet. Then, you are expecting to become pregnant again, in short order.'

'Well . . .' I blushed.

'I congratulate you. But Almack's has not been the same without you, this last year. Should anything occur to change your mind . . .' She smiled and squeezed my hand. 'Or perhaps I should say should anything *not* occur to change your mind. You know you are always welcome. Remember what I told you – now that you have done your duty and given your husband an heir, the world is your oyster.'

I almost weakened and confessed to her that she was nearly three years out of date – if only for the pleasure of seeing her expression – but I again resisted the temptation. 'You are very kind,' I said. 'But I think it is time we rejoined the others.'

I had no intention of accepting her invitation, resolved as I was not to sin again. But my resolve depended upon Edward, and it ended that very night. It was two o'clock when the last of our guests departed. Edward thereupon went into the library for a last glass of brandy, looking vaguely surprised when I followed him. 'I wanted to thank you,' I said. 'It was a most enjoyable party.'

'I thought so,' he agreed. 'Not even the presence of that detestable woman could spoil it.'

That was like a slap in my face, as he had to know that Jane was one of my closest friends. But I did not let it upset me, although I also had had more than enough to drink. 'Now I lack only one thing to make me the happiest woman in the world.' I moved further into the room, closing the door behind me.

'And what is that?' he asked, opening a book.

'The joy of being held naked in your arms.'

He raised his head. 'Oh, really, Jane, the things you come out with.'

'Should I not wish to go to bed with my husband? Do you not wish to share my bed?'

'It is obviously not practical at the moment.'

'Why is that? Oh, I know there may be a little milk scattered about, but surely that will not be an inconvenience.'

'Sometimes you are positively vulgar.'

'I beg your pardon. Will you not at least share my bed, if I promise not to mention sex?'

'My God!'

'I have been vulgar again. I apologize.'

'You have been downright indecent.'

At last my temper burst. 'Well, then,' I said. 'I shall have to go and be indecent by myself.'

I doubt, living as he did in a world which was not prepared to accept that women could have carnal thoughts, much less feelings, he had any idea what I meant. Nor was I the least successful in my lonely bed; I was too angry. Yet I still refused to accept that the physical side of my marriage was over, and kept telling myself that it was but a mood, perhaps brought on by too much drink (although in my experience this usually enhances a man's sexual desire, if not necessarily his performance). Next morning we were coldly polite to each other, but there was nothing unusual in that. However, when I chanced to go upstairs to my room,

I was taken aback to discover his man in there, collecting everything that belonged to his master. On returning from our honeymoon Edward had established one of the spare bedrooms as his dressing room, which was entirely according to the rules of society. Not many men wished a wife and her clothes and cosmetics cluttering up where he was trying to dress; and the same may be said of the wives. Also, when Edward was dressing he was always attended by his valet, who would have been quite out of place in my bedroom, and during my pregnancy he had preferred to sleep in there as well. Again, there was nothing unusual in this. However, as he had shared my bed on a regular if far too rare basis before my pregnancy, there were quite a few of his things lying about, and now every last one was being removed. 'Why are you doing that?' I inquired.

'I am carrying out his lordship's instructions, milady.'

There was clearly nothing to be gained by questioning him more closely, so I waited until Edward returned that evening. Then I remarked, 'I found Barrett in my bedroom this morning.'

'I hope it was not inconvenient.'

'He was moving your things into the spare room. He said you had told him to do that.'

'Yes, I did. I feel it would be more convenient for you not to have my things about.'

'But I like having your things about. I like having you about – and your things are at least a substitute, even if a poor one.'

'You are being absurd. As usual.' A quite unnecessary addition. 'It will be best for both of us, you'll see. I am merely trying to make your life more convenient.'

Talk about hypocrisy! I wrestled with my desires and my conscience for a few more days. Then I ventured, 'I should like to go to Almack's next Wednesday night. It must be a year since I was last there.'

I held my breath as I waited for his reply. I really did not know what I should do if he refused permission. But he said, 'I think that is a splendid idea. It is not good for you to mope about the house. Wednesday . . . yes, there is a late night sitting of the House. I shall be able to drop you, and Carpenter will pick you up.'

'Thank you, Edward,' I said.

★   ★   ★

What was I looking for? Perhaps there was a vague hope that George might be there, even if in my heart I knew that we had run our course. Besides, believe it or not, I did not wish an affair at that moment. I just wanted to be out of the house, and away from Edward's deadening company. I wanted to laugh, and engage in animated conversation, and drink champagne, and dance . . . and above all, be openly admired, instead of constantly denigrated. And so I went to Almack's – where I was greeted as an old friend by the chief flunkey, who himself escorted me up the stairs to the ballroom and remained at my side, pointing out to me the new gas lighting which was certainly very bright, while my card was delivered to Lady Oxford, as on that unforgettable first night. And as on that night, Jane hurried across the vast room to greet me, while all eyes turned towards me.

'My dear,' she said, 'I am *so* happy you have returned to the fold. And I have someone I want you to meet.' She escorted me to where the great ladies were seated, and I was again greeted most heartily. 'Princess Esterhazy,' she said, 'I would so like Jane to meet Prince Felix.'

'Of course,' Princess Esterhazy agreed. 'He is right here.'

'Felix . . .,' she said. I turned, and gazed at Felix Schwarzenberg.

So much rubbish has been written about Felix and myself, mainly by ill-informed gossip-mongers, that it is time to set the record straight. I am not going to attempt to deny that we behaved scandalously, or at least, I did. Throughout our initial relationship, Felix behaved as what he was – a gentleman, though sadly the accent needs to be placed on the man. He found himself in possession of the most beautiful woman of his time, but as he had been a connoisseur of beautiful women throughout his life – he was seven years older than me – he found it difficult to believe that any woman would seek a lifelong love affair, and certainly not a girl of just twenty-one. Completely out of his depths, for all his confidence and experience, and hamstrung by the requirements of his birth and his family's expectations, not to mention his own ambitions, he did, I firmly believe, the very best he could in our circumstances. Because of his initial ardour, I could not, at that time, believe that he would so cruelly betray me, in more ways than just playing with my love.

And me? When I met Felix, I was at the lowest point of my life, up to that moment. I had just been most humiliatingly rejected by my husband – who, so far as I could see, now that I had produced the required heir, had no more use for me at all except to act as his hostess. My guilt over my affairs with George Anson and Fred Madden, which I had been prepared to expiate by becoming the most faithful and obedient of wives, had turned into a mood of bitter defiance. And I was only just twenty-one years old.

None of these are intended as excuses for what happened: they are possible reasons. But I can definitely say that, contrary to what has been written and said, I did not fall in love with Felix at first sight. I certainly liked what I saw. In the first instance it was the uniform, for it appeared that Lady Jersey, while happy to snub the Great Duke, had not been prepared to treat an Austrian prince, son of that country's most illustrious soldier, with similar disrespect – especially as he was the protégé of one of her fellow patronesses. Thus the man in front of me was in all the glory of blue breeches and tasselled black knee boots, crimson tunic heavily laced with gold thread, matching cape thrown carelessly over one shoulder . . . He lacked only a sword (which had been discarded simply because it would have been such an impediment to dancing) in order to present the most romantic picture imaginable. But then there was the man himself. Taller than me, which was an immediate relief, he had the most dashingly handsome features, topped by a mass of curly black hair – and he wore a moustache. I was so taken aback, I instinctively looked for a club foot; but he had the most perfect body, ideally displayed by his tight-fitting hussar uniform, the breeches of which were like a second skin, leaving no doubt that he had splendid legs . . . and was singularly well endowed. His voice was melodious but yet powerful, and he spoke English with just enough of an accent to make it interesting. 'Lady Ellenborough . . .,' he said. 'The most beautiful woman in England!'

I looked at Jane in some concern, never having been approached so boldly before, and certainly not in the presence of my predecessor in that role. But she merely smiled. 'His Highness has a way with words,' she remarked.

Felix had bent over my hand. Now he straightened. 'Will you

dance?' I glanced down at my card, which was held in the same hand as my fan. 'Ah!' he said. 'May I?'

I gave him the card. As I had just arrived, it was blank; and I watched in consternation as he wrote his name across the two pages of cardboard, from the bottom left corner to the upper right. 'Your Highness!' I protested.

'To you, fair lady, Felix. And we need to get to know one another, do we not?'

I again looked to Jane for support, but she merely smiled again and left us to it. I do not know what she expected, or perhaps even hoped, of this so obviously arranged meeting. She had to be aware of Edward's dislike for her, and no doubt reciprocated his feelings; and she certainly knew of my interest in Byron, because I had told her of it. But whatever she anticipated, in a matter of days the relationship between Felix and I escalated out of her control – and out of the control of anyone else, including ourselves. This had absolutely nothing to do with my feelings at that moment. I was delighted to be waltzing in the arms of the most handsome man I had ever met, and he danced superbly. But I remained embarrassed, and somewhat miffed, by his calm assumption that I was to be his for the evening; and, equally, by the way he looked at me (he had the most passionate dark eyes which made me feel I was already naked in his arms) and the way he held me, which was far closer than was customary or even decent.

I searched desperately for words; and as always happens on these occasions, descended into banality. 'Are you really a prince?' I asked.

'Are you really a lady?' he countered.

That question could be taken in several ways. I decided to take offence. 'I am Jane Elizabeth Law, Lady Ellenborough,' I told him, as haughtily as I could.

'Then I most humbly apologize – not least because you are also a member of the famous Coke family.'

He had obviously informed himself about me – which, as we had never met, and he could not possibly have known I would be attending Almack's that night, was highly flattering. But no one had told him the proper pronunciation of my family's name, which he had made sound as if it rhymed with cloak, suggesting that Grandpa was some kind of fuel for a furnace. 'The name is pronounced Cook,' I explained.

'But it is spelt C–O–K–E, is it not?'

'And is pronounced Cook,' I insisted.

'Ah, English! What an unfathomable language!'

'And my unmarried name was Digby,' I told him, 'which is my actual family.'

'That is also confusing. Now I . . . I am simply Felix Ludwig Johann von Nepomuk Friedrich, Prince zu Schwarzenberg.'

I understood that I had just been thoroughly put down – and also that I was out of my class, at least as regards names. 'Then I must apologize to you,' I said.

'That will never do,' he objected. 'We cannot spend the rest of our lives apologizing to each other. Let us make a pact that whatever either of us may say or do, we shall never apologize to each other. Will you agree?'

I could not help but laugh. 'If you wish. That is supposing we ever meet again.'

'Oh, we shall do that,' he assured me. 'I am resolved on it. Time and again.'

This was really travelling at an unacceptable speed – and without the slightest regard for any opinion I might have. I would have abandoned him there and then, but I had not demurred when he filled my card, and to cease dancing with him might have left me bereft of a partner for the rest of the evening. Besides, his arms were such a delightful place to be. So we danced through the night, and by the time I left the gossips had already deduced that we were lovers. Gossips, of course, are always some distance ahead of the truth. They had ascertained, at least to their own satisfaction, some years before that George and I had shared more than cousinly chats. This being established, they had discovered no reason to reassess the situation, being quite unaware that we had seen very little of each other over the past year, and certainly had not shared a bed in that time. There was even a rumour going around that George was the father of my child, which I found extremely offensive. Now, to their great delight, they deter-mined that George had been replaced, well before I had made a decision as to his replacement. It so happened that that year's Derby, England's premier horse race, was won by a mount called

Cadland, which beat one called The Colonel into second place. As a result, Felix found himself being called, behind his back, Cadland, as having achieved a similar success over Colonel Anson!

The Derby is run in June, and by the time it took place the gossips were absolutely correct in their estimation of the situation. But still, it did not happen immediately. Needless to say, Jane played her part in precipitating events: perhaps inadvertently, but I never could be sure. Two days after that unforgettable night – when I was still recalling all too readily the touch of Felix's hand, the pressure of his body against mine and, above all, the magnetic glow of his eyes – she invited me to one of her tête-à-tête teas. 'I would say that you had a considerable triumph, on Wednesday,' she remarked.

'He is about the most forward man I have met,' I said.

'He is that. But you found him attractive.'

'He is an attractive man,' I admitted. 'His self-confidence is startling.'

'He has every reason to be. His family is one of the oldest and most noble in Austria. It is even connected to the royal house.' She paused to see my reaction to this, but she must have been disappointed: I entirely shared my grandfather's views on royalty. 'And then, of course,' she went on, 'there was his father's triumph.'

'What was that?'

'My dear, Prince Schwarzenberg was in command of the allied armies at the Battle of Leipzig in 1813. That was the decisive battle of the wars.'

'I thought Waterloo was the decisive battle of the wars.'

'That is an English concept, because our side was commanded by the Duke – with a little help from the Prussians, to be sure.' Being a profound Whig, she was, of course, no admirer of Wellington, a profound Tory. 'But the Continental view is different and, shall I say, more realistic. They hold that no matter what happened at Waterloo, even if the Duke had been smashed, Bonaparte would still have fallen in short order because of the vast armies being raised against him in Austria, Russia and Sweden, while he was operating with merely the remnants of the Grande Armée, which had been utterly shattered at Leipzig two years before – by Prince Schwarzenberg.'

This was a totally new and un-English view of recent history;

and however true, I was not sure it was one I wanted to accept. 'Was Prince Felix present at this battle?' .

'I have no idea. He was only thirteen at the time. The point I am making is that he has a family background of unlimited wealth and power and success; and since his father's death and his inheritance, he has unlimited prospects. Especially as, apart from his family background, he is known to be a protégé of Prince Metternich.' Again she paused to gaze at me with arched eyebrows.

'Prince Metternich,' I said. 'Isn't he the Austrian Prime Minister?'

'My dear, he is the Austrian Chancellor. You could describe him as the Austrian equivalent of Wellington. But he is even more powerful. In Austria, the Chancellor's position is not at the mercy of either his own party or the ballot box, but only of the Emperor. Oh, what a man! I met him, you know, when he was here in 1815. So handsome, so *soignée* . . .' She gave a little sigh, leaving me of the opinion that the prince had been amongst her lovers. 'What I am saying,' she went on, 'is that to be taken up by Metternich is a guarantee of success. Thus young Schwarzenberg has already been an attaché at Berlin and Rio de Janeiro. That is in Brazil, you know. South America.'

I did know this, as I am sure Jane knew. What she possibly did not know was that I had spent my life dreaming of visiting such faraway places, while – apart from that mad dash to Gretna (when I had not been in a state of either mind or circumstance to admire the view) and our visit to Switzerland, when I had been too young – my entire world remained limited by the Wash, the Cotswolds and the English Channel. As I have said, I do not know whether Jane was engaged in putting me off or luring me on, but she now capped her homily by adding, 'I'm afraid that, during these travels, he indulged in a large number of affairs. It seems the ladies just cannot resist him. Not that he has ever, apparently, considered marrying any of them.' She fanned herself vigorously. Byron reincarnated! From that moment I was lost.

But still capable of rational consideration. If Felix was, as Caro Lamb had said of Byron, mad, bad and dangerous to know, even to flirt with him would be risky in the extreme. I contented myself with placing him amongst my dreams, telling myself that things would turn out as they would turn out, though knowing all the while that they would turn out exactly as I chose. For London society was really very limited. Apart from the weekly gathering at Almack's, at the various dinners and receptions and balls to which one was invited one met the same people over and over again. Which is why a new face was regarded so highly. I had had a glimpse of this when I had first made my entry into society, and I would have seen a lot more of it had I not been wooed and won so rapidly, and had I not been married to a man who regarded all social intercourse not primarily concerned with politics to be a waste of time. Thus there was absolutely no chance of my attending any parties, not to mention Almack's, without encountering Felix again and again; and once it was known that I was back in circulation, I was bombarded with invitations, most of which I accepted – always on my own, Edward never showing the slightest inclination either to accompany me or to stop me attending. His behaviour as my husband indeed again attracted a great deal of adverse comment, and not only from his enemies.

In his defence, I must say that he continued to have a great deal on his mind. For as the Reform Debate grew hotter, his political ambitions were coming closer to fruition. With King Prinny ailing, the heir to the throne was his brother William – popularly known as Sailor Bill, as he had served in the Navy as a young man. Like his brother, he had almost nothing to recommend him save his birth, but he was known to have Whiggish leanings, which could turn out to be a disaster for the Tory administration that had ruled the country for a generation.

In an effort to pre-empt events, and to obtain the continuation of royal support, the Duke began to consider introducing a Reform Bill of his own. But this was unacceptable to many of his colleagues, who resigned from the Cabinet. Edward, although he was in principle as opposed to reform as anyone, saw his opportunity, backed the Duke to the limit, and was duly rewarded. Although he did not actually achieve what he wanted, the Foreign Secretaryship, he was appointed Lord Privy Seal – which, as it carried a seat in the Cabinet, was the next best thing.

But long before then, he had lost me for ever. Only a couple of weeks after my meeting with Felix at Almack's, and my revealing tea with Jane Harley, I attended a reception given by someone whose name quite escapes me. It was one of those horrendous affairs where five hundred people are crammed into a space perhaps sufficient for a quarter of that number. Thus one descended from one's carriage into a crush, fought one's way into the midst of an army of footmen and flunkeys, found one's way up the stairs to the withdrawing room, wriggled one's way through a screaming, shouting, grabbing mass to reach the buffet, secured – if one was lucky – a glass of champagne and a canapé, endeavoured to drink without having the glass dashed from one's hand and to eat without being choked by a sudden embrace or push, resisted clutching paws and hungrily sought kisses, while endeavouring to retain one's hat and jewellery, not to mention one's very gown, all the while maintaining a fixed smile, interspersed with a happy giggle, until it was possible to leave again, which involved another battle royal, and one regained the safety of one's carriage, feeling as if one had been ridden over by a cavalry charge – and all, quite often, without having even seen, much less exchanged, a word with one's host or hostess.

So there I was, having allowed myself to be forced against a wall, if only in search of an opportunity to breathe, when I suddenly found a man standing in front of me and looked up, at Felix.

He had a glass of champagne in either hand. 'I saw you from across the room,' he said. 'And thought you might be thirsty.' He had found his way through the throng without spilling a drop!

'That is very kind of you,' I said, and drained the glass. Apart from my thirst, this was a sensible move, as a moment later someone barged against his back and he was thrust against me. As I was in the act of stretching out my arm to place the empty glass upon a nearby table I was totally defenceless; and when I managed to close my arms, it was with Felix inside my embrace.

He did not seem to be in a hurry to move. Well, neither was I. This was the safest I had felt all evening. 'Are all London parties like this?' he asked.

'Most,' I replied. 'They are absolutely dreadful.'

'I think they have their compensations,' he argued. I looked up, and he looked down. Our faces were only inches apart. 'I have an overwhelming urge to kiss you,' he said.

'Well, you cannot do it here,' I told him. 'Think of the scandal.'

'But if we were elsewhere?' I had been hoist by my own petard.

'Are you enjoying yourself?' he asked.

'The party? Not in the least.'

'Why do you not leave? My carriage is outside. I could take you home.'

'My carriage is also outside.'

'It can follow.'

'I do not think that would be a good idea. I live some miles out of town. Why do you not let me take *you* home, and *your* carriage can follow.'

He regarded me for several seconds before bursting into laughter. 'You are the most remarkable woman. A lady does not take a gentleman home.'

'Ah. Well, then, some other time, perhaps. I do not wish to hurt your sensibilities.'

'I would not dream of allowing you to. For you, I shall make an exception. Do we leave together, or separately?'

I looked past him at the throng. 'I suspect that if we once lost sight of each other we might never meet again.' So we left in company.

This was perhaps thoughtless of me, as we were seen by a great many people, thus adding to the speculation that already existed. But I was not in the mood to care about that, I was too excited. As with the opening of my liaison with George, I did not know what was going to happen, just as I did not know what I *wanted* to happen. It was the thrill of the chase that attracted me, with me playing the quarry in view of my sex. The question was how I would be caught, and what would be my fate.

The event far exceeded my expectation, although it got off to a shaky start. Our carriages having been summoned, I informed Carpenter, my driver, that we were going to give this gentleman a ride home. William, a bright lad who was utterly devoted to me, never even blinked, although the prince's carriage was immediately behind mine. I turned to Felix and said, 'You will have to give us directions.'

'Harley Street,' he replied. For a moment I was struck dumb, which caused him to add, defensively, 'I am told that it is quite a good neighbourhood.'

'Oh, it is,' I assured him. 'I know it well. What is the number?'

'Seventy-three.'

Practically opposite my parents' house! At least I knew that they were not in town at the moment. At the same time, my quick-thinking mind was already roaming over the possible advantages of such a situation, however dangerous it appeared at first consideration. 'Number seventy-three Harley Street, William,' I said, and allowed myself to be helped into my seat. With Felix sitting beside me, we moved off. And a moment later I was in his arms.

This was also a rather public business. My equipage was a phaeton (my version was known as a high-flyer, an evocative description). A light four-wheeled affair with a pair of horses, built for speed rather than comfort, it had only a single seat, for two passengers, and was open in the front. When seated, one looked at the back of the driver. William, to his credit, never attempted to discover what was happening behind him, although he must have known that something was going on – for even if there were no more than a few gasps, there was considerable rustling, although largely disguised by the clip-clopping of the horses' hooves. But, the equipage lacking side panels, we were certainly exposed to the vulgar gaze. Fortunately, there were not a lot of people about at nine in the evening, and those that were had no means of identifying the couple grappling with one another inside the carriage, or reason to suppose that a crime was being committed – and I was certainly not crying rape. In fact I was enjoying an experience of which I had only dreamed. Hitherto my love life, such as it was, had consisted of a well-defined duty on the part of my husband, and groping uncertainty on the part of Fred Madden and Tom Burrows; even George, who had had more access to my body than anyone else, had always approached me with desperate haste. Being an English gentleman, I do not think it ever crossed his mind that I might have feelings of my own that needed to be expressed, and exploited; and I, even after my eye-opening chat with Jane Harley, had remained unsure just how far those feelings could go, and how they could be properly released.

Felix's approach was in a different class. His lips were gentle, as was his tongue, but it was none the less demanding and pervasive and utterly mind-consuming, especially as while he was kissing me his fingers were playing gently with my half-exposed breasts – not immediately seeking my nipples, but stroking the flesh. When he left my lips his mouth joined his fingers, while his other hand extracted my shoulder from my gown and thus allowed the strap to slip down my arm entirely, to expose his goal. This delicious attention I had of course experienced before. What made Felix's ministration so different to any other was his utter confidence that he was doing exactly as I wished. As indeed he was.

But we had barely started on our journey through paradise. While still sucking my nipple, his hand left my shoulder and began working on my skirts, sliding them up my leg to allow his hand beneath them to caress my stocking, and then move up. Here I felt I should stop him, not because I did not enjoy what he was doing, but because I did not see that what I assumed he had in mind could be practical on a narrow seat, and with William only inches away. I did not wish to speak – because of William's presence – so I put my hand over his, clasping it tightly. He allowed himself to be checked, for the moment, raising his head to whisper, 'You taste delicious.'

'You have been sucking my milk,' I whispered back, wondering if that would terminate his advances there and then. I could not imagine Edward's reaction to such a confidence – but then I could not imagine Edward ever sucking a woman's nipple, unless, perhaps, it belonged to Miss Harriette Wilson. 'I am but four months a mother.'

For a moment he did not move, then he said again, 'You are delicious. All of you.' And set about discovering if this were true. Once again ecstasy, or as close to it as I had yet been at any time. His fingers, moving gently upwards, encountered my garters and went beyond. Here again was cause for alarm, for on warm evenings, when about to dance or be crushed, I had entirely aban-doned such encumbrances as drawers. Thus in a moment he was touching the gates of my personal heaven. This also had happened before, on a handful of occasions, but always with studied care-lessness on the part of the man. Now again, certainty – both of intent and of my reaction. I gasped, and reached for that always tantalizing horizon . . . and, at that moment, the carriage stopped.

'Number seventy-three, milady.' William said.

I sprang back, even though Felix was reluctant to release me, and endeavoured to straighten my skirts. Felix at last raised his head. 'You enchant me.'

'And you, me,' I assured him, trying to stop panting. So near and yet so far! But there was another matter that concerned me: in all our wrestling I had not had the time or indeed the opportunity to reciprocate. 'But you . . .'

'I can be patient, up to a point. Will you come in?'

But this was simply too sudden. 'I must . . . go home.' And think about things, I reflected, although I did not say so.

'I must see you again.'

So much for thought, or caution. 'Oh, yes,' I said.

'When? You must give me your address.'

'That is not possible. I mean, for us to meet at home. I come up to town most afternoons.'

'You mean you would come to me?' Not for the first time I had surprised him. 'My God. But . . .'

'Yes?' I was suddenly anxious.

'It is no matter. I share my rooms with another officer. But Dietrichstein is a good fellow and will make himself scarce.'

'And your servants?'

'Give me a time, and I will see that they are also absent.'

'Two o'clock.'

'I shall count the seconds.' He kissed my hands and stepped down.

I waited for him to enter the house, giving my heart time to settle down and my breathing to return to normal, although beneath my skirts I still seethed. Then I leaned forward and said, 'I rely utterly on your discretion, William.'

'You have it, milady,' the faithful lad replied. Perhaps he too was a dreamer, of what might be? I did not care. I knew my dream was about to come true.

Easy to say, from a considerable retrospect, that this was the most utter madness. Nor could I delude myself that, at that moment, it was anything other than sheer lust: I knew that he wanted the use of my body, and I knew that I wanted him to have that use. Again in retrospect, it is possible to claim that all the great love affairs of history have grown from a powerful physical attraction that has developed into an ongoing desire to share one's all with the man of one's choice. None of these reflections concerned me at the time, nor did I consider the absurdity of refusing to stay with him that night, at least for an hour or two (which would have been perfectly safe, as we had left the party so early), while agreeing to visit him on the morrow. I was in a state of some confusion. But I did wish a few hours for reflection, and perhaps to exercise a woman's privilege of changing her mind. I was not then in love with Felix; I was, as always at that period of my life, in love with the *idea*.

But, equally, as always, I did not neglect practicalities and necessities. 'You were home early last night,' Edward commented at breakfast.

I had in fact been in bed, although by no means asleep, long before he came in. 'I got bored with being stamped on and jostled,' I said.

'The price of beauty, my dear.'

I stared at him with my mouth open, wondering if this was an advance, and what I should do if it were. But he was not looking at me, and a few minutes later prepared to leave the house. 'I thought I might visit Harley Street today,' I remarked. 'I do not think that Papa's house is being properly looked after.'

'Doesn't he have a man of affairs to see to that?'

'Men of affairs deal with affairs. And they are men. They have no interest in an extra layer of dust.'

'True,' he agreed. 'Try not to be too critical.' And he left for Westminster.

I had several hours to kill, and they seemed to pass very slowly. I had a bath, and spent more time than usual at my toilette. This was not lost on Lucy – who submitted several heavy sighs as she brushed my hair – but she dared not comment, however certain she might be that I was off to misbehave. I was dressed and ready, and William had the phaeton at the door, when there was the clatter of hooves and another equipage drew up. 'I am not receiving anyone today,' I told Lucy. 'Please inform Mowlem.'

But Mowlem was no match for my visitor, and a moment later I was confronted by Steely. 'My dear Jane,' she said. 'How well you look. I hope you don't mind my dropping in, but I was in the area . . .'

Of course she was lying. There was no possible reason for her to be in Roehampton except to visit me. 'It is always good to see you, Steely,' I said, doing a bit of lying myself. 'Have you come to stay?'

'That is very kind of you. I would so like to see Arthur. I trust he is well?'

'He has a sniffle.' Poor Arthur always had a sniffle. 'But by all means visit the nursery. Lucy, tell Mowlem to put Miss Steele's boxes in the Blue Room, and inform Mrs Blundell that we have a guest for the next . . .' I looked at Steely.

'I should not dream of staying more than a day or two,' she promised.

'The next few days.' Lucy hurried off. 'And now, dear Steely,' I said. 'I must ask you to amuse yourself for the next few hours. I shall see you at dinner.'

'You are going out? Up to town? May I come with you? I should enjoy that.'

'So would I,' I lied with a straight face. 'Unfortunately, I have a business appointment. I will see you at dinner.'

At the time I was not interested in what she might make of my snub. Although I was intensely irritated by her unwanted appearance at such a time, I was above all else bubbling with anticipated excitement. Perhaps she observed this. But then William and I were away, and I was taking off my gloves and putting them on again, wondering what I might be doing in an hour's time. When we were about to enter Harley Street, having come up Wimpole Street, I tapped William on the shoulder. 'Stop the coach, William. I have an urge to walk the rest of the way.'

He brought the horses to a halt. Of course he knew where I was going, and what I would be doing when I got there; but I trusted him absolutely, and with reason. He alone of all my servants never let me down.

'Perhaps you could find something to do for a while.'

'Certainly, milady. How long a while? Half an hour?'

'Ah . . .' Half an hour was all the time I had ever spent with George, as William no doubt recalled, but I had such hopes of this afternoon . . . 'I think an hour would be best,' I said. 'And you will pick me up here, not at the house.'

'Of course, milady.' He got down from his seat to assist me, and I squeezed his hand before I raised my parasol and walked slowly up the street. I was well-known in this vicinity, and was greeted by several people, all of whom naturally assumed I was proceeding to my parents' house. I had to suppose that eyebrows might be raised if I was seen standing in front of the door of No. 73, instead of No. 78. But in fact Felix had been looking out for me; and as I drew abreast of the door of No. 73, it opened and I was whisked into the interior before anyone could have blinked twice, and into his arms.

We were in the downstairs hall, but true to his word Felix appeared to have emptied the entire house. We kissed and stroked and fumbled our way up the stairs and into his apartment, which possessed a large, bright front room with a huge window looking out on to the street. There were curtains, but these were drawn back to allow the maximum amount of afternoon sunlight to enter. That this light also illuminated the interior of the room, and whatever or whoever was in it, did not occur to me.

Still in great and, to me, slightly disturbing haste – I had suffered this so often before – we undressed each other, Felix showing great familiarity with the intricacies of my stays. This was a new experience for me, and a most enjoyable one, as it was to be lifted in his arms and carried, naked, into his bedroom and laid on the bed. Once again I anticipated disappointment; but instead of immediately looking for an entry, he resumed where he had left off the previous night, commencing with my breasts and then working his way down to my pubes . . . with his mouth! The touch of his lips, and that of his hands, sliding sensuously up and down my legs, was the most stimulating I had ever known; while to approach me the more comfortably, he was lying with his legs above my head, which meant that his genitals were readily available. Never had I been in such a happy position. He seemed to relish my touch, and within seconds I was entering heaven at both ends, as it were. I thought I had ruined everything when he ejaculated all over my face, but he laughingly cleaned me up and assured me that I would not have long to wait. By then I no longer cared whether he managed to enter me or not; but when he did, I knew yet more rhapsody. For unlike any other man I had ever met, he was in no hurry. His strokes were long and slow and powerful, and I swear I climaxed twice more before he was again spent.

But there were yet more delicious surprises in store. He attended to us both with a damp cloth, and then we lay together, talking and sipping wine. We both wanted to know so much about the other. I had to be discreet, and Felix did not press me as to former lovers or my relationship with my husband; but he seemed fascinated by what I told him of life at Holkham, and equally interested in my views on British politics. 'Will your Parliament be reformed, do you think?' he asked.

'Not if my husband's people have their way. On the other hand . . . some people say that if something is not done, there may be a revolution,' I ventured.

'And if there is, do you not have one of the most formidable armies of our time, the most formidable fleet in the world, and your greatest living soldier to deal with it? Prince Metternich always says that hanging one or two malcontents restores order, in either army or country.'

Now we were perhaps getting too serious for a couple lying naked on a bed. 'Tell me of your travels,' I begged. 'Tell me of Rio. I should love to go there.'

'Why, so should I.'

I raised myself on my elbow. 'But you were attaché at the Portuguese court.'

'Yes, but that was after it had returned from South America. I was at Lisbon.'

'Oh! You will think me a goose.'

'If you were a goose, my dearest Aurora, I would eat you, very slowly.' And he commenced to do just that.

It was four hours before I left Felix's house. William was waiting patiently, but he felt constrained to remark, 'You have lost your parasol, milady.'

'So I have,' I acknowledged. 'I will fetch it the next time I am up.' Which we had agreed would be as soon as I had got rid of Steely.

'Of course, milady. But perhaps . . .' He blushed. 'Your bonnet . . .'

There was a small glass in my reticule, and I examined my appearance. I looked, from the neck up, as if I had been dragged through a hedge backwards. And I was going home to Steely! But I really did not care. I was in love. The cynic will observe that this was still pure lust – and I cannot deny that I was eager to renew the experience – but already a deeper feeling was creeping in. Felix had revealed himself as far more than a consummate lover. He was a kind and gentle man, perfectly mannered, exquisitely educated, fluent in half a dozen languages and capable of profound thought, with perhaps a fascinating suggestion of ruthlessness, when needed. In short, he was my romantic ideal of what a man should be.

But I did not dare carry my desires to their logical conclusion; that remained a concept too enormous and too outrageous for serious consideration. I merely determined to enjoy myself while I might, rejecting any opinion but my own. Indeed, on that very first day I had to see off Steely, who could discern that I had hardly been in a business meeting, and who soon departed in a confused and clearly disturbed state of mind. As she was returning to Forston, it is very likely that she conveyed her misgivings to Mama, but I doubt that Mama took her seriously . . . at that time. Although my mother clearly still recalled the Tom Burrows incident, I do not believe she ever knew, and certainly never accepted, any rumours of George and I, even if the matter had been brought up by her sister; and, to dispel them, she had the evidence of her own eyes that I appeared a contented and indeed happy wife and mother.

But people were emerging from every direction to suggest to Edward that he sit up and take notice. Even his uncle, the Bishop of Bath and Wells, who had married us four years before, felt called upon to suggest to his nephew that there was talk to be rebuffed. For his part, Edward, who operated on such a low emotional level as regards sex, simply could not conceive that I would so inconvenience myself as to indulge in an affair – with all of its necessary secrets and subterfuges, so irritating to a man of business. And, as always, there was a great deal of business to be done. If the threat of the imminent death of the King seemed to have receded, and with it the immediate necessity to tackle parliamentary reform, a new critical matter had arisen: that of

Catholic emancipation. This issue had been confounding the
nation for a generation, and had even brought down Pitt. But,
although their often bloody attempts to overthrow the monarchy
and the Established Church were much to be condemned, the
Catholics' suppression had meant the exclusion from office of a
great many talented men. I therefore applauded the Great Duke's
determination to do something to alleviate the situation.

However, needless to say, he ran into rank after rank of opposition, and there were resignations and upheavals. As before, these
benefited Edward. Since he did not consider it worth his while
to discuss politics or religion with me, I have no idea what opinion
he actually held on the matter. But by dint of pursuing his rigid
policy of supporting the Duke at all times, that autumn he
found himself President of the Board of Control for India, and
busier than ever. And therefore even less interested in social
tittle-tattle, even when it concerned his wife. Indeed, his sole
intrusion into my life that year was his decision to have my
portrait painted.

Of course I did not object to this. But soon enough I objected
to the artist, or at least his ability. His name was James Holmes,
and he came highly recommended. He was, in fact, often employed
by the King, but from my point of view he had an even better
artistic pedigree: he had painted the famous and so romantic
portrait of Byron in Grecian costume, which had induced me,
as a girl, to fall in love with the poet.

Perhaps his true talent lay in painting men. He certainly made
the most awful mess of painting me! He elected that I should
wear what he called peasant costume: a skirt and loosely laced
bodice, and nothing else so far as any spectator could perceive.
More embarrassing still, obviously well up on London gossip, he
made me recline on a settee, with one hand to my head and
holding what could have been a love letter in the other, regarding
the world with what might best be described as a come-hither
look. I would not say that he did no justice to my beauty: he
caught my hair and my hands and my complexion very well, but
my expression was altogether too calculating to be attractive. Ah
well, maybe he saw more in me than I at that time recognized
in myself! Edward thought the painting was splendid, but I was

more pleased with the little prints which, now that I had returned to society, again began to sprout in the shops – and I was flattered when I was included in *Heath's Book of Beauty*, which was published that same year.

The Scandal

Meanwhile the gossip increased in intensity. My detractors had plenty of mud to fling, but I should stress that there was nothing intrinsically different in my public appearances with Felix to those I had shared with George. We preserved such discretion as we considered necessary. Thus although we invariably attended the same parties, we always arrived in our own coaches ... however often we left together. Admittedly, we spent several afternoons a week in his apartment, and soon ceased to bother what the other occupants of the house thought of it; but none of these ever let us down, Felix's flatmate, Count Dietrichstein, being the soul of discretion. As was William, who not only drove me to and from every assignation, but also acted as a go-between for messages regarding any unforeseen changes of arrangement, which were left at the Windmill Inn in Wimbledon − midway between Roehampton and Westminster − either by William for Felix, or by Felix's man for me.

But nonetheless the inescapable fact was that wherever Felix was to be found, there was I beside him − whether riding on Rotten Row or boating on the Thames, waltzing at Almack's or dining with friends. Indeed it soon became accepted that there was no point in inviting Felix to any function unless I was included too, for he simply would not attend without me. I may say that our popularity was not based solely on my beauty and Felix's good looks or our joint notoriety. Felix possessed a splendid singing voice, as did I, and we were often required to entertain the other guests after supper, playing the piano and accompanying ourselves, to rapturous applause.

It was quite the most socially successful summer any couple has ever had. Our greatest triumph was at the Jockey Club's annual ball − an auspicious occasion because, for the first time in months the King felt well enough to appear in public. As may be supposed, vast crowds turned out for a glimpse of their monarch, but in the event they spent their time looking at Felix and me, seated as always next to each other, and clearly concerned only with each other. Which is not to say that we did not have our differences, and our valleys as well as our peaks. I did, certainly, whenever Felix was seen or reported squiring other ladies. He always claimed these were official duties – but knowing him as I did, I could not help but be doubtful, and when he was seen with one particular female (at this distance in time I cannot recall her name) I got myself in quite a tizzy, and complained of his inconstancy to Jane. I felt I could do this not only because she was my mentor in love matters, but because I had no doubt that she had engineered the whole romance. This was a mistake. Although Jane was utterly sympathetic, I had overlooked her propensity for gossip. Before I could draw breath, all of London was regaling itself with the story of how I had been abandoned by my lover and was bitterly upset. At least this had the virtue of bringing Felix back to my side!

But all the while, the wheels of more than gossip were turning. One observer of the scene, a detestable Austrian diplomat, named Aponyi, who joined the London Embassy about this time, apparently recorded in his diary – the contents of which he was fond of confiding to others – how I had told him that I was forced to suffer the anger of an insensate jealous husband. Apart from the fact that I do not recall conversing with Aponyi more than once or twice at Almack's (and even then only briefly), and that I have never been in the habit of confiding my personal affairs to comparative strangers, the idea that Edward was ever jealous of anyone save a rival for a political appointment was too absurd to be considered. But it is an example of the wild tales that were being circulated. More to the point, my nearest and dearest were at last becoming agitated. I was distressed to receive a letter from Mama begging me to assure her that the rumours she was hearing were untrue. I assured her that they were greatly exaggerated (what is an exaggeration is a matter of opinion and I was, of course, entitled to have my own). Clearly this did not satisfy her, for it was after this exchange that Steely paid a visit to Edward, with the usual request that he should devote more attention to his wife. This was the most utter cheek from someone who was not of his social class, and she was properly snubbed.

★   ★   ★

The year 1829, which was now upon us, proved to be one of the two most disastrous years of my life. When it began, I was at the top of the tree, in every way. I was popular, if considered slightly risqué; I was squired by the most talked-about man in London; and we had then shared our romance for eight months, surrounded by rumour, it is true, but in no way condemned or even apparently observed by my husband, who was the one person who truly mattered. By the end of the year I was an outcast, a fugitive from all polite society.

Yet the year began on a high note. 'A new year!' I said to Felix, as we lay together in his bed on a January afternoon. 'What would you like, most of all, to happen this year?'

'I would like to spend a night with you. One night, in which you would not have to sneak away like a thief.' He rose on his elbow in turn. 'Does your husband never go away?'

'Not for the night. And even if he were to do so, it would not be possible. Our servants, with perhaps two exceptions, are all his more than mine.'

'Can *you* not go away for a night?'

'Only to my parents or my grandparents. And if I were to have you invited as well, that would be to shout our love to the world.'

'I would like to be able to do that. But as we cannot . . .'

'There is a possibility,' I said.

'Poor Arthur really is not very well,' I told Edward that night at supper.

'He never does appear to be very well,' he agreed.

'Dr Cowley thinks he needs careful building up.'

'He'll get that at Eton.'

'Eton is still a dozen years away. I think we should start planning now.'

For once he looked directly at me. 'Planning what? His name is down.'

'Planning what to do about his health, Ouzey. I would like Wilson to take him to Brighton, for a few days.'

'When do you wish this to happen?'

'Well, as soon as it can be arranged. If possible, next month.'

'My dear girl, no one goes to Brighton in February!'

'That's just it. The Norfolk will be empty. In fact, I thought

I might go down myself, just for a few days.' I gave him a bright smile. 'I think it would be a good idea if I got to know my son a little better.'

'Hm,' he commented. 'Yes, you are probably right. Parliament opens again on the fifth. I shall be rather busy with this Catholic emancipation business for some days. Will you arrange it?'

There are no lengths to which a woman will not go to lie in the arms of her beloved. But I was not being entirely deceitful. Due to the unchangeable custom of upper class households, I did not know little Arthur at all well: an hour an evening, often when I was dressing to go out and therefore considerably distracted, did not make for intimacy. I would therefore be killing two birds with a single stone, satisfying my desires and my maternal instincts at the same time. So the necessary letters were written, and Felix was appraised of my dispositions. Then on the sixth of February, a Friday, I drove down to Brighton, Edward not having returned at all the previous night, and Arthur having been in residence at the Norfolk for the previous week. I left Roehampton early and arrived in the middle of the afternoon, to be greeted warmly by the manager and staff – and shown to the same suite in which I had honeymooned! This left me feeling quite remorseful. In fact, after a pleasant hour spent with Arthur, who I found much improved and hardly sniffing at all, I sat down and wrote Edward a very tender letter, acknowledging my faults and begging his forgiveness for them. This may have been a mistake, for when all my private affairs were divulged to the curious public, shortly afterwards, the letter was held up as a supreme example of female hypocrisy. But the sentiments it expressed were genuine. And having written it, I felt much better.

Not that I had the slightest intention of changing my arrangements. It was too late for that! Felix arrived just in time for supper – travelling with an enormous carpet bag embroidered in gold thread with the initials FS, which was somewhat disquieting. But I did not think it in any way compromised us (unless questions came to be asked, which at that moment I did not anticipate happening); and his room was at the other end of the hotel, a matter of several staircases and passageways away. We greeted each other courteously, but did not converse;

I then retired early, telling Lucy that I was quite exhausted and intended to sleep in on the morrow, and was therefore not to be disturbed. She of course knew exactly what was going on, and was like a cat on hot bricks.

Then I got into bed, and waited. And waited. It was well after midnight when at last my unlocked door was opened, and then locked from the inside, Felix for some reason removing the key and laying it on a table before arriving at my bedside. 'I was beginning to suppose you had changed your mind,' I remarked.

'I would have come sooner, but I was accosted by some impudent servant who wished to know my business at this hour. I damn near twisted his ears, I can tell you. But in our circumstances, I deemed it best to make some excuse and went back to bed. I had to give him time to stop prowling about before I could come again.'

'And he had stopped prowling about?'

'Well . . . I didn't see him.'

'Well, then, let us forget all about him,' I said. 'We have so little time.'

What time we had we put to excellent use. We did not sleep a wink, and when he finally left me, just before dawn, I was as exhausted as I had pretended to Lucy. It had been perhaps the happiest night of my life, and one I have remembered in every detail for over fifty years.

Felix left the hotel again that morning – we did not publicly say farewell – and I remained in Brighton for another week, spending most of every day with Arthur. When I returned to Roehampton, with him, I was in an entirely contented frame of mind.

Three months later my world collapsed. I discovered myself to be pregnant.

I had always taken all the precautions, as recommended by Lucy, that had seemed either necessary or appropriate. That is, whenever I shared a bed with a man, I douched vigorously as soon as possible afterwards. I had not, of course, done this after Edward's visits and had thus happily conceived, even if it had taken some time; but it had worked perfectly throughout my liaison with George, my brief affair with Frederick, and the entire period – very nearly a year – during which I had been seeing Felix. But I had become somewhat careless; and after Felix left me that February morning in Brighton, instead of immediately attending to myself, I had remained in bed and, indeed, fallen asleep. Carrying out my instructions that I was not to be disturbed, Lucy did not appear until I rang for her, which was the middle of the morning, and the delay had been fatal. At the end of that month both of us had understood that something might be amiss, though I had missed periods before. At the end of March it was a cause for concern; and by the end of April there could be no doubt about the situation. 'Oh, ma'am,' Lucy said. She was starting to sound like Mama.

'Tell me what's to be done.'

'Well, ma'am, you have three options.' She paused, conspiratorially. With reason. 'One is to drop the babe.' I stared at her. She blushed. 'You know, ma'am . . .'

'I know what you mean. But is abortion not against the law?'

'Well, ma'am . . .' she was obviously considering reminding me that to bear an illegitimate child was also against at least all social and moral laws, certainly when one was married. 'I know a woman . . .'

I shuddered. 'What are the other options?'

'One would be to tell the father.' She knew as well as I did that the babe could not possibly be Edward's.

I had no doubt that Felix would have to be told, but I had not yet formed an opinion as to what he could do, or what I wanted him to do. 'And the third option?'

'To put the situation before Lord Ellenborough.'

'You can't be serious!'

'Well, milady, some husbands do accept such a situation rather than cause a scandal. And . . .you could be strongly placed.'

'I'm afraid I don't see how that can be possible.'

'Well, milady, do you remember your wedding night?'

'It is not something I am ever likely to forget.'

'Well, milady, after his lordship left your room . . .' and she told me what, apparently, had become common knowledge below stairs at the hotel. I listened to what she had to say with a mixture of chagrin, humiliation and outrage. On the other hand . . . might it be possible to tell Edward and still remain his wife? I had the example of Jane Harley, and, indeed, several others before me. But I knew such a *laissez-faire* attitude would not work in my marriage. Morals had altered considerably in the more than twenty years since Jane's heyday and were indeed well on their way to the present lamentable state of affairs, when, although it is as prevalent as ever, vice is never supposed to exist. This was as regards women. For men, life proceeds on its merry way, at their dictation. Edward might have been guilty of the most disgraceful behaviour on his wedding night, and there was the business of Harriette Wilson, but I knew that while he might be criticized for his conduct it was not likely to ruin him. And what our domestic situation would be like if I threw that business in his face as an excuse for my own adultery, did not bear contemplation.

I was already considering other possibilities. It was *not* a possibility that Felix, so gallant and honourable, would ever let me down, any more than he would consider allowing his child to be flushed down some miserable drain. 'We will adopt the second option,' I said, and wrote him a note requiring to see him as soon as possible. Time enough to make a decision after that.

Over the past month we had not, in fact, seen as much of each other as I would have liked, Felix having apparently been occupied with various diplomatic duties. In addition, it seemed that Dietrichstein had at last become edgy over the rumours surrounding us – which naturally encompassed him, if only as our accomplice. Felix had therefore moved out of Harley Street to another apartment, in Holles Street. I had continued to attend him there, but with much less ease, as I could no longer pretend I was visiting my parents' house and merely sidestep, as it were. To avoid prying eyes I had to approach from the street behind, thus being required to find my way through noisesome dustbins and lines of washing. This had not disturbed me; but our less frequent meetings did. Now, having dispatched William to the Windmill Inn, I was surprised, but gratified, when he returned, bearing me a note, also asking for an urgent meeting. Could Felix know the situation? However, my gratification was short-lived, when I read further and discovered that our meeting was not to be at his rooms, but at the pub itself. This was not the sort of lovers' tryst to which I was accustomed. Nevertheless, I attended the meeting, and we found ourselves seats in a corner of the lounge, hopefully out of earshot of any of the staff or other customers. 'My darling,' he said, holding my hands. 'I have sad news.'

'Not from Austria, I hope.' I was immediately concerned that some member of his immediate family might have died.

'Yes. I am to return to Vienna.' I stared at him with my mouth open. As far as I knew, military attachés were usually left in place for at least three years, unless something dramatic happened. He had been watching my expression. 'I am afraid Esterhazy has been listening to gossip. Or at least his wife has. He has had me into his office several times over the past month, telling me to end our relationship.' So those had been his 'diplomatic' duties. But I was entirely reassured when he continued, 'When I refused to consider it, he seems to have written to Prince Metternich. Now I have received a command to leave London . . . to leave England, and return home.'

'Vienna!' I said, my fertile brain wondering if this was not the answer to all of our problems. I was still naïve enough to consider them to be ours. 'I shall so love to visit Vienna.'

'Eh?' He appeared agitated.

'I shall come with you.'

'You cannot. Think of the scandal.'

I squeezed his hands. 'We shall have to ride that. I must come with you. I am with child.' Never have I seen a man so consternated. 'I did not intend it,' I said, feeling the first stirrings of alarm.

'But . . . did you not take precautions? I mean, well . . . it has never happened before.'

'I know. I did not act soon enough after our night together.'

'But . . . what are you going to do?'

'I have told you. I will accompany you to Vienna.'

'What about your husband?'

'I shall leave him.'

'And your son? Your title? Your place in society?'

To a man like Felix it was incredible that I could consider abandoning any of those. He did not realize that I did not give a fig for my title or my place in society. My son . . . Jane Harley's admonition at that first tea party kept ringing in my ears – but I had forgotten that, like so many people fond of disbursing advice, she had never actually had to act on such advice herself. 'I will work something out.'

'Jane!' Felix looked into my eyes with all the intentness of his powerful gaze. 'You cannot accompany me to Vienna.' He licked his lips. 'It would ruin me.' I could not believe my ears. 'It would end my career. In Austria, these things are not forgotten or forgiven, ever.'

I freed my hands. 'I thought you loved me.' My brain was in a whirl.

'I do,' he protested. 'I adore you. I worship the ground on which you walk.'

'But not sufficiently to risk your career.'

'Without my career, what would I have to offer you? I would be an outcast from society. I would not be received at court. Jane . . .' He took my hand back again. 'We must be patient.'

'Patient?' I cried, causing heads to turn in our direction. I lowered my voice. 'In a couple of months my condition will become obvious.'

'But everyone will suppose the child will be your husband's.'

'Everyone, perhaps. But there is one person who will know it is not. Edward has not slept with me for over a year.'

He produced a handkerchief and wiped his brow. 'I had no idea! You did not tell me.' So was it now to be all my fault? 'What will you do?' Not a suggestion of the word, we. 'You will have to . . .' he bit his lip.

'How can you think of such a thing? This is our child.'

'Ah . . .' For a moment he trembled upon the brink of an indiscretion that would have ended our relationship there and then. It might have been better had he uttered the fatal words, 'Can you be sure it is mine?' But he thought better of it. 'Well, of course, we must see what can be done.' At last, the word 'we'. My heart pounded. 'You will have to ask your husband to allow you to take a holiday. On the Continent would be best.'

'Vienna!'

'Not Vienna. I have explained that that is not possible. You must go to Switzerland.'.

'And you will join me there?'

'Ah . . . It would be better if I did not, at least for a while. I would beg you not to tell your husband, not to tell anyone, that you are pregnant. You should go away and live in retirement until the babe is born. That way you will leave all your options open.'

'My options? I only wish to be with you.'

'And I have explained that that is not practical at this time. Your best option will be to return to your husband after your delivery.'

'And our child?'

'We will put it out for adoption.'

'Adoption? My baby?'

'Do not fret. We will be able to reclaim it when we are ready. After a year the scandal and the gossip will have died down, no one will be able to prove anything against either of us, and we will be able to plan our future without the burden of notoriety weighing on us.'

He was making this up as he went along, I knew. I had done the same thing when planning my elopement with Tom Burrows. How did one reclaim a baby once it had been adopted by someone else? And a year . . . apart? But I so wanted to believe that it would all turn out all right. I looked into his eyes. 'Do you really love me, Felix?'

'I have said so. I adore you.'

'And will we be able to be together again? When the scandal has died down?'

'I swear it. If it is at all possible.'

A prevarication that made a nonsense of the oath. But I still only wanted to believe that it would be all right in the end. 'Will you write to me?'

'Every day.'

'And I will write you, every day.' I left in tears.

But these had dried by the time I reached Roehampton. This was necessary, because although Edward was not yet home, his brother Henry was staying with us. A decent enough fellow, who obviously could make nothing of his brother's marriage, he was always very pleasant to me and I suspect was in the ranks of those who felt that Edward had been neglectful of me. However, I had to suppose that when the chips were down, he would be a faithful supporter of the name of Law. And the chips would have to be thrown down without delay. I decided to set things in motion that very afternoon; and received my second unpleasant surprise of the day. 'Go abroad, ma'am?' Lucy asked, when I told her that we would be doing some travelling. 'You mean, out of England?'

'That is what abroad means, yes.'

'Oh, ma'am. I couldn't do that. England is my home. And over there, there's all them foreigners.'

I realized I might not only be about to lose husband, child and home, but personal maid as well. I felt quite put out. 'I hope you understand,' I said, 'that if you refuse to accompany me where I wish to go, I no longer have any use for your services.'

'Oh, ma'am!' For a moment she looked quite concerned, and I hoped she might change her mind. Then she recovered her composure. 'But you will give me a good reference, milady.'

The little witch was threatening me! But she was in a position to do so: she knew every secret of my life as a married woman. 'I may,' I told her.

I dressed quietly, left my hair loose – I felt this made me more appealing – and waited for my husband to come home. He was both late and in a bad humour. I gathered that all was not well at Westminster; but as he never discussed his affairs with me, and I was in any event preoccupied, we spoke little over supper. Henry did his best to make conversation, but was not very successful. After the meal, at which I had drunk sparingly – a single glass of wine – I said, 'I would like to have a word, Edward.'

'Please be brief,' he replied.

'In private.'

'Oh, good lord!' But he left the table and went into the library. I smiled at Henry, then followed and closed the door. 'Now, really, Jane,' Edward said. 'I am not in the mood to be troubled by domestic crises. If one of the servants has misbehaved, I expect you to deal with it. Tomorrow is going to be a vital day. I don't suppose you have taken the trouble to keep abreast of affairs, but my successor as Lord Privy Seal is to be selected, and there is a move in favour of Chandos. This I will not have.'

At this juncture I could have said, I would know more about, and have more interest in, politics if you ever troubled to share your thoughts with me. But I was determined to stick to what was, to me, the more important matter. 'I would like to go abroad.'

He had been pouring himself a glass of port. Nor did he stop. But he said, over his shoulder, 'Oh, really Jane. Please be serious. Arthur is perfectly well here.'

'I am sure he is. I am speaking of myself.'

He turned to face me. 'You wish to go abroad. Is this some madcap scheme like that undertaken by your absurd cousin?'

I kept my temper. 'I just wish to be away from here for a while.' I took a deep breath. 'Away from you.'

'Now you are being ridiculous. A lady does not travel without her husband, and you know that I cannot leave Westminster at this time.'

'I said, I wish to be away from you.'

He snapped his fingers. 'So the rumours are true.'

I had to be sure of my ground. 'What rumours?'

'That you have developed an attachment to Schwarzenberg. You wish to follow him to Vienna.'

'I had not thought of going to Vienna,' I lied. 'I just wish to be alone, to think about things.'

'Well, I am afraid I cannot agree. Whether you are in Vienna or not, he'll find a way to join you. Next thing you'll be committing an indiscretion.'

I briefly reflected on the facts. He knew about the gossip, but he did not yet know that I had slept with Felix. Or anyone else, it seemed. Of course the evidence that I had done so would be obvious soon enough, but for the moment all I had to do was to remain calm. 'I will give you my word that I will not go near Prince Schwarzenberg.' This of course did not preclude the possibility of Felix coming near me.

'And I have said that you will not go near the Continent. You are being a very silly little girl. Now go to bed and wake up with this mood behind you.'

I was speechless with rage. Not only had the interview, for which I had steeled myself, not gone the least according to plan, but to be treated as an errant schoolgirl at the end of it . . . ! I almost told him the truth there and then. But my instinctive caution restrained me. As Felix had said, one should keep one's options open for as long as possible. I lay awake, making plans, but did eventually sleep, and came down to breakfast with my mind composed. Edward seemed to have entirely forgotten our discussion. 'I may be late,' he said. 'This damnable Privy Seal business.' He then kissed me lightly on the forehead, and left the house. I was never to lay eyes on him again.

★   ★   ★

I do not believe he planned this; I certainly didn't. But Edward, if a taciturn and inwardly-turned character, was also a far deeper one than I had ever suspected. He had in fact taken in all I had said, and all I had virtually admitted, and no sooner had he reached London than, parliamentary business or not, he set in motion an investigation into my relationship with Felix, as well as taking steps to restrain me from any more, to him, absurd behaviour. He had, indeed, commenced this last exercise before he had even left Roehampton. Ignorant of this, I certainly did not intend to see him again for a while. Once he was safely off the premises, I went up to my room and told Lucy to pack. 'Just a single box, with a few of my good things,' I told her. 'I will send for the rest later.'

She looked more doubtful than ever, but did as she was told. I then rang the bell, and when Mowlem appeared, told him to inform Carpenter that I would need my carriage in half an hour, and also that I wished my box to be taken down at that time. I had sufficient money to see me across the Channel and to keep me until Felix could send me some more, as I had no doubt he would as soon as I let him have an address. But to my consternation, Mowlem never moved, and instead gave a gentle cough. 'I am afraid that will not be possible, milady. His lordship has given instructions that no boxes are to leave your room, and that no carriages or horses are to leave the estate.'

I'm afraid I goggled at him. It had never crossed my mind that Edward could be so decisive. Nor would I immediately accept defeat. 'I have given you an order, Mowlem.'

'And I must obey his lordship, milady.'

I nearly struck him, but decided against it. Instead I went downstairs to see for myself. I was sure that if I could once gain the stables, William, at least, would obey me. But it appeared that I could not even leave the house, and was surrounded by anxious and nervous servants, headed by Mrs Blundell. I saw no point in antagonizing these poor people, who were bound to carry out their master's instructions upon pain of dismissal – and who, in addition, were undoubtedly experiencing that extreme uncertainty any servant must feel when there is a domestic upheaval that may leave their jobs in doubt. I was saving all my wrath for when, as I naturally anticipated would happen, Edward came home that evening. If necessary, I was determined, I would tell him about my pregnancy, even if that meant going against Felix's recommendation. Felix had never envisaged that I would find myself a prisoner! I assuaged my fury by writing him a letter, bringing him up to date on events, and then settled back to wait, only to find myself confronted by my mother.

I was utterly surprised, and distressed, because Mama was so obviously distraught. 'Oh, my dear girl,' she said. 'My dear, dear girl!' She held me close, and whispered in my ear. 'We must talk.' For we were surrounded by servants. I showed her into the library, a place of such memories for me, and closed and locked the door. 'Jane,' she said. 'Tell me it is not true.'

'Tell you what is not true?' I countered. I had no idea how much she knew of the situation, although I gathered that she did know something. Even so, I could not understand how she had so promptly got in the act, as it were.

She sat down, and I poured her a glass of sherry, then took one myself. I suspected we both needed it, or would shortly. 'I received a note from Edward this morning,' she said. 'Saying that you had announced your intention of leaving him for that, that Austrian . . .'

'Prince?' I suggested.

'He asked me to come down and see you, and, well, talk some sense into you. Tell me it isn't true.'

I needed to buy a little time. 'Are you saying that Edward got a note to Forston and you got from Dorset to London all in a single half-day? Have you wings?'

She waved her hand. 'I was staying at Harley Street, Jane . . .' Which Edward had clearly known, but I had not. 'Say it isn't true,' she begged again.

I sat beside her, choosing my words with care. 'I asked Edward to allow me to go abroad for a season, and he refused.'

She gazed at me with enormous eyes. 'Is that all? He gave the impression that there was a crisis.'

'Well, Prince Schwarzenberg's name came up. So we quarrelled. Now he will not let me leave the house. Can you believe it?'

Mama, as always, stuck to essentials. 'But, this Prince Schwarzenberg . . .'

I drew a deep breath and took the plunge. 'I love him, Mama. I cannot live without him.' For all the rather cavalier manner in which he had left me to face the onslaught on my own, I was speaking the exact truth . . . at that moment. Opposition has always inspired me, and I felt like Byron's Manfred, standing on a cliff top, waving his sword at the lightning and defying the gods to do their worst.

Mama's mood was somewhat different. 'Oh, my God!' she said. 'Oh, my God! You can't be serious!'

I was tempted to tell her what lay beneath my gown, but again my instincts told me to be cautious. Parents, especially when backed by husbands, have more powers than is often supposed. It was entirely within the bounds of possibility that were they all to unite against me, I could be pronounced of unsound mind and forced to undergo an abortion. I knew Mama loved me too much ever to wish to harm me, but in this instance she might well feel she was saving me from an unthinkable fate. I determined that no one should know of my condition until abortion would be out of the question. And so I said, 'I am very serious.'

'But why? Is Edward unkind to you? Does he beat you? Does he not allow you sufficient funds?'

'He is very generous with his money, Mama. As to being unkind, that has to be according to one's interpretation of the word "kind". And as for beating me, would that he did. He has not laid a finger on me for well over a year.'

Her mouth was open. 'You mean . . .'

'What I have just said.'

'But why? You are beautiful, charming . . .' She ran out of words, being unwilling to delve into a subject she had never discussed with me before. 'Has he found out about Tom Burrows?'

'I have never told him.'

'Then there is no reason for what is happening.'

'Yes, there is,' I insisted. 'I do not love him any more. In fact, I am not sure that I ever did.'

'Oh, really, Jane. How many married couples do you know who are still in love with each other after a year or two?'

'Are you saying that you are no longer in love with Papa?'

'Of course I still love your father.'

'And do you still share a bed with him?'

She blushed. 'Well, certainly . . .'

'Then you are claiming that you are uniquely blessed? Why should I not expect, and claim, the same happiness?'

'Because . . . because to do so will be to ruin your life. It will bring disgrace on the family. It will . . .'

'I am truly sorry, Mama. But it happens to be my life. And it is the only life I shall ever have. You must give me the chance to live it as I choose.'

She understood that she was making no progress on that front, and changed tacks. 'You believe that you are in love with Schwarzenberg. Is he in love with you?'

'Oh, yes.'

'And if you leave Edward and go to him, do you expect him to marry you?'

'Whenever it is possible, yes.'

'How can it ever be possible, Jane? The Austrian nobility, and that includes the Schwarzenbergs, are Roman Catholics. They do not recognize divorce. For as long as Edward lives, they will consider you his wife, unable to marry again.'

That was a point I had not considered, and it came as a nasty jolt. Why had Felix never put it to me? Surely because we had never discussed marriage, until yesterday. And yet we had not really discussed marriage then. I had assumed it would follow, in the course of time, and he had chosen not to mention it for the time being. 'Felix will work something out,' I said, loyally.

'Then may I ask you this. How long has this liaison been going on?'

I saw no harm in admitting this, now. 'Just over a year.'

'And when did you determine that you no longer loved Edward?'

'Oh, before that,' I said, carelessly.

'But a year ago you had just given birth to his child!'

'That is when I fell out of love with him.'

'I'm afraid I cannot understand . . .'

'It is simply that once Arthur was born, Edward informed me that our conjugal relations would cease.'

'And thus you decided that you were no longer in love with him. My dear girl, all marriages go through these patches. And do not bring up the subject of my relations with your father again.

I was perhaps fortunate in that he was away so often, and for such long periods, on his ship that when we came together it was always as if we were newly-weds. Believe me, Jane . . .' She held my hand. 'I know how easy it is, during a period of difference with one's husband, to imagine oneself in love with some handsome fellow of whom one knows very little. But all infatuations pass, and so do all marital differences. And you are a mother! Please, Jane, for the sake and the love of us all, give yourself time to get over this madness.'

However much I was certain she was wrong, and that I would never stop loving Felix, or he me, these were still powerful arguments – the most formidable being the question of the Roman Catholic attitude to divorce. I realized that I did need some time to consider, and to plan more carefully than was my habit. In addition, I could see that Mama was really distressed, and she was, after Felix, the person I loved most in all the world. I did not, at rock bottom, lose any of my ultimate resolve, but I did weaken to the extent that I agreed to give myself some more time to think. And thus found myself plunged into a series of situations I had never anticipated.

The sequence began that evening. Mama was still with me (she had brought some clothes with her and was clearly intending to see the crisis out at my side) and I was awaiting the return of Edward with some apprehension. Meanwhile Henry tried to keep out of our way, not a difficult task as we spent most of the afternoon in the nursery. To my surprise, but not, it seemed, Mama's, we were joined, just on dusk, by Aunt Anne Margaret. She had spent a busy day: for Mama, the moment she received Edward's note and determined to come down to see me, had got in touch with her sister, who happened to be at her own London residence, and asked her to visit Edward – both to obtain some more information as to the true state of affairs and, if possible, find out what he might regard as an equitable solution. This she now claimed to have done. 'He would like to hear from you, Jane,' she said. 'I feel sure that a letter, properly couched, would effect a reconciliation.'

I would hate to accuse my mother's sister of deviousness, but she was certainly guilty of wishful thinking. She had even more reason than Mama to wish to keep our domestic linen from being washed in anything other than the strictest privacy. She was afraid that if Edward and I fell out in public over my extramarital activities, George's name, and that of the Anson family, would be dragged through the dirt. Nor were her fears entirely unfounded, for when it became known that Edward was seeking a divorce, several people, Countess Lieven amongst them, openly proclaimed that George was to be named as the co-respondent. At the time, under pressure from every quarter, not least my own family, and with increasingly confused emotions, I agreed to do as she suggested. The letter I wrote was not very coherent. I tried to be affectionate, and asked for his discretion, but I had to repeat my wish to be given some time to myself, for reflection, as I put it.

In the event, that letter proved another mistake. Edward did not trouble to reply – I am not sure he wished to receive it, and that Aunt Anne Margaret had not made the whole thing up – and it was later used at the divorce hearing as more evidence of my duplicity. The fact was that, as I have said, Edward had already put in hand investigations into the various rumours; and had already, by the time he received my letter, come into possession of various facts which indicated to him that I had not told him the whole truth about the affair. This was mainly servants' tittle-tattle, such as the wretched account of a girl named Ann Lewis – whom I vaguely remembered as a maidservant of Felix's – as to how I would arrive at Holles Street by the back door; and that of some dreadful person named John Ward, a servant in one of the houses situated opposite No. 73 Harley Street, who claimed to have looked from his drawing-room window into Felix's drawing-room window and seen Felix lacing my stays! I was thus already damned, although I did not know it, and although Edward – always the cautious lawyer by instinct – had not yet undertaken a legal investigation but was already considering his options.

However, I had more immediate problems. Aunt Anne Margaret had also come to stay, and the next day they were joined by Steely. I therefore had quite a formidable force arrayed against me – no support at all, the entire household, including Lucy, continuing to regard me as if I were a reincarnation of Lucrezia Borgia.

What made my position more difficult was that Mama and

Aunt Anne Margaret were the two women in all the world I least wished to offend or distress. I cannot say the same for Steely, who was her usual objectionable self: she was incapable of understanding how any woman, having been forced to undergo what she considered the ritual sacrifice of yielding her body to her husband, should wish to undergo it again with someone else, especially when to do so was a criminal act. Mama and Aunt Anne Margaret, while far more broad-minded, and *au fait* with the ways of the world, had never, thanks to their own happy marriages, been exposed to such temptation, and therefore could not understand how I could risk home, happiness and family for the sake of passion. And as I was resolved not to confide my condition to them until it was irreparable, they increasingly came to the conclusion that I was merely being stubborn.

This stand-off lasted a week, with daily recriminations, lectures and pleas, and was a most tiresome business. By the end of the week I was worn to a frazzle, as were they. Fortunately, by the end of the week, Edward was intimating that he would like his house back – he did not specify that the return of his property should include his wife – and it was necessary for us to make immediate plans. But my seniors continued to temporize. They would not let me leave the country, as this would bring matters to a public head, and still hoped that I would reconsider my position – and theirs. But they wanted me as far away from London as possible, and at the same time also as far as possible from any cross-Channel packet port, just in case I was tempted to defy them and do a moonlight flit. I was therefore packed off to the seaside village of Ilfracombe in Devon, where Aunt Anne Margaret had a cottage. This was humiliating, but it was made all the more so because, as the family did not feel that I could be left to my own devices, Steely was deputed to be my companion. Actually, I was glad of her presence, at least initially, for I was feeling desperately low, and became lower by the day. My entire situation was because of my love for Felix, and, I believed, his love for me. I had written to him on the morning after my interview with Edward, and I continued to write to him every day, as we had promised to do. And I never received a reply! I kept telling myself that he would be having a great deal to do, setting up his new establishment, but with every day I reflected more and more that if he loved me as much as I loved him, he would surely find the time to drop me at least a reassuring note.

In these circumstances, I needed to talk to someone. Steely was as good as anyone, from my point of view. As I gradually unfolded the whole story she appeared to be totally shocked, but she could not gainsay the evidence of her own eyes that I was definitely pregnant. She later claimed that I was hysterical with guilt. I was certainly depressed at this time, but to describe my mood as hysterical more indicates her emotions than mine; and whatever I felt, it was not guilt, merely desperation at not hearing from Felix. However, as a result of her reports, letters were exchanged with Forston, and at the beginning of July we left Ilfracombe for Minterne House. Waiting for us there in Dorset were both Mama and Papa, a disconcerting experience. Poor Papa was completely out of his depth, as I am sure he had never been at sea, and gazed at me as if he could not believe I was his daughter. Mama was more in control of herself than when last we had met, although she was as shocked as everyone to learn that I was five months pregnant. But there was another aspect to the meeting. Edward had announced he was suing for divorce. There can be no doubt that the news of my condition had reached him as well – how I would not care to say – and in his view his honour and position demanded nothing less. There could now therefore be no objection to my leaving the country, and in fact it was agreed that the sooner this could be arranged the better. The question was how and where, and in whose care I should be. My own feelings were pique that I should be treated like an unwanted parcel lying about the place, but it so happened that when in the very depths of angry despair I was uplifted by two events that put a very different complexion on my situation.

The Fallen Woman

I had of course informed Felix that I had left Devon for Dorset, and now at last I received a reply, full of love and concern for my well-being. Why he had been so long in writing he did not say, but he did recommend that I leave England just as quickly as possible. He suggested Basel as the best place for me to await my confinement. Indeed, he offered to arrange a house for me to rent during my stay there. This suited me well enough: Basel is just about as close to Austria as one can get. But I would have agreed to anything just to hear from him. Yet it was disturbing that although he was seeking to control my life, even if from a distance, he made no mention of any financial support. Even more disturbing, he told me under no circumstances to come near Vienna, or indeed set foot on Austrian soil; this, he said, would irretrievably ruin his reputation and his prospects. Had I been in the mood for sober reflection his point of view might have made me very angry indeed – but having given up all for his love, I wanted only that. I showed the letter to Mama, who in turn showed it to Papa, and I could tell from their expressions that they were immediately considering how I should be supported and how much might be involved.

But only a few days later I received a visit from a Mr Freshfield, who apparently was acting for Edward, and who was clearly on official business, for he carried a well-stuffed satchel. I received him in the garden, where we could be in private, although I was well aware that we were being overlooked by every window at the back of the house.

Poor Mr Freshfield was in a state of high embarrassment, endeavouring to look at me without ever looking at my stomach. 'His lordship has required me to inquire as to your ladyship's intentions,' he began.

'I am to leave the country.'

'I am sure that is wise. He also requires me to inquire into your financial arrangements.'

'I have none. I will rely on my parents.'

'His lordship feels that will not do. He feels that, as the mother of his son, it is now and always will be his responsibility to ensure that you are never forced to live in any lesser comfort and security than you do now.' I could not believe my ears. 'I am therefore empowered by his lordship to make you the following offer. Lord Ellenborough will immediately provide you with one thousand pounds, to cover your removal expenses and the cost of establishing yourself in a new home.' I gasped. 'He will also provide you with an income, throughout the term of your life, of five hundred pounds every year, to be paid in two half-yearly sums of two hundred and fifty.' I was speechless. There simply had to be a catch. 'Is this agreeable to you?'

'It may be,' I said. 'When you tell me the conditions.'

'There are only two.'

'Ah,' I said. 'This generosity is dependent on my not seeing Prince Schwarzenberg. I will not agree to that. So . . .'

'No mention has been made of any gentleman, milady. Lord Ellenborough specifically required me to inform you that he has no desire or intention of controlling or influencing your future activities. Your annuity is to be for the rest of your life, regardless of what you may choose to do with it or with yourself. I may say that it is to be secured upon his lordship's estate, and will be continued even should anything untoward overtake him.'

Almost I scratched my head, still seeking hidden traps. 'But there are two conditions?'

'His lordship requires you to undertake to leave England, and never during his lifetime return.' He paused, giving me an anxious look. 'You have said that this is what you mean to do?'

'And the other?'

'That you promise never to see your son again or make any attempt to do so, or even to write him a letter or make any attempt to contact him. On this one matter your annuity is vulnerable.'

I sat absolutely still for some seconds. It is easy to say that I should have told him I could not accept such a condition, and I have been condemned for not doing so. But such condemnation has emanated entirely from people who have never themselves had to face such a situation. The reality was that whatever my answer, I was not going to be allowed to see Arthur again, except perhaps fleetingly. Certainly to attempt to interfere with his life as he grew older, and able to understand what had happened, would be to subject him to a great deal of unhappiness. He was the future Lord Ellenborough. With such an inheritance, and such a father, a glittering political career lay before him, in which any suggestion that the fallen woman who was his mother still interfered with his life could only be a severe, perhaps an insuperable, handicap. Those facts being evident, by refusing to accept Edward's terms I would be condemning myself to a life of penury to no purpose. Whereas by accepting, what a vista of freedom was opening in front of me! I realized that it would be the first true freedom I had known; there would be no one to criticize me, at least to my face, or to restrain me, and I would still have a child, already stirring in my womb . . . and Felix! If such feelings arouse the sentiment that I was a heartless mother, I will accept that criticism – but only from those who have themselves suffered my experience . . . and chosen differently. And been but twenty-two years old when faced with the decision.

Besides, I was a romantic – and for all my ability to look facts in the face, still dealt in dreams. Was it not possible that in the course of time Edward might die, and Arthur, inheriting his estate, might come across this biannual payment to a woman he would not remember, but who he would easily identify as his mother, and wish to seek her out? He would have to be an unnatural child not to wish to look upon the face of the woman who had given him life – and if he were to seek me, I could hardly be accused of breaking my word to his father. Ah, dreams! 'Milady?' Freshfield asked, becoming concerned at my lengthy reverie. 'What answer am I to give his lordship?'

'Am I allowed to see my son a last time? To bid him farewell?'

'I'm afraid not, milady.'

I sighed. 'Very well, then. I accept.'

It was his turn to sigh, with relief. 'It will be necessary to sign a paper confirming the arrangement,' He touched his satchel. 'I have it here. May we go into the house? We will require a witness.'

'Will my father be acceptable?'

'Oh, indeed. He would be ideal.' Because that would make

Papa responsible for my keeping my word, even in the unlikely event that one day I might no longer need my annuity.

Papa, like the entire household, had been waiting, one might say with bated breath, both to learn the reason for our meeting and its outcome. He read the document produced by Freshfield, his expression registering a mixture of concern at what I was being required to swear and relief that the unhappy business should be so adequately resolved, and at no cost to himself. 'You are content with this, Jane?' he asked.

'Yes, Papa,' I assured him. 'I am content.'

We signed, as did Freshfield. Then he delved into his satchel again. 'I have here a cheque for one thousand, two hundred and fifty pounds.' Proving that Edward had never doubted that I would accept his terms. 'The subsequent payments will be made as arranged. All I will require from you, milady, is your address at the time.'

We shook hands, and he left, whereupon I was delivered to the family, who commented on either Edward's cruelty or his generosity, according to their point of view. But as with Papa, the over-whelming sentiment was that of relief that the business was being so quickly terminated – and even a touch of envy, that I, now quite well off, should be leaving England and the scandal behind, while they were going to have to sit through all the gory details of the divorce.

That night I wrote Edward a letter of thanks, even suggesting that he had been too generous. My sentiments were genuine enough. As I had never had control of any money of my own (save for my pocket money as a girl, and that I had not always found sufficient), I had absolutely no idea of what it might be going to cost me to live. But £1,250 in my pocket, and a further £500 a year, seemed an enormous amount of money. Of course I must confess that in protesting his generosity I had very much in mind that the agreement between us had been signed and witnessed, and could not now be altered or negated as long as I kept my side of the bargain.

I did not mention Arthur at all.

That done, it was simply a matter of arranging my departure as rapidly as possible. It was decided that I should travel incognito, to avoid the risk of any muckraking journalist discovering what I was at and making himself a nuisance. The name chosen was Madame Einberg, which sounded suitably Austrian and was definitely not English; Papa had no problem securing a passport. I wrote Felix to inform him of my plans and new identity, and he promised to meet me in Basel just as soon as he could. This made me very happy.

Then we got down to details. Now that I had reached agreement with Edward, and in effect pleaded guilty to whatever he chose to charge me with, I no longer had any fears of blackmail. Thus I did not renew my offer to Lucy but dismissed her from my service, without a reference. 'But my dear,' Mama expostulated, 'you cannot travel by yourself . . . in your condition.'

'I will employ a maid on the Continent,' I said.

'But until you do . . . Miss Steele will accompany you.' Not again! But I knew I did need assistance.

Then came the unhappy business of farewells. I may say that my brothers, although both fully grown young men (indeed Edward was coming up to twenty-one), had not been included in our various family conferences, and were not produced to say goodbye to their errant sister. Neither were there any Ansons about to bid me adieu, save, briefly, for Aunt Anne Margaret. She was not at all happy with the situation, as there could be no doubt that there was going to be a divorce hearing, and no one could tell what names might be dropped. George did not even write me a letter.

Nor was there any word from Holkham, both Grandpa and Step-grandma having apparently written me off. And needless to say there was no communication from any of the great ladies who had introduced me to London society, not even from Lady Oxford. I had broken their rules and shattered their mould into a thousand pieces. I was more saddened at the thought of having to leave my pets, but Mama promised me that she would collect them and take them down to Forston and care for them until I was sufficiently settled for them to be sent to me.

Steely's and my first destination was Brussels, and it was a most tedious journey, first across the Channel to Ostend and then several hours by coach. It was the end of August, and we travelled in the midst of an army of English holidaymakers – which made it necessary, as my face had become very well known over the past few years, for me to be veiled when in public – while my condition (I was now close to seven months gone) did not make for comfort. And needless to say Steely, whose views of 'abroad' were not so very different to Lucy's, was not the ideal travelling companion.

But I was buoyed up both in anticipation of seeing Felix again and of my coming delivery; I so longed to regain my figure and my energy . . . and my passion. I was thus irritated when we remained in Brussels for a fortnight. This was because Steely took a long time to find a maid she felt would be acceptable to me. What she meant was acceptable to her! Equally, I had to be acceptable to my maid – for contrary to the generally held English opinion, Continental manners and morals, if perhaps different in detail to ours, are not the less strict. It did not take a genius to work out that a young woman claiming to be married who was travelling with a single companion and very obviously pregnant was in flight, whether from her husband, her family, her lover or the law, and thus probably disreputable. On the other hand, I was offering a generous wage, and eventually we found someone willing to throw in her lot with me. Her name was Emma; only a year or two older than me, she was prepared to adventure and quite pretty, with fair hair and a vivacious temperament. I liked her on sight, and took her into my employment over Steely's protests (she would no doubt have preferred someone older and less 'giddy', which was certainly her opinion of me).

This led to a final parting of our ways as regards any permanent relationship, though it was bound to happen anyway. I definitely did not want her to be cluttering up the place when Felix arrived, and I think even she understood that she would be a large fifth wheel to our coach, especially as she knew she could never approve of, much less like, the man who she considered had brought me into infamy. In any event, she was anxious to get home. If I had not enjoyed Brussels because I was not in the mood to enjoy any place except where Felix could join me, she did not like Brussels because it was Brussels. Every time we left our hotel we walked past the famous statue of a naked little boy relieving himself into a fountain, and she found this extremely off-putting. So, after sharing a few mutually insincere tears, we parted, she to return to England and the divorce court, where she gave extensive evidence (I cannot say on my behalf, though she of course had to tell the truth as she saw it); and me to my destiny.

Which did not seem ready to receive me. Emma and I reached Basel without difficulty, and found the house Felix had rented for me comfortable if a trifle small, situated in a pleasant neighbourhood. We immediately made contact with both a doctor and a midwife, who examined me and announced that there should be no difficulty with a body as strong and healthy as mine. Then there was nothing to do except await Felix's arrival. Needless to say, this did not happen. There was a letter waiting for me saying that he was delayed but would be with me in a matter of days. But the days soon became weeks, while with every day my belly grew and I became less and less physically attractive and more and more despondent. News from England was scarce, the immediate gossip concerning me being apparently overshadowed by the enormous catastrophe of the death of the King's pet giraffe! I did not know whether to be relieved or insulted by this example of the inconstancy of public interest.

Quite apart from the non-appearance of Felix, there was absolutely nothing to do. Basel is a pretty town, very ancient, having actually been founded by the Romans, and situated dramatically close to the Black Forest; but like all essentially tourist resorts, while it flourished in the summer months, in the winter, which was now upon us, it became an inwardly-turned place of private entertainment. In my condition I would not have been able, in any case, to attend such events, but it was galling to be entirely excluded from all polite society. I filled my sketchbook but even that soon palled – one can only draw the same mountains a limited number of times – and while I found some amusement in watching the local lads indulging in their peculiar hobby, which consisted of climbing up a convenient snow-covered mountain and then sliding down, standing upon two narrow planks of wood strapped to their feet, this seemed to me to be at once a dangerous and absurd, rather than stimulating, pastime.

To my various discontents was now added concern for my baby. Dr Schmitt had suggested that it would be due about the beginning of November, which fitted very well with my own calculations: my night at the Norfolk in Brighton, from which I dated my pregnancy, had been 6 February. But November dawned, with not a stir, and without Felix. I became increasingly agitated. And then, on 10 November, he appeared.

I cannot say how many very pregnant women Felix had come into close contact with before me, but I doubt it had happened very often, Austrian society being far more strict than ours in these matters. He was certainly totally taken aback by his first glimpse of me in six months – for which he cannot really be blamed (to use a vulgar expression, I was as big as a house). Subsequent reflection leads me to the conclusion that, although he never admitted it, he had deliberately delayed joining me until after my expected delivery. But he carried it off very well, kissed me enthusiastically, and immediately began issuing orders and giving instructions. Emma was in total awe of him, for as always he travelled with no concept of anonymity, and was clearly not Monsieur Einberg; and for the first time she realized that she was moving in the very highest circles.

For my own part, I was naturally in seventh heaven – in more ways than one, because, whether as a result of Felix's arrival or not, two days later I was delivered of a bouncing baby girl. 'She is enchanting,' Felix announced. 'We shall name her Mathilde.'

'Mathilde?'

'It is the name of my sister. Did you not know?' I am sure he had told me, but I had forgotten. 'Since the death of my mother, she has been the female head of the family,' he explained.

'And she will wish our baby to be named after her? She knows about us?'

'I have no secrets from Mathilde. I have said, she is like a mother to me.'

I was not sure I liked the sound of this. On the other hand, if she was the key to my acceptance by his family . . . 'I look forward to meeting her.'

'Ah,' he said. 'Yes. Now, my darling, I have the most tremendous news.'

'You have arranged our wedding?'

'Oh, my dearest, you know that cannot be considered until after your divorce, and that may take some time.'

'But it will happen? Will I have to become a Roman Catholic?' Remembering Mama's warning.

'These are all things that will have to be considered,' he said. 'But first, my news. I am being posted to Paris. Do you know it?'

'I spent a night there, with my family, oh . . . a long time ago. I should love to see it again.'

'And so you shall.'

'You mean I can come with you?' Oh, bliss.

'Not with me. That would cause talk. But there is no reason why you should not live in Paris while I am there. I will arrange a house for you.'

'And you will come to visit every day!'

'Well . . . as often as I can. This is a very important posting. I am going to be very busy.'

'Tell me about it.' I had to appear at least interested.

'Why, it is simply that France is on the verge of another revolution.' I was taken aback by this. Having heard so many tales of life in Paris during the Terror, I was not sure that I wanted to become involved with tumbrels and guillotines. 'Their king, you see, Charles, has become somewhat heavy-handed, and there is talk of a Bonapartist restoration.'

'But isn't Bonaparte dead?'

'Oh, indeed. But he left a son, the Duke of Reichstadt, who actually lives in Vienna. Well, his mother was our Princess Marie Louise, don't you know.'

'And you would like him to become King of France?'

'God forbid! One Bonaparte in a lifetime is sufficient. No, no. We would like Charles X to continue as king; but if the opposition to this grows too great, then he must be replaced by another member of the royal house, someone with whom we can do business. Whatever happens, France must remain a monarchy. But the situation is very difficult. Like you, a lot of people assume that we would want to have Reichstadt on the throne. So, you see, there is a lot of work to be done, keeping everyone happy and making sure affairs turn out as we wish.'

I could have asked him at this point, what about keeping *me* happy? But I *was* happy at the thought of us being together in Paris, freed of all restraint.

★   ★   ★

But first, there was the registering of my babe – we decided to keep the christening for Paris – who was officially named as Mathilde Einberg. This attempt at anonymity did not make me very happy, and as far as I could see was equally unnecessary, as Felix, obviously the proud father, made no effort to conceal his identity. I did not like the name Mathilde, anyway, and so called her Didi. But she was a most delightful child.

And then Paris! Felix went on ahead, both to commence his new duties and to see to my accommodation. In fact he left Basel immediately after Didi's birth; and although he returned in the new year, it was only for another brief visit, to assure me that all was prepared for my arrival. These fleeting moments together did little for my now very bereft sexual impulses; but just to know that I was a part of his life left me contented enough. And in February Didi, Emma and I were on our way.

I cannot say that Paris on my second visit presented a very welcoming appearance. As Felix had warned me, revolution was in the air; people stood around on street corners muttering, and one generally felt safer indoors than out. However, the house Felix had secured for me, on the Rue de Grenelle, in Faubourg St Germain, was comfortable enough, though, as in Basel, a trifle small. But my arrival in the city, my observations of the political scene and considerations of my comfort were all immediately overshadowed by a letter from Mama (who I kept informed of my various changes of address), telling me that little Arthur had died.

I was totally shattered. He had always been a delicate child, but he had been so carefully attended by his nannies, if, sadly, not by his mother, that I had never doubted he would grow up into a healthy if perhaps frail man. Nor, it seemed, had he died of any lung complaint that might have been expected from his persistent sniffles. Instead, he had succumbed to a convulsive fit. Mama could not tell me what had caused the fit, or what, if any, was the medical diagnosis. In February of 1830, regardless of what I had promised Edward, I was still legally Arthur's mother and it was all I could do to prevent myself from dashing back to England, at least to kneel by my son's grave. However, I knew that would accomplish nothing save for partly assuaging my own conscience, and with my usual clarity of vision I also understood that I might place myself in a difficult and perhaps irretrievable position. Indeed, with the death of Arthur I was not at all sure of my status, but to my great relief the first of my biannual cheques arrived only a week later. Call me mercenary if you will, but surely, if one were driving in one's carriage and had an accident, as a result of which one's companion was so badly injured as to lose an arm, it would be utterly pointless, no matter how near and dear that companion might be, to cut off one's own arm in sympathy. I wrote Edward a letter of condolence expressing my own grief, to which he never replied, and then concentrated on my remaining child.

Didi was christened a week later, and given the name Mathilde Selden, another absurdity that would have irritated me had I had less on my mind. The name was chosen by Felix, and I had no concept that the wheels of my betrayal had already been set in motion. For while I was being torn between grief over Arthur's death and delight at being able to see Felix every day or every night, without fear of interruption or betrayal, in the comfort of my own home and the warmth of my own bed, I was not aware that my divorce proceedings were being held in London. In most countries of the so-called civilized world – that is, Western Europe – divorce is unobtainable for ordinary folk. Kings can indulge in it for the sake of obtaining an heir, but even then it has to be bound up in some discovery of consanguinity, no matter how far in the past – another example of human absurdity, for as the same holy fathers who forbid the ending of marriage except on these grounds also require us to believe that we are all descended from Adam and Eve, clearly we are all the result of incestuous unions. The English, being more inclined to litigation than any other nation on earth – or more civilized as they would have it (on the Continent, the only redress open to a husband who discovers that his wife has committed adultery is to kill her or her lover, or both) – permit such a marriage to be legally terminated, supposing the husband is important enough and wealthy enough to undertake the procedure (it is of course unthinkable that a wife should, or could, ever seek a divorce from her husband). And if not permitted to shoot the co-respondent, the husband does have the right to claim sufficient damages from him to at least cover his own costs. In fact, there was a rumour that Edward had claimed the enormous sum of £25,000. I do not know if this was true. Felix never mentioned the claim, and I very much doubt if it was ever admitted.

The point is that such a case can only be heard by the highest court in the land, and that it needs to be proved beyond a shadow of a doubt. This necessarily leads, in the absence of the two guilty parties, to the public airing of every scrap of dirty linen than can be found. During the first hearing, before the House of Lords, reportage was forbidden, and my attorney – a Mr Dampier (recruited by my family) – on instruction attempted to limit the damage by refusing to call any witnesses to rebut the plaintiff's contentions, thus in effect pleading guilty on my behalf. This being so, the Lords felt constrained to grant the petition, although not without several derogatory comments on the way Edward had neglected me.

However, the ordeal was only half over. From the Lords, the case had to go to the Commons for confirmation. These gentlemen insisted upon hearing all the evidence again, and this time there were no reporting restrictions. Thus detestable people like Ann Lewis and John Ward retold their sorry tales. And they even dug up Robert Hepple, the flunkey on duty at the Norfolk during our night there, who had wished to discover Felix's business when he sought my room. Hepple, it turned out, had not retired but waited to see if Felix would try again, and then followed him surreptitiously and looked through the carelessly unblocked keyhole of my room! Why such people are not locked up as peeping toms defeats me. At least, being under oath, he could not claim to have *seen* anything taking place, but he did insist that he had heard incriminating sounds from the bed. Oh, the wretch! What a contrast was the behaviour of William Carpenter, also required to give evidence, who refused to concede anything more than that from time to time he had dropped me on the street rather than at a destination, because of my wish to walk for a while.

Also figuring prominently as a witness, as I have mentioned, was Steely, mainly to relate how I had tearfully confessed to her that Felix was the father of the child I was carrying, but adding a great many other things besides. Oddly, Lucy was never called, although she would have been in a position to offer the most incriminating evidence of all. I do not know the reason for this, but I suspect she was up to her tricks and informed Edward that she might be obliged to relate the events of our wedding night if Mr Dampier got to learn of them, which could easily be arranged. I imagine this earned her a satisfying pay-off to keep her mouth shut.

I may say that my case was taken up with great vigour, not by my attorney (who remained under instructions to have the business over with as rapidly as possible) but by several members of the House – who, as had happened in the Lords, attempted to put at least part of the blame upon Edward for his neglect of me. By dragging things out these people did me no good, and the end was inevitable. At the beginning of April, my marriage was proclaimed at an end.

The news of the outcome of the divorce case reached me before anyone else in Paris, and was extremely welcome. Even more welcome was the astonishing information, conveyed to me by Mr Freshfield, that I was to receive a further £350 a year, again payable half-yearly. This was the sum agreed upon by Edward to the court, and accepted by them. No mention was made of the earlier agreement between us, and this second payment was to be made without any restrictions whatsoever. For a few days, indeed, I was in a state of some agitation for fear that it was intended to replace that earlier, so generous settlement. But Mr Freshfield assured me that it was *in addition* to the earlier agreement. Edward's motives for offering this additional sum and endeavouring to keep our arrangement secret were, I suspect, due to the censure he had received for what was felt to be his role in the breakdown of the marriage – which made him realize that were the terms he had imposed on me to be made public, he would receive more censure yet.

Whatever Edward's motives, I was now a relatively wealthy woman, which I found very enjoyable. In fact, my first couple of months in Paris were most pleasant. This despite the fact that I rapidly discovered that I was *persona non grata* as regards Parisian society. My reputation had preceded me, and although I left my card at all the important houses, even at the Court, I received no invitations. This did not greatly concern me – from what I heard on every side, the Court was unlikely to be there very much longer – but I will confess to feeling hurt when Princess Aloisia Schoenburg, Felix's younger sister, refused to see me. Felix promised to reason with her, but nothing came of it, and I was not prepared to beg; yet the fact remained that her attitude clearly influenced that of the rest of Parisian society.

I received a further snub when Lady Blessington, a detestable woman who had the effrontery to use a caricature of me in one of her scurrilous novels, threw a great reception for my cousin William, now a captain in the Royal Navy and on a visit to Paris, and thought fit not to invite me. Nor did William even call upon me, which I considered very poor form, on the part of a first cousin who was also a childhood playmate. I decided to write the Ansons off – and merely shrugged my shoulders when, later this same year, I received news that George had got married, to Isabella Weld-Forrester, who had taken my place as the reigning beauty of the day (only the best for George!) and who, according to my correspondent, was a woman of spotless virtue. The correspondent who found it necessary to point this out was, needless to say, Steely.

But even I was forced to feel a pang of regret when soon afterwards Cousin William got himself killed in an accident on board his ship. Two of my three childhood playmates had come to an untimely end. How far away did dark corridors at Holkham and the ghost of Great-Aunt Mary seem then.

But these events were in the autumn. In the spring, Paris has always cast a magical spell over poets and lovers alike, and I was both. I had regained my figure and my beauty, I was rich, and I was able to receive my lover whenever he was able to come to me, which was almost every day. True, by the end of April my notoriety had grown, as full reports of the divorce proceedings reached the Paris newspapers – but I did not give a fig for that. Felix was somewhat put out by a cartoon depicting him lacing my stays, based on the evidence of the foul Ward, but I persuaded him to laugh at it. For the rest, although I remained barred from polite society, we attended the theatre and the opera (where we were the cynosure of all eyes), we frequented the cafes of the Left Bank, and on occasion we even danced in the streets. Indeed, everyone else was doing it. For the Parisians, all of this frantically gay activity was no doubt intended as a relief from trepidation concerning the explosion that was obviously coming, as the King tightened his repressive measures; but for me it was an unending delight. Which ended abruptly, when I received a visit from the Marquess of Londonderry.

Dear Robert, as will be recalled, was Edward's cousin-in-law first time around. Again, as may be remembered, we had liked each other on sight; and indeed we remained friends all of our lives. Robert was a totally different character to Edward, and had been a regular attendant at Almack's, where we had danced together often enough. I was delighted to see him, even if a trifle concerned as he was clearly very agitated. 'Robert!' I cried, embracing him. 'What brings you to Paris?' I could think of no reason for him to visit me, save a domestic tragedy. I felt quite breathless.

'Actually, I am here on Edward's behalf.'

Now my thoughts began roaming over a number of unpleasant possibilities, such as my ex-husband having gone bankrupt, thus leaving me also in that unhappy condition. But I kept my face and my voice under control, showed Robert to a chair, sat beside him, waved at my butler to bring some wine, and asked, 'I hope he is well?'

'Oh, very well, thank you. Actually . . .' He looked embarrassed and accepted a sherry with some gratitude. 'He sent me to see Schwarzenberg.'

'Whatever for?' I was decidedly alarmed, as Felix would be very put out if Edward started dunning him for money.

'Well, you see . . .' Robert looked more embarrassed yet. 'He feels, I feel, well, we all feel, that the fellow ought to do the right thing. By you.'

I put down my glass. 'What exactly do you mean?'

'Well, dash it all, he put you in this position – and now that your divorce is final, well, you can marry again. Can't you?'

'You mean you proposed marriage on my behalf.' I didn't know whether to laugh or be angry.

'Well, I explained to him that it was the only gentlemanly thing for him to do.'

'I see. And what did he reply?'

'There's the rub. He said it was impossible.' My head came up. 'He offered a whole host of reasons,' Robert said. 'For one thing, he and all his family are Roman Catholics, and you are a Protestant.'

'He knows that I am perfectly willing to convert.'

'Are you really? I say! But I think the more important problem is his family. It's very old, you know.'

'Oh, really, Robert. Surely every family on earth is the same age!'

'What I meant was, its nobility is very old. Schwarzenbergs have been counts and princes since before anyone can remember. Their reputation is spotless, and must remain so . . .'

'You mean their women have always had spotless reputations,' I pointed out. 'That can hardly apply to their men. Anyway, I thank you for your efforts on my behalf. May I ask why you have come to tell me all this? Did Edward also instruct you to do that?'

'No, no. He did not suggest I call. Indeed, I doubt he would approve. But Jane, dear Jane, I had to come. I hate to see you wasting your life on, well, frankly, a cad. Please don't take offence,' he added, as my face froze. 'I seek only your happiness.'.

'I have taken offence,' I told him. 'But as I know you have acted in good faith, I will forgive you. Will you stay to dinner?'

'Ah . . . that would be very nice. But I really must be off. There is a packet out of Calais tomorrow night.'

'As you wish. Perhaps you will thank Edward for me. But I do assure you, and him, that no matter what Felix may feel called upon to say publicly, we are going to be married as soon as it can be arranged.' He did not look the least reassured.

My optimism was based upon a fact known only to me and Emma: I had just missed my second period. Within a month I was able to confirm to Felix that I was again pregnant with his child. He seemed pleased, and I did not tell him of my visit from Robert. With a growing family on the horizon – and also because, Paris having become used to my presence, and the titillation of my divorce having subsided under the pressure of more important events, I now felt that I could start entertaining – I decided I needed a larger and more centrally situated house. I therefore left St Germain for the Place du Palais des Députés, so named because these gentlemen held their meetings in an old royal palace on one side of the square. The house I rented, No. 99, was exactly opposite, and was about as central as you could get. My plans for entertaining, however, were rudely disarrayed – by the arrival of the anticipated revolution.

This occurred roughly a month after we had learned of the death of King Prinny. I imagine this caused quite a stir among the English residents of Paris – I was not actually on speaking terms with any of them – but it certainly interested me, not on the King's account (he had long outlived any usefulness he had ever possessed) but because I could imagine the turmoil that would be ensuing at Westminster with the accession of Sailor Bill, and the almost certain ousting of the Tory administration at the required election. However, within a month what was happening across the Channel was completely overshadowed by what now happened in Paris. I awoke one July morning to the noise of gunfire, ran to the window and looked out at a crowd of men, and women, tearing up the paving stones and erecting barricades. This, I understand, is an age-old pastime of the French when they become agitated. But the agitation without was nothing compared to the agitation within. Emma who, in common with the other maidservants, was having hysterics, rushed in to present me with my pistols and begged me to save her. Didi was much calmer, taking her lead from me. But my butler was just as excited as Emma, and his footmen were hurrying about closing shutters and loading muskets and pistols, apparently determined to defend me to the last.

However, I doubted that a handful of pistols would repel a mob, and therefore adopted the only sensible course of action: I had Emma unpack the large Union Jack with which I always travelled (I intended that it should be draped over my coffin), and hung it from our upstairs windows. This raised a cheer from the mob, and soon I was disbursing coffee and cognac (tearing up cobbles is a thirsty business). Felix arrived to make sure that I was all right – and seemed quite put out to discover that not only did I not need rescuing, but that I was in charge of events, at least in my locality. In fact, as revolutions go, this was a very low-key affair. There was some more firing and barricades were erected all over the place, but it appeared that not even the Army wished to fight for Charles, and by the end of July France had a new king – a Bourbon to be sure, named Louis-Philippe.

Acceptable to the mob because his father had actually voted for the execution of King Louis XVI (his cousin!) before being guillotined, in turn, during the Terror, Louis-Philippe was offered, and accepted, the crown on the basis that he would rule as a constitutional monarch. Overnight, Paris shrugged off its tensions and became gay again, its enthusiasm kindled by a military triumph – the capture of the pirate city of Algiers, long the scourge of Mediterranean shipping. The French had been besieging Algiers for several years, and the ultimate victory had finally been achieved during the summer – a fact that Charles had been relying on to restore his popularity. But that had been beyond repair, and it was Louis-Philippe who reaped the benefit.

By the time all these political matters had reached their climax, I was five months pregnant and no longer in a condition, or mood, to socialize. Thus largely confined to my house, and not receiving casual visitors, I depended mainly on Felix for news and company. But as the summer wore on, I began to see less and less of him. I knew that he was very busy, sorting out various political intrigues. And indeed threats – for Louis-Philippe was not immediately accepted throughout the country, and Austria was desperate that he should be, and that France should settle down again to being a good neighbour, with all possibilities of either a nationalistic authoritarianism or Bonapartism removed. Equally, because of my pregnancy, Felix and I were no longer able to make love. But soon I began to hear increasing whispers, from my servants, that my lover had been seen at various receptions and at the opera with other women – one especially, Madame d'Oudenarde, being mentioned quite frequently.

I raised the matter with him, and was not entirely content when he put forward the same excuse as he had in London – that squiring women was a part of his job. However, I was reassured by his insistence that he would far rather have me on his arm than any other woman in Paris, but as that was not possible, both because of my condition and because I was not yet socially accept-able . . . Which led on to the real issue. My pregnancy was going to end in a few months, and my non-acceptability would end the moment we were married – which I anticipated would happen as soon as my figure had returned to normal.

Felix promised that it would be so. He swore that he had converted his sister Mathilde to the idea – she was far more important than the younger sister, Aloisia – and that the only obstacles remaining were his brother Frederick and Prince Metternich. Frederick had just entered the Church, and was filled with religious prejudice against such abominations as extramarital sex and divorce. But as he was Felix's brother, I was given the impression that he would not sustain his opposition for very long, especially if I became a Roman Catholic. I found it difficult to appreciate the importance of Metternich's opinion as regards Felix's private affairs, but apparently the chancellor controlled every aspect of Austrian life, social as well as political. Indeed, his disapproval could close every door that mattered in Vienna, and without his wholehearted support there would be no possibility of my being accepted at court. But Felix seemed certain that Metternich could be brought round, especially when he learned that I was carrying a possible Schwarzenberg heir.

With this I was content, trusting, much as I adored Didi, that I would not have another daughter – and shortly before Christmas I gave birth to a son. 'We shall call him Felix,' I said. Felix was delighted, and told me he would be writing letters to his sister to prepare the family for the news, and what would surely follow. But within a few weeks of his birth, little Felix developed a cold, which must have spread to his lungs. One morning in January, he was found dead in his cot.

Even more than with the death of Arthur, I was shattered. As I have explained, such was the domestic situation obtaining in upper-class English households I had really seen very little of my first son, but the situation had changed completely once I was on my own. I spent a large part of every day with Didi, overseeing every aspect of her life, and was doing the same with Felix. And then he was gone. His father appeared to be as distraught as I was, and for the first few days after the baby's death and hasty interment we were very close. 'Have you written to your family?' I asked.

'There has been so little time. And I will have to consider what I should say.'

I held his hand. 'Felix, darling, I will bear you more sons.'

'Of course. But still . . . it will have to be considered.'

I let it go, for the moment. But inside me there was beginning to churn a combination of distrust, despair . . . and, I am afraid, anger. But what could I do? I had given up all for this man. My reputation was irretrievably ruined; I had supposed that by fleeing England I could regain a measure of social standing, but that belief had been dispelled by my reception – or perhaps it would be more accurate to say, my non-reception – in Paris. Now, I was the mother of Felix's child, his acknowledged mistress, so that there was no man able to approach me romantically, even had one been willing to risk the social eclipse that might have followed.

But more than any of these considerations, I was still in love. Felix remained the only man I had ever loved without reservation – and as far as I could see, or wanted to see, he would remain the only man I would ever wish to love. Without him, I had nothing left in my life; indeed, without him I felt I could have no life. It should be remembered that that spring, of 1831, I was still only twenty-four years old. I was also in a condition of utter misery over little Felix's death, and could only endure life in his father's company. But this became increasingly rare. The excuse was the same as always, pressure of work: but the reports reaching me of his evening activities with various beauties became increasingly disturbing.

I needed distraction, so I reverted to the plan I had had the previous year, and began throwing select soirées. They soon became popular – and while I never did attract any of the important female members of Parisian society, I certainly attracted the men. My house became quite a rendezvous; indeed there was seldom an evening when someone did not drop in for a glass of wine and a gossip. My guests came from all quarters of society, and several of them have since become quite well known – among them Victor Hugo and a handsome and interesting young woman three years older than me, named Aurore Dudevant. I found her interesting both on account of her name, so like the nickname I had once been given and because, again like me, she had abandoned her husband to run off with a lover. Perhaps I should have studied her experience more closely, for he had deserted her after a couple of years. She was now living with a writer named Jules Sandeau, with whom she had collaborated on two novels. She confided to me that she was now engaged in writing a novel of her own, which she did eventually publish the following year, under the name of George Sand, and which was a tremendous success. After that she became famous, not only for her writing but also for her lifestyle – which included the habitual wearing of masculine clothing – and for her innumerable lovers, who included the popular Polish pianist and composer Frédéric Chopin.

Also included among my guests, quite often, was Prince Alfred Schoenburg, husband of the detestable Aloisia, and thus Felix's brother-in-law. He was a charming fellow and a witty conversationalist. I enjoyed his company but was decidedly put out when he hinted that if I should ever tire of Felix, he would willingly take his place as my protector. That was quite insulting, as it indicated that he regarded me less as a woman who had given up all for love than as a woman who would accept the company of any man willing to pay her bills – in effect, a courtesan! I rejected him quite brusquely. My most famous visitor, however, was a grotesquely ugly novelist – somewhat vulgar, at least in his dress – named Honoré de Balzac, who was already the toast of the Parisian literary establishment. I cannot say that I cared for him greatly.

Unfortunately, also amongst my callers, who should turn up but the abominable Aponyi, who had been seconded from London to Paris. He gushed over me, brought me up to date with London gossip, and was eager to hear all about my life. Naturally I did not discuss Felix with him – except to reiterate, as I did to everyone, that our marriage was simply a matter of time – but I did discuss many subjects and many people with him. Had I known that every word I said was being recorded in his diary for repetition to anyone who would listen to him I would have been more circumspect – and had I suspected that in his craving for gossip he chose to discern things that simply were not there, I would have forbidden him my house.

As I have said, my guests were mainly men. When they were accompanied by women, apart from Aurore Dudevant, these were more often than not prominent actresses, who had no social positions to risk; and indeed I suspect there was the occasional courtesan amongst them, although I insisted that everyone behave with absolute propriety when within my walls. But it was the men who mattered, whose conversation I enjoyed; and it would have been strange had I not flirted with them. Apart from the fact that they wished to flirt with me, I was well aware that at those very moments Felix was undoubtedly flirting, at the very least, with some high-born lady. For my own part, I certainly never allowed any man more than a squeeze of my hand. I was thus taken entirely by surprise when one morning in May Felix arrived – to my initial pleasure, as I had not seen him for several days – and remarked, 'And how is the brothel today?'

It is possible that he was being facetious, but it so happened that I was out of sorts that morning, and my feelings were accentuated as I was conscious that I had not seen him for over a week. 'I think you should apologize,' I said, quietly enough.

But he was in an aggressive mood. 'Apologize for what? Do you not entertain all and sundry?'

'I entertain those who amuse me.'

'As do their antics, no doubt.'

I was beginning to grow angry. 'Any gentleman, or lady, who enters my doors, behaves with complete propriety at all times. I am not responsible for, and am not interested in, what they do outside of my house.'

'Ha!' he commented. 'You'll be telling me next that you do not spend hours alone with this fellow Tabourier?'

Jacques Tabourier was a very pleasant young French officer who had obviously fallen head over heels in love with me. As he called at odd hours we had certainly spent some time alone together, but as with all my other male guests I had never permitted him more than a touch of the hand. But by now I was well on my way to losing my temper. 'Do you, then, maintain spies in my house?'

'Then you admit it!'

'I admit nothing, because I have nothing to admit.'

'You expect me to believe that?'

'Yes, I do. Just as you expect me to believe that when you escort Madame d'Oudenarde to the opera, and then home again, you do no more than kiss her fingers. May we now end this futile conversation?'

'Futile? You are betraying my bed!'

I slapped his face. It was not something I intended to do – but his accusation was so outrageous, when I compared his behaviour, both as regards promises and conduct, with my own utter loyalty to him, that I quite lost my head. Having delivered the blow, I stared at him, open-mouthed, half expecting him to hit me in turn. Instead, after gazing at me for some seconds, his cheek suffused from my blow, he turned and left the house.

I was furious, and at that moment glad to see the back of him. But next morning I had regained my composure, and wrote him a note, apologizing for my behaviour and inviting him to supper. I anticipated a great reunion, and was utterly taken aback when my messenger returned to say that Prince Schwarzenberg had left Paris. I had no idea what to do, save to be patient and await his return; I could not believe he would have run off just because of a spat — it had to be official business. I waited for two days, then wrote to him again. This time the news was devastating. 'The Prince's rooms are closed, milady,' my messenger said. 'And to let.'

Still I refused to panic; I found it difficult to believe that he had abandoned the daughter he seemed to adore. 'Take the message to the Austrian Embassy. Ask them to keep it for the Prince, and at the same time ascertain when he will be returning.'

The reply to this was crushing. 'Prince Schwarzenberg is no longer at the Embassy, milady. He has returned to Vienna.' I later learned that he had actually fled to one of his family's castles, but that made very little difference. I still could not accept that he would have done such a thing, without a word of explanation, just as I could not accept that he would react so violently to a lover's quarrel. Presumably for a member of the Austrian aristocracy to have his face slapped was the ultimate insult; and to have it done by a woman, thus preventing any opportunity to seek revenge by means of sword or pistol, was more devastating yet. I have no doubt, that had he challenged me to a duel, with my skill and coolness, I would have ended the business there and then — and it might have been better had this been possible.

But what had happened was far more devastating for me. I had devoted my entire life to this man, and now he had just walked away from me. For a few days I couldn't move, or think. My house remained shuttered as if I had suffered a bereavement — which, as far as I was concerned, I had. All callers were turned away, no doubt providing an inexhaustible subject for gossip, with Aponyi offering his version of events as absolute fact. But after a week I pulled myself together. I wrote to Felix, again apologizing and asking for the courtesy of an explanation of his behaviour – but as I had no idea where he was and the Embassy would not enlighten me, I had to send it to his family address in Vienna, and doubted he would receive it. Then I had to consider my own position. I had come to Paris simply to be with him. Apart from him, I had no friends in the city, only hangers-on and gossip-mongers. I had no wish to remain for their titillation. Going to Vienna, where my heart was, would expose me to ridicule – or worse, if the Schwarzenbergs were as powerful as everyone claimed. To return to England would be to break the terms of my agreement with Edward. Where was left?

In my despair and confusion, I actually consulted a fortune teller, hoping for a glimpse of the future. This lady, who called herself Madame Normande, was quite famous, as she had, from time to time, been visited by Bonaparte. The story goes that she fell from favour when she predicted that he would be defeated by Wellington! Whether this was true or not, I quickly determined that she was a quack, as she held my hand and stroked it in a rather unpleasant manner, before saying, 'My dear, I see for you the most exciting future. You will have countless lovers before *the one*. Some of these men will be very powerful. Why, I see a king in your bed. No, no, two kings. But wait . . . three kings. You will be loved by three kings.' I had never heard such clap-trap in my life! Quite apart from the fact that I knew I was never going to love any man other than Felix, the idea of my ever getting together with a king, especially in my non-existent social position, had to be absurd. As for three . . .!

But my visit to Madame Normande had left me more confused and uncertain as to my best course than ever. I swallowed my pride and wrote to Mama, begging advice.

The King

She wished to see me, but could not at that time come to France, and suggested we meet in Dover. As it was going to be a brief visit, I did not see that I would be breaking my word, which had been never again to *live* in England. I took with me Emma and Didi, as Mama had never seen her granddaughter. I was rather taken aback to find that she was accompanied by Steely, but in fact the meeting went off very well. Mama was enchanted with Didi, and she was also prepared to put the past behind her and be as positive as possible. 'Bavaria,' she recommended. 'Munich. That is the place for you to settle until, well, you have determined what you wish to do.'

'I know no one in Munich.'

'Yes, you do. Don't you remember Lord Erskine? He is an old friend of the family. You met him at dinner on more than one occasion, before your marriage.' I hoped he had not been one of my prospective suitors. 'He has recently been appointed ambassador to the Bavarian Court,' Mama said. 'And writes most glowing accounts of the country. I know he will be happy to welcome you.'

'What of Bavarian society? Will they accept me?'

'I am told that they are more liberal in their outlook than us,' Mama said.

Thus, casually, can the entire course of one's life be changed for ever.

I decided to take her advice. I could hardly do otherwise, as I had no alternatives. We spent a pleasant if sad day together – Mama had to inform me that both Gibraltar and Turpin had died, she thought they might have pined for me – then we embraced and I returned across the Channel.

Fortunately the journey from Paris to Munich was not a long one. I was met by Lord Erskine himself, together with his wife, who, despite having a large and boisterous – and most enjoyable – family, found room to put me and Didi and Emma up for a few days until I took possession of the new home they had secured for me to rent. I became especially friendly with their daughter, Gabrielle, who was only a year or two younger than myself. The house I rented was decorated and fitted out exactly as I wished. If all this movement and resettlement sounds an expensive business, it was! But as I still possessed most of Edward's original capital settlement, and the cost of living in Munich was considerably less than in Paris, my finances soon recovered. And Munich, I rapidly discovered, was a pure delight.

It had been the capital city of the Wittelsbachs for a very long time, through the centuries when the Electors of Bavaria had played a prominent role in the political and military history of Europe; and like so much of Germany, it had been sucked into the grasp of Napoleon. This had had one positive result: the then Elector, father of the present ruler, had been created a king. Since then, at the behest of the present king, Ludwig I, the Bavarians had over the past few years indulged in an extravaganza of building, turning an already pretty city into a beautiful one. In this sense Munich was very like Paris, where work was still going on erecting the Arc de Triomphe. And in Munich, as in Paris, left-wing political views were flourishing.

I felt I could be happy here, if I was ever going to be happy again. But the future lay uninvitingly empty of everything I desired from life, save for the care and upbringing of Didi. Mama had been over-optimistic about the liberality of Munich society, and even Erskine's sponsorship could not open doors to me, although I fell into the habits and customs of the locals readily enough. I went for a ride in the park every morning; and most afternoons sat at one of the green-topped outdoor tables at Tombosi's, the most popular restaurant in the city, to sip tea and watch the passers-by – the boulevard outside the restaurant being the centre of the daily promenade in which everyone who considered himself or herself anyone took part. The promenaders in turn watched me. But none was bold enough to speak with me, although I had no doubt that they all knew who I was. I was therefore the more surprised when one afternoon, about a fortnight after my arrival, I was sitting at my usual table, and was approached by quite a group of people, who had been strolling down the boulevard. Now they stopped, at the behest of their leader, and followed his example in staring at me. I found this very bad form. A surreptitious glance at a beautiful and perhaps notorious woman is perfectly acceptable, but a downright stare is rudeness.

I summoned the waiter. 'Who is that person?' I inquired.

He positively blanched. 'That is His Majesty, milady.'

His Majesty? I turned back again in consternation. I had never seen a king strolling along a street. I had never heard of one doing so. And his entourage, if large, did not appear to consist of bodyguards; indeed, it was composed of both men and women, all fawning on his every word. As for the man himself . . . he was of medium height, well built, with regular features, wore a moustache, carefully trimmed and shaped, had receding dark hair, and was very well if modestly dressed. And now he was coming towards me! I hastily stood up, while the waiter stood to attention behind me. A king! The King!!! Shades of Madame Normande! But that was impossible. The King came right up to me. 'Lady Ellenborough?' he inquired, to my dismay positively shouting the words, so that every head in the restaurant turned – not that there were many not already looking at us.

I gave a brief curtsy. 'That is my name, Your Majesty.'

'Why,' he said, still speaking far too loudly. 'You are everything they say of you, madam.'

I wasn't sure I should accept that. but I did not feel I could afford to take offence: I was a guest in his country. 'I am sure the reports have been exaggerated, sire.'

'They have not been accurate enough, madam. Not accurate enough. You are quite beautiful.' So he had been referring to my looks rather than my reputation. I began to like him. 'I am your devoted servant, madam,' he went on. 'I should like to have a conversation with you.'

'I am at *your* service, sire.'

'Yes. We will hold a conversation. Good day, madam.'

I curtsied again, and he set off again, followed by his people. But one of his gentlemen remained behind. 'May I have your address, madam?'

I gave it to him, and he wrote it down, and nodded. 'May I ask how His Majesty knew my name?' I inquired.

'He stopped in his walk and asked, "Who is that utterly divine creature?" Those were his words, if you will pardon me.'

'I do pardon you. And one of you knew who I was?'

'Of course, madam.'

'Then . . .' I hesitated, having to choose my words with care.

'His Majesty had heard your name, madam. Now, if you will excuse me.' He bowed.

'There is one thing more. Does His Majesty always speak so loudly?'

'Sadly, madam, His Majesty is afflicted with poor hearing. A childhood illness.'

'Ah,' I said.

I left the restaurant and took myself to the Erskines' residence, where they listened to my strange encounter with a mixture of amusement and concern. 'I'm afraid the King is a law unto himself,' Erskine said. 'Basically, he is a very nice fellow, but there is no check on his decisions, or his . . . shall I say . . . whims. Sadly, there is a history of insanity in his family.' I began to feel a little concerned myself – as he could see. 'I am not suggesting that the King is mad. But he is certainly given to eccentricities.'

'He worships beauty,' Lady Erskine said. 'Beautiful buildings, and beautiful trees and flowers – well, you only have to look at the way Munich has been transformed since he came to the throne. Only six years ago, and he has practically redecorated the city.'

'He also worships beautiful women,' Erskine put in. 'Do you know, he has a portrait gallery, containing paintings of all the handsome women in his kingdom? These were commissioned at his expense, you understand.'

'And also at his command,' his wife reminded him.

'Well, my dear, he is the King.'

I did not consider the worship of beauty, and certainly the worship of beautiful women, to be proof of eccentricity, much less madness, but I was still trying to ascertain where I stood. Or possibly might be required to lie, if La Normande had been at all accurate in her prognostication. I still could not believe it. But if she had been right . . .? She had spoken of *three* kings! Well, one has to start somewhere, I supposed. But did I want to start, anywhere? Since my first meeting with Felix, I had never looked at another man with anything more than politeness, and I had no desire to do so now: I was still hoping for a miracle, still believed that it had to happen. Nor, even in my girlhood dreams, had I ever considered the bed of a king. On the other hand, as Erskine had just intimated, how did one refuse a king? How did one *dare*, when one was living in his country? Most important of all, how did one dare go against a prophecy, certainly one so redolent of romantic adventure? 'Are all these beauties his mistresses?'

'Oh, good heavens, no,' Lady Erskine said. 'There are more than thirty of them. That would be beyond the capability of any man.' She flushed. 'Well . . . anyway,' she added brightly, 'most of them are ladies of spotless reputation.' Her flush deepened. 'Oh, my God! My dear, I do apologize.'

'I can forgive everything except hypocrisy,' I assured her. 'Is there a Queen Ludwig?'

'Very much so. But . . .' Erskine looked at his wife.

'Queen Theresa was once described, by Napoleon himself, as the most attractive princess in Europe.'

'By Napoleon?' I queried.

'Well, yes, it was more than twenty years ago. She still retains much of her looks. But . . .' It was her turn to look at her husband.

'She and Ludwig fell out, soon after his succession,' Erskine explained. 'This had nothing to do with any peccadilloes he might have had. But the Queen holds a most liberal point of view as regards politics and personal freedom. She and Ludwig shared this attitude before he became king, but then he discovered that ruling a country does not admit of too much liberality. Don't misunderstand me, Ludwig is not in any sense a tyrant; and as far as one can gather, he is beloved by his people. But there was some trouble at the time of his accession, and the Queen took the side of the malcontents. Ludwig does not appear to have forgiven her. She has her own apartment in the palace and still appears beside him at official functions, but I do not think he ever visits her bed.'

'Are there any children?'

'Several. But all born before his succession and his separation from the Queen.'

I found all of this even more intriguing, although it did not seem to involve me to any great extent. If King Ludwig wished to admire me, I was happy to be admired. If he wished me to sit for a portrait, I was happy to do so. Apart from these passing thoughts, and still unable to bring myself to believe Madame Normande's prophecy, I was content to enjoy my privacy and wait to hear from Felix. I had no doubt that I would, once he had got over his absurd pique. I duly sat in my usual place at Tombosi's the following afternoon, and the next; but Ludwig did not appear, and I assumed that he had had second thoughts on learning more about me. I was thus totally surprised when, on the third day after our meeting, just after I had returned from the restaurant, and was playing with Didi in the garden, my butler, Manfred, appeared, looking distinctly flustered. 'Milady,' he said. 'The King is here!'

Emma gave a squawk of alarm. And I leapt to my feet, terribly aware that as I had been sitting on the grass with Didi my dress was both stained and crushed; and that, as I had carelessly discarded my hat on returning, my hair was coming down, untidily. To all this had to be added a sudden pounding of my heart, which I knew was pumping blood into my cheeks. As with his promenade along the street, I had never heard of a king calling unannounced on a private household in the middle of the afternoon. Kings summoned, they did not come to you. 'Is he alone?'

'There is a carriage at the front, milady.'

'Oh, good lord!' How public could one get? 'Please ask His Majesty to take a seat, and I will be with him in a few minutes. Serve wine.'

I turned to the door into the house, and paused in fresh consternation. Ludwig stood there. 'I did not come to drink your wine,' he said. 'I came to drink in your beauty.'

My hand had instinctively gone up to my head to push hair from my eyes. Now I attempted to curtsy and all but fell over. He hurried forward to take my hand. 'You have me at a disadvantage, sire,' I said.

'You can never be at a disadvantage, Lady Ellenborough.'

I sought defences where there were none. 'That is no longer my name.'

'Then we shall discuss your name, shall we not?' He looked past me at Emma and Didi. 'What a charming child!'

I accepted the unspoken command, while endeavouring to remain in control of the situation – this was, after all, my house. 'Take Mathilde inside, Emma,' I said. Didi was clearly bewildered; as she was not yet two years old, she of course had no concept of kings. 'And then, Manfred, please bring the wine.' The servants bowed, both to me and to the King, and hurried off.

'Will you sit, sire?' I indicated a rustic bench that stood beside the lawn.

He seated himself, obviously expectantly, so I sat beside him. 'May I ask . . .?'

'Mathilde is my daughter, sire.' If he wished to be my friend, he would have to accept me warts and all. 'Her father is Prince Felix Schwarzenberg, and she is named after his sister.'

'And Prince Felix is here with you?'

Obviously he would already know the answer. 'The Prince is in Austria, sire.'

'But you are expecting him to join you?'

How much else did he know? 'I am hoping he will do so, sire.'

'To marry you?'

These direct and very personal questions were disconcerting, but I had resolved on a course of telling the absolute truth, so I repeated, 'I very much hope that too.'

He studied me for several seconds. 'The Prince must be a very wealthy man.'

'Sire?'

'Well, when one neglects the greatest treasure one possesses, it can only be because there is so much else to be protected.'

At that moment Manfred returned with the wine. But he left again, immediately, before I had had the time to collect my thoughts. 'Your Majesty is too kind,' I mumbled.

'I am making excuses for the fellow. Do you still love him?'

I met his gaze. 'Yes, sire.'

'Then he surely does not deserve you. Did you really give up everything for him?'

'That is one way of putting it.'

'Thus you say you no longer have a title. What are you to be called?'

I took a step into the dark. 'My name is Jane.'

'Jane,' he mused. 'I would like to call you, Ianthe. That is Jane in Greek.'

'I think it is entrancing, sire. I shall be Ianthe, from this moment.'

'Now *you* are flattering *me*. My name is Ludwig. I would like you to call me Ludwig, when we are in private.'

'Ludwig.'

'You do not like it?'

'It is too harsh. I would prefer to call you Lewis.'

'You mean Louis. The French equivalent.'

'No, sire. I mean Lewis, the English equivalent.'

Once again he gazed at me for several seconds, then he smiled. 'You are enchanting. Lewis it shall be. I would like to see your bedchamber.'

Not for the first time in our brief acquaintance, I was totally taken aback. 'I'm afraid it is not very tidy,' I ventured.

'That will be ideal. I wish to learn about you. I wish to *know* all about you.' This, given the Biblical connotation of 'knowing', was quite the quickest and most direct seduction I had ever heard of. But I did not see that I could refuse him – after all, he was the King. And what was more, he was *my* king. My first king! I had La Normande much in mind. I rose and escorted him up the stairs, past the scandalized eyes of my servants, and showed him into my bedroom, which was, as it happened, absolutely spick and span, as I had not been in it since my visit to the restaurant. I stood to one side while he wandered around the room, picking up objects and studying them, then replacing them, uncorking one of my bottles of perfume to inhale the scent, and finally arriving at the bed, which he tested for softness before sitting on it. I had remained standing by the door, but now he waved his hand. 'Why do you not close that, Ianthe?' I obeyed. 'Join me,' he said.

I crossed the room. As so often in the past, not at all sure what I wanted to happen. He patted the bed, and I sat beside him. 'Tell me about your childhood.' This I did, in, shall I say, a bowdlerized version, reflecting that I needed to be brief. But I had talked for the better part of an hour, wondering when the main act, as it might be considered, was going to begin – when he suddenly leaned over and kissed me on the cheek. 'You understand that

I cannot invite you to Court. Protocol. Etiquette. I most humbly apologize for this.'

I had to reassemble my thoughts, these having been concentrating on memories of Holkham. 'Of course I understand, sire . . . Lewis. I had never expected such an honour.'

'So we shall have to meet here.' He got up, and I did also. He went to the door, and there paused and looked at me. 'How many men have you slept with?'

Another mind-jolting surprise. 'Ah . . . five.' I had certainly slept with Tom, although perhaps not in the sense that the King meant.

'Your husband and Prince Schwarzenberg . . . and three others?' He held up his finger. 'I do not wish to know their names. Only to envy them.' He kissed my hand and went down the stairs. I almost tumbled behind him, feeling I had to see him out – but at the same time unsure whether he wished me to stand in the doorway and expose us, together, to the gaze of any passer-by. In the end, I remained in the house, although I reflected that any passer-by who observed the King leaving my house could only draw one conclusion. In this, I was absolutely right. I later learned that from that day everyone in Munich assumed that I had become the King's latest mistress.

Had I been aware of this, I would have been extremely put out. I was still dreaming of a reconciliation with Felix, and could not feel that any prospect of this would be enhanced by his learning of my liaison with another man, even if that man was a king. I was in any event totally confused by the whole business, having never been approached in such a fashion before. I could not even be certain that I *had* been approached, in a sexual context. But if I did not wish Felix to have any suspicions regarding my faithfulness, I equally could not help but feel that what was sauce for the gander was equally sauce for the goose. I had no doubt at all that Felix had shared various beds since our separation. Indeed, I had no doubt that he had shared the bed of La Oudenarde, even while we had been in Paris together. And this was a king!

But I did not know if it would ever happen. I attempted to maintain as balanced an approach as I could to the situation, and forbade my servants to speak of the King's visit – though that was like King Canute forbidding the tide to come in. And I cannot deny that I was greatly flattered by the King's interest, and hoped to see him again privately – so much so that when two days passed and he neither came to visit me nor walked past Tombosi's, I did what many might consider a very forward, and perhaps foolish, thing: I wrote him a note expressing my pleasure at having been able to entertain him. To my great delight he replied, and thus we began a correspondence that lasted as long as our friendship.

And my advance had a more tangible result, for a few days later he again called. This was earlier than the first time, and I had just returned from my morning canter in the park. For the first time since leaving Paris, I was feeling in quite an elated state – for two reasons. One was that I had received an invitation to a soirée at the house of one of the King's ministers. I did not know whether this had arisen from gossip linking my name with Ludwig's, or whether indeed it had been his direct command that I should be taken up – but I hastened to accept and hoped that it might end my social purdah. The second reason was that I had that very morning been joined in the park by a most charming and handsome man. Riding is one of the few pastimes that permit an approach to be made without an introduction; thus a gentleman was quite entitled to bring his mount alongside mine, to compliment me on my mare and my seat. 'You handle her superbly,' he said. 'Would I be right in assuming that I am addressing Lady Ellenborough?'

I was not going to argue the point with a complete stranger, especially when he presented such an attractive prospect – tall and handsome, with the most splendid deep-red hair and moustache, the whole shown off by his hussar uniform. I swear that had I never met Felix I would have considered him the most compelling man I had ever seen in the flesh. 'You have the advantage of me, sir,' I said.

He saluted. 'Karl von Venningen, at your service, milady, now and always.'

I found this very flattering, and returned home intending to have Manfred obtain some information on him – only to be joined by Ludwig before I had even had time to change my clothes. 'Your Majesty,' I cried, as Manfred was hovering. 'What a pleasant surprise!' Which was not absolutely true, but I understood that the King had to have priority.

He kissed my hand and then led me up the stairs. 'Will you

take wine?' I asked, a trifle desperately. He seemed to be moving with a great deal of determination.

'Later,' he said, entering my bedroom, this time without so much as a by-your-leave. I followed and closed the door, standing in front of it. I had handed my hat and whip to Manfred, but knew I was looking somewhat tousled. As before, the King sat on the bed; and he gazed at me for several moments.

'I must ask you to forgive my appearance,' I said.

'I love your appearance. Undress for me.'

'Sire?'

'I wish to look at you. I have thought of nothing else for the past three days.'

My brain began to spin. 'I usually have a bath after my ride.'

'Splendid. I will watch you. But I wish to look at you, first.'

As usual, I was suffering from extremely mixed emotions. I could not help but be offended at the way he commanded me, as if I were some serving girl. But equally, I reflected, it is a king's privilege to command – and he certainly did not mean to insult me, it was just his way of speaking, and acting. As to what he had suggested might follow . . .

Complying with his command, I undressed – a slow business, as I lacked Emma. He watched me intently, neither speaking nor moving, at least visibly, until I stepped out of my drawers, then he beckoned me. I stood in front of him, and he drew little patterns on my sweat-damp flesh with his forefinger, circling my nipples, moving from my breasts down to my stomach, slipping through my pubic hair, before coursing round my thighs to do the same with my buttocks. I turned round to facilitate his investigation: I found what he was doing quite entrancingly sensuous.

'You were fashioned in Heaven,' he said.

'There are those who would say I was fashioned in hell.'

'We are surrounded by people who cannot see,' he remarked. 'This complexion, it is like the purest and richest milk, with just a hint of strawberries. What do you do to maintain it?'

'Why, nothing, sire, save for some creams. And I wash it, regularly.'

'There is not a woman in my court, or in my country, I suspect, who does not have some blemish. If it is not the residue of an attack of smallpox, it is an unsightly mole. You are perfection. And your teeth! They are like a collection of priceless pearls.'

'Again, I brush them regularly.'

'Sit beside me.' I obeyed, now in the grip of a considerable passion. I was about to be mounted by a king! Or was I? He put his arms round me, and caressed me some more, but made no move to remove any of his own clothing – and I did not feel I could initiate any progress in that direction, however consumed I was with a mixture of desire and curiosity. Then he kissed me – on the mouth, certainly, but with no great thrust – before releasing me. 'Tell your maid to draw your bath.'

Another of those moments of extreme uncertainty. Did he find my sweaty body repulsive? Up till then he had seemed to be enjoying it. I got up, rang the bell, and wrapped myself in my dressing gown. 'She will be embarrassed,' I suggested. Although Emma had been in my employ for more than two years, we had never attained the same measure of intimacy as I had once shared with Lucy. Now . . . she was indeed embarrassed. But then so was I. Bathing, when closely observed, is a far more intimate affair than actually having sex with anyone – when, in most cases, observation does not come into it at all, only feeling. Ludwig certainly observed, so that once again I anticipated a conclusion of this first stage of our relationship; but after watching me being dried, he kissed my hand and left – leaving me in an even greater state of confusion than before.

The next morning I received a huge bouquet of violets, with a card bearing the royal crest but no message. I was still contemplating these when Manfred announced that I had a caller. I studied the card: *Baron von Venningen*. Oh dear, I thought. But I couldn't turn him away. 'Milady!' He kissed my hand. 'Please forgive this intrusion.'

'You are most welcome, Baron,' I assured him, not for the first time being forced to be economical with the truth. I showed him to a chair, and Manfred presented a tray of sherry. The Baron sipped the drink with a slightly critical expression: I do not think he had ever tasted it before. 'It is an English drink,' I explained. 'Made in Spain.'

'I see,' he said, clearly not seeing at all. 'It is very nice.'

'Some people find it too dry.'

'No, no. It is very nice.' We gazed at each other. 'I called,' he explained in turn, 'to inquire if you are attending Baron Bardoch's soirée.'

'As a matter of fact I am.' Now how did he find that out, I wondered?

'Have you an escort?'

'Do I need one?'

'It is better to attend such functions with an escort. Will you permit me . . .?'

Why not? I asked myself. He was perfectly right: it is far better to have an escort on a public occasion. 'I should be flattered,' I told him.

Ludwig called again the next day. He was now such a regular visitor even I began to realize that all Munich, perhaps all Bavaria, knew of our relationship. That the rumours might have spread beyond Bavaria concerned me less than it should have done, because there had as yet been no impropriety between us. He liked to look at me; and to touch me, but never with any great passion. He had, thus far, made no attempt to bed me. But, at the same time, he wrote me most affectionate letters, and sent me repeated bouquets of violets – to match my eyes, he said. Thus assuming we were no more than very good friends, I asked him if he knew Baron von Venningen.

'I know the Baron,' he agreed. 'Why? Do you know him?'

'If I knew him, dear Lewis, I would not need to be told of him. I have met him, riding in the park.'

'And he made advances?'

'No, sire.' I realized I might have been indiscreet. 'You must forgive me, but I suffer from an insatiable curiosity about people I meet.'

'Did you have that about me?'

'Of course.'

'And to whom did you turn for enlightenment?'

'To the only people I then knew in Munich: the Erskines.'

'And what opinion did they express?'

'They said you were a very good man.' Which was true. 'And that you would prove a good and faithful friend.' Which was my own interpolation.

He was pleased. 'That I shall. Venningen! He has estates all over

Bavaria, Austria and Hesse-Darmstadt, and also Baden. Since his father's death, he is the head of the family, and spends his time managing his properties. Very successfully, so I understand.'

'When I met him he was wearing uniform.'

'Oh, he is a colonel in the Austrian army, although they are not fighting anyone at the moment. Some men suppose that uniform flatters them. He is also unmarried.' He shot me a glance.

I conceived that I had achieved a minor triumph in that I seemed to have aroused a spark of jealousy. But I hastened to reassure him. 'That is of no interest to me, Lewis. I am resolved not to marry again, unless it is to Prince Schwarzenberg.'

'Your constancy does you credit,' he remarked, somewhat drily.

Karl von Venningen duly escorted me to the soirée, and I was very well received. I will not say that I have never looked better, but I looked very well, with a new gown and my hair dressed as I chose rather than as custom dictated. As had happened so often in the past, the men clustered around me like bees round a honey pot, and the women whispered behind their fans. Clearly they were unable to reconcile my appearance on Karl's arm with the rumours surrounding my relationship with the King. Karl was delighted, and over the next couple of weeks escorted me to the opera and the theatre, as well as regularly joining me for my daily ride in the park. With my mornings and evenings thus occupied, and my afternoons subject to ever more regular visits from the King, I hardly had a moment to myself. Obviously my notoriety grew, and I could tell that the Erskines were concerned, though we continued to be the best of friends.

As for my two admirers, I managed at that time to keep them both happy. Karl was always the perfect gentleman, never seeking to do more than kiss my hand. He never inquired into my relationship with the King, and indeed his name was never mentioned between us. The same could not be said of Ludwig, who appeared increasingly suspicious of my escort. But as I explained, I had to have an escort, unless I was to lock myself up and never go out. '*You* cannot take me anywhere in public, dear Lewis. I understand and accept this, much as I would so love to be seen on your arm. I am always here waiting for you, when you can spare the time to visit me. Baron Venningen fills a purpose — nothing more.'

This seemed to reassure him, and he kissed me most passionately. I thus felt I could look forward to a busy social winter.
Then, just as the days began to grow shorter in October, I received
a letter from Felix!

I read the letter and then again, my heart pounding so much I
thought I would swoon. There was more than a page of endearments, of apologies for his unseemly behaviour, of his urgent
desire to see both Didi and me again, and of his wish to end my
long wait for legitimacy. How could I ever have doubted him?
In fact, I had never done so, in my heart, however I might have
been surrounded by scepticism on the part of my friends and
relations. I could hardly wait for Ludwig's next visit to show him
the letter. 'He writes a pretty hand,' he remarked.

'He has made me the happiest woman in the world.'

'He certainly seems to be intending to do so,' the King agreed,
still with no great enthusiasm of his own. 'Will you receive him?'

'Well, of course I will receive him,' I said. 'I so want you to
meet him.'

'I don't think that would be a very good idea. In fact, I do
not think it would be a good idea for your prince to come to
Munich at all.'

I could not believe my ears. 'I thought you were my friend.'

'I am more than your friend, Ianthe. I have only your well-
being, your happiness, at heart.'

'But you will not permit me to receive the man I am going
to marry.'

'I think it is most important that you receive him. I merely
do not think it would be a good idea to do it here, where you
are surrounded by gossips. I suggest that you go to one of my
castles. I think Berg would be the ideal place. It is isolated, and
is situated on Lake Starnberg, a lovely place.'

'And you will let me use it? Oh, Lewis . . .' I held his hands.
'I shall be for ever in your debt.'

'I wish only one thing from you in return. I wish you to sort
out this affair once and for all. Insist that he act the man and the
gentleman. Refuse to be fobbed off with any more promises.
Make him agree to an immediate marriage, or end it. Will you
promise me that?'

'Oh, I do, Lewis, I do!' I was feeling that way myself, but I knew it would not come to that. It never occurred to me that Lewis might have his own reason for not wishing Felix to come to Munich, in that it might be considered a humiliation for him were a foreign prince to arrive to court a woman everyone supposed was his mistress, and then carry her off.

I told no one I was leaving Munich, much less the reason. I simply gathered up Emma and Didi, and some clothes, and departed. The distance from Munich to Berg was only about twenty miles, and we covered it in a few hours. The schloss was a delight – situated on the east side of the lake, a considerable body of water, and surrounded by quiet woods. Separated by these from the little town, it was utterly peaceful and private. Ludwig had sent messengers ahead, so that we would be welcomed and our every comfort seen to. I had of course written to Felix informing him where I was to be found – Ludwig had allowed me to send my letter in the diplomatic bag to Vienna, so that it would be delivered virtually overnight. I settled down in contented anticipation of his arrival. Never had I felt so at ease with myself as I did on the day after our arrival, when I went for a long walk, entirely by myself, through the woods, no longer having to rely on dreams and now able to make concrete plans. I found this so enjoyable that I repeated it the next day, returning to the castle just about noon – to find an air of some agitation. 'There is a visitor, milady,' said the butler, who awaited me.

My heart pounded so rapidly I almost fell. I hurried up the front steps, discarding my hat and gloves as I did so (they were rescued by the good fellow) and went into the knights' hall – to find myself facing Karl von Venningen. For a moment we were both lost for words. I was the first to speak. 'What are you doing here, Charles?' By now, between ourselves at least, I habitually used the English version of his name.

'I should ask the same of you. Why has the King sent you here?'

'His Majesty has granted me the use of this house for a while. How did you know I was here?'

'Surely you know by now how impossible it is to keep a secret in Munich. He has sent you here to separate you from me!'

'From you? Why should he do that?'

'Because he knows that I am hopelessly in love with you.'

I sat down on one of the old high-backed, and quite un-upholstered, chairs. 'You have told him this?'

'Well, of course I have not told him. But it is obvious to everyone.' Except me! But then, I had not even considered the matter. 'Oh, Jane, Jane.' He fell to his knees beside my chair. 'I adore you. I fell in love with you at first sight. Jane, I care nothing for the King's displeasure. Marry me! I will not let him harm you.'

'Lewis would never harm me.'

'Then why has he sent you away?'

'He has not sent me away,' I insisted. 'He has lent me his house for a few days.'

'Then will you marry me?'

I stood up. 'I cannot.'

'Because you are in love with the King?'

'I am not in love with the King!'

'It is widely known that you are his mistress . . .'

'That may be widely known, but it is widely mistaken! The King is my very good friend, but I have never slept with him.'

'He comes to your house almost every day and accompanies you to your bedroom – and yet you have never slept with him?'

I made a mental note to do some sorting out of my servants, when I returned to Munich. 'We like to talk, in private. He comes to see me, because protocol prevents me from visiting him.'

'Will you swear that you have never shared a bed with him?'

I was at once offended and concerned. Offended because of his importuning; concerned because, although I had never had sexual intercourse with Ludwig, I had certainly been on a bed with him, naked. I took refuge in offence. 'I do not see that you have any right to demand anything of me! I have told you that I have never had sex with the King, and I am not in the habit of telling lies.' I was stretching a point – not for the first time in my life, nor, I have to confess, the last – but he was immediately contrite.

He rose himself and followed me – I having moved a few feet across the room – and again held my hands. 'Then marry me! I will give you anything and everything you wish from life. And you will make me the happiest man on earth.'

Has ever a woman received a more gallant proposal? But . . .

'I cannot,' I repeated. 'I am in love with another.'

He stared at me. 'Not Schwarzenberg? Still!'

'I love Felix now, and I will love him always. He is the father of my child, and he is the only man I will ever marry.'

'And he is going to marry you?'

'That is why I am here. Felix is coming here to make the final arrangements.'

He released me and left the room.

I expected him also to leave the castle, and felt very sorry for the situation. But I could not see that I was in any way guilty. If he was attracted to me, that could be said of a great many men; I had never felt under any obligation to marry any of them. But he did not leave. And as I did not feel I had the authority to have him thrown out, I was forced to entertain him to dinner. We sat at opposite ends of the long table, attended by a score of footmen and a couple of butlers – and hardly exchanged a word. Until the meal was over, when he asked. 'When do you expect the Prince?'

'At any moment.' It was no great distance from Vienna to Berg.

'Then I must wish you every fortune in the world,' he said, kissed my fingers, and went up to his room. He was so noble and gallant I nearly wept. However, I did not consider any man *that* noble and gallant, and locked my door. But it was never tried. The next morning he had gone.

That day was a very long one. I spent some time playing with Didi, who was now walking vigorously, then had one of the horses in the stables saddled and went for a ride. I then returned to the castle, bathed and dressed, and had a lonely dinner. The same pattern followed the next day, and I became increasingly agitated – with, I have to confess, sentiments that were profane rather than sacred. It was six months since I had properly known a man, and the thought of lying naked in Felix's arms was consuming my mind.

It was on the third day that a horseman arrived from Munich bearing a letter addressed to me, which had been delivered to the government offices in the diplomatic bag. It had obviously been forwarded by Ludwig, but there was no covering note.

I retired to my bedroom to read it, but already knew what it had to contain. My fingers trembled as I broke the Schwarzenberg seal. *My dearest Jane . . . pressure of business . . . unforeseen circumstances . . . unavoidable . . . will make other arrangements and keep you informed . . . undying love . . .* I did something I had never done before: I lifted a vase, which stood on the table beside my bed, and hurled it to the floor with all my strength.

That brought people hurrying from every direction. I sent them away, and then lay on my bed, fully dressed, and wept my heart out. But even while in this paroxysm of misery, I could still try to think. Why, why, *why*? He had written to me, after six months of silence. Throughout that time I had waited patiently, and at last he had responded – only to thrust me into the depths of despair. Had he learned of my intimacy with the King? But gossip had been current since mid-September, and Felix had not asked for this meeting until mid-October. He had surely heard all the rumours before writing me, and the extravagant terms in which he had professed his love for me had not suggested a jealous lover. But suppositions of my own seemed irrelevant compared with a contemplation of what had happened. I had been told on all sides that my behaviour in London had ruined my life, and I had snapped my fingers at my critics – believing that the moment I became the Princess Schwarzenberg my reputation would be entirely restored. Now I was simply an abandoned woman of ill repute. I swear that had it not been for Didi I would have ended it all, by diving into the lake.

The future was unthinkable. Only Ludwig's friendship seemed at all tangible; and having expressed my hopes so confidently, I did not even see how I could face him. I do not know for how long I lay there, wallowing in my misery, but it was the middle of the afternoon when there was a tentative knock on my door. I had been lying on my stomach. I rolled over and sat up. 'Yes?'

'It is Emma, milady.'

I pushed hair from my eyes. 'Come in.'

The door opened. 'The gentleman has returned, milady.'

I had to think for a moment before I understood whom she meant. 'Oh, good Lord!' I stammered. 'Tell him to go away. I am not receiving anyone today . . . Or tomorrow . . . Or next week . . .' She uttered a cry of surprise, as she was gently moved to one side – and I gazed at Karl von Venningen.

I watched him, still gently, push Emma through the door and close it behind her. Then he locked it. I found my voice. 'What are you doing here?'

He came towards me. 'I knew you would need me.' I looked at the letter, which lay on the bed beside me. 'I do not know what is written there, but I can guess. No one writes a letter who intends to come himself.'

Which coincided with my own thoughts. But I was still in a fog. 'How did you know there was a letter? Did you not return to Munich?'

He sat beside me on the bed. 'I remained at the inn in Berg. I wished to be here, to comfort you, should you be disappointed . . . in your reunion. When the messenger stopped for a drink on his way here, I engaged him in conversation, and knew at once what had happened. So I followed him.'

'Unbidden.' I was doing my best to be angry with him. But such devotion . . .

'I was commanded by my heart. That cannot be refused.'

Easy to say that what I did next was not something I should have done, or would have done, had I been in full command of my senses. I was not in love with Karl. But I was desperately unhappy and desperately afraid of the future, desperate for affection and desperate for love. Desperate! And I knew that he loved me, and not just for that moment. Indeed, I would say he was one of the two men in my life who genuinely loved *me*, as opposed to my beauty or my aura. It was a tragedy for both of us that I never could reciprocate that love; but I could reciprocate the physical manifestation of it. And never more than at that moment. I had built up so much desire during the loneliness of the past six months, rising to a crescendo over the past few days. Thus I surrendered to my emotions without restraint, and threw myself into the business of forgetting the past, at least momentarily.

In fact, it was a great deal more than momentarily, or even hourly. Karl was if anything more virile than Felix; and unlike Felix, he had had just sufficient amatory adventures to know what he was about without becoming blasé. In a matter of seconds, we were both naked and rolling about the bed in each other's arms. I played with him and he played with me. He kissed away my tears – and did a good deal else besides – and entered me with gentle persuasion; then we lay together, panting but not speaking, until we set to again. Afterwards, I felt like a bath. 'I will see you downstairs in an hour,' I told him. 'Have they given you a room?'

'Not as yet.'

I put on an undressing robe, rang the bell, told Emma – who had spent much of the past couple of hours hovering outside my door, no doubt in case I needed assistance – to summon the butler, and informed him that Baron von Venningen would be staying for a few days.

'Of course, milady,' he agreed, 'but I do not know where the Baron is. He entered the schloss, I know, and I believe came up the stairs . . .' He might not have been sure where exactly Karl was (as the Baron was carefully keeping out of the line of fire, as it were), but he must have been able to tell – from my tousled hair, my blotched complexion, my extreme *déshabillé* and, above all, the laziness of my eyes – where my impetuous caller had been.

'The Baron is presently occupied, but will be with you shortly,' I told him. 'Have his room prepared.'

The Trap

By the time I had dressed and gone downstairs, Karl had done the same, was drinking wine, and had changed from lustful lover into masterful male. 'We shall be married as soon as possible,' he declared. 'There are one or two problems. My mother, well, she is very old-fashioned. And there is the business of your being a divorced woman and a Protestant. But I promise you that these difficulties will be overcome.'

His remarks induced a very strong feeling of *déjà vu*. But I had also changed from the role of wanton woman into my more normal clear-headed condition of being able to look facts in the face. I accepted a glass of wine, and laid my hand on his. 'You are the kindest, most gallant man I have ever met,' I told him. 'But we cannot marry.'

'Why not? Who is to stop us? Not the King.' He paused for a moment, then said, 'I'll have none of that.'

I did not pick up on that pause, as I should have done: I was, as usual, concentrating on the immediate facts. 'You have just said that there will be difficulties, with your family. Am I not right in understanding that since the death of your father you are responsible for the prosperity of all your estates and the welfare of your brothers and sisters, and of course your mother, all of whom will oppose our union?'

'I have told you that I will deal with them. As you have just said, I am now the head of the family.'

I sighed. I really did not wish to hurt this man. But equally, I could not deceive him. 'I cannot marry you, Charles, because I am still in love with Felix.' At that moment this was not strictly true; although it was true that if Felix had walked into the room at that moment and beckoned me, I would have gone to him without hesitation.

He was frowning, and his cheeks were reddening. 'You cannot

still be dreaming of Schwarzenberg? After the way he has treated you?'

'I am sure there were very good reasons for his inability to come.'

'But . . . you let me . . .'

'I am sorry. I thought you enjoyed it.'

'Of course I enjoyed it. But . . .'

'I am glad. I enjoyed it too. Very much. And I needed it, so very badly.'

'My God! Then you are nothing but a whore, after all.'

'I think,' I said evenly, 'that you had better leave.' He did so. I wept again that night.

I remained at Berg for several more days. I needed yet more time to think, to ponder where I was going and what I was going to do. I bitterly regretted quarrelling with Karl, even if I could not in all honesty regret having had sex with him. But the incident meant that I had lost my only practicable escort. The question of Ludwig loomed larger. As I was staying in his house, surrounded by his servants, I had to presume that he would very shortly know everything that had happened. On the one hand, I also assumed that he would be pleased to learn that my relationship with Felix was definitely at an end. On the other, he had never really approved of my friendship with Karl, and I had no idea how he would respond to the knowledge that I had slept with him. At that moment, Ludwig was my only lifeline.

I determined that only the most complete honesty would see me through this crisis, and so sat down and wrote him a long letter, telling him everything that had happened. This having been posted (I knew he would probably receive it the same day), I had Emma pack our bags and returned to Munich. I was in a state of some apprehension, half expecting him to be waiting for me. But he was not, nor was there any message. Next day I resumed my usual routine, riding in the morning and drinking tea at Tombosi's in the afternoon, but there was not a sign of him. I spent an anxious couple of days, not wishing, indeed not daring, to write him again. Then, on the fourth day after my return, he called.

I was in a considerable twitter as he strode into the hall,

past the bowing Manfred. 'You are as beautiful as ever,' he remarked, as if surprised that this should be so. He kissed my cheek, and went straight upstairs. This was his usual procedure, which was a relief; but at the same time it indicated that he wished to be alone with me, and I still did not know his mood. I therefore followed with increasing trepidation, closed the door, and stood in front of it. He patted the bed beside him, and I sat down. 'Did you have a pleasant time in Berg?' he asked.

'Did you not receive my letter?'

'Yes, I did.'

'Then you will know I did not.'

'Indeed. Your letter gave a quite different impression.'

I licked my lips. 'I was overwrought.'

'I was quite upset when I read it. I suffered a nervous headache and had to retire early.'

'Oh, Lewis!' I held his hand. 'I am so terribly sorry.'

'Did you not know I would be upset?'

'I thought you wished the matter settled.'

'I am speaking of this act of immoral madness with Venningen.'

He sounded really angry, but he did not look it. 'I was so upset, and lonely, and miserable . . . If only you could have been there, dear Lewis!'

He glanced at me, and said in a low voice, 'I am here now.'

Simple to say that in view of the prophecy this moment had been bound to come. But equally I at last gained an insight into the peculiarities of his behaviour. He had wanted to have sex with me from the moment he first saw me. But his pride forbade him from doing so as long as I considered myself irrevocably bound to Felix. I have never been sure whether he possessed inside information, either that Felix would not come, or that if he did he would again refuse marriage, but I am sure he felt certain that after I had seen Felix – or not, as the case might be – I would be all his. Instead, I had turned to another; simply because the other had been there at the crucial moment, and he had not.

I was surprised that he forgave me. In my heart, I have often wondered if he actually did. But he certainly wanted me, on his terms. For my own part, I needed him, so desperately; and not just for sexual or emotional reasons. I felt that my whole life depended on his support – without suspecting how important that support would actually be – and I was prepared to give him anything he wished. Which was surprisingly little. Ludwig liked to touch, but not to be touched. This was nothing like Edward's repugnance for what he considered vulgarity. It was simply that the King wished to be about his business without distractions. And he preferred to look even more than to touch. This meant that he did not regard intercourse as the essential end of any amatory encounter – as close encounters of this kind are, by their very nature, too close for contemplation. He was absolutely orthodox in his approach, and I had not yet been introduced to the ultimate pleasure that can be obtained from sexual coupling – and even if I had, I would hardly have dared to suggest contravening the requirements of the Church and manners to a king!

Thus, I embarked upon the most decorous affair of my life. We might almost have been an old married couple. I knitted him an embroidered night cap and gave him a nickname, Basily; and he gave me a little dog, a dachshund. Having been used all my life to large dogs, of the hunting variety, I found Bonzo something of a curiosity, but he was very sweet and loving.

And so, contentment. If there were no moments of overwhelming passion, there were no troughs of deep despair – and, at that time at least, no quarrels. Nor, for the first time in my life, did I have to undergo any criticism, either to my face or behind my back. The King would do as he pleased; and the Bavarian people were happy for him to do so, as long as he let them get on with their own lives.

This business was so foreign to my essentially passionate nature that I do not suppose that in normal circumstances it would have lasted more than a few months, but at that time the security Ludwig offered was what I both wanted and needed, and I was content. Needless to say, Ludwig wished me added to his art gallery, and so I sat for a portrait by the court painter, Josef Stieler. I cannot pretend it is one of my favourites. It made me look older than I was (in December 1831, I was not yet twenty-five) and gave me an expression rather like that of a faithful dog begging a favour – which is not in any way indicative of my character. But Ludwig seemed pleased enough.

It was in the new year that our cosy romance started to unravel, when I received a visit from Karl.

I was sitting in the winter parlour before a roaring fire when Manfred brought in the card. Ludwig had been and gone, Didi had been put to bed, and I was enjoying a glass of sherry, which I nearly spilled. I instinctively looked at the door, expecting to see him already there, as was his wont. But on this occasion he was waiting to be summoned. I all but sent him away, which would certainly have been the prudent thing to do. Alas, prudence has never been one of my virtues. 'You may show the Baron in, Manfred,' I said.

Karl approached me cautiously. Well, I had every right to be very angry after the way he had insulted me. But he was so handsome, and unlike Felix he had not stayed away and written me a letter. 'Can you forgive me?' he asked.

'Should I?'

'No. But I beg you to do so.'

I myself poured him a glass of sherry. 'Tell me what you have been doing.'

'I have been dreaming of you.'

'And during the day?'

'I have been dreaming of you all day, too.' What was I to say to that? He put down his glass to seize my hands. I hurriedly put down my glass as well. 'Jane, Jane . . . marry me.'

'Dear Charles. I have explained . . .'

'That you still love Schwarzenberg. Very well, I accept that. But marry me.'

I was dumbfounded. 'You would marry me, knowing that I love another?'

'And always will,' I felt compelled to add.

'Always is a very long time. I will be patient.'

For someone in my position, this was a quite remarkable proposal. Karl was a very wealthy man, considerably more so than Edward had ever been. And however much the stiff-necked snobs might continue to snub me, as the Baroness von Venningen I would occupy a far higher place in the social scale than I had ever done as Lady Ellenborough. Nor, on the terms he was offering, could he or anyone else ever accuse me of duplicity,

as I had told him, plainly, that I did not love him. And yet I
hung back. I will not deny that I still hoped the letter had
been the truth rather than a lie, and that Felix would yet wish
to claim me. Perhaps it was a more noble sentiment, that whatever the prestige and security now offered me, I could not
inflict a loveless marriage on this so devoted man. And could
I inflict a loveless marriage on myself?

But how to tell him? I temporized. 'You must give me time
to consider,' I told him.

These exhausting emotional decisions apart, it was a pleasant
winter. For all the continued opposition to me, I had steadily been
making friends. The Erskines were loyal. I also became friendly
with Countess de Cetto, who I had met at Bardoch's soirée. People
like these entertained me to discreet supper parties; and if not all
of the female guests approved, their husbands certainly did.

In my spare time I explored the many magnificent works of
art to be found not only in Munich itself but in the surrounding
country, and for the first time stood before the statue of Princess
Uta in Naumburg Cathedral. This stone sculpture was painted,
originally, and remains so, even after hundreds of years. Never
have I seen such a combination of beauty and strength. I quite
fell in love with her, and am sure that my memory of those
powerful features has played a part in the development of my
own character.

I should say that during these months my sex life had virtually ceased to exist, in real terms. Ludwig, as I have said, preferred
to watch and play. Karl, apparently, preferred to talk. I found this
odd, when I recalled his ardour that afternoon at Berg – and put
it down to his desire not to offend the King, as he understood
that I had no secrets from my royal lover. But I was no nearer a
decision regarding marriage when, at the end of March, Ludwig
announced that he was leaving Bavaria for a few months, to visit
Italy. 'It is a business matter,' he explained.

I was amazed. In my experience, and according to my knowledge of English history, kings did not leave their kingdoms to
visit foreign lands, except on state occasions or to wage war: that
the first Georges had regularly perambulated to and from Hanover
had merely been to move from one of their domains to the other.

I would dearly have liked to ask him what this personal business matter was that could extract him from his responsibilities, and even from me, for such a lengthy period; but I did not wish to presume, and he made no effort to tell me.

It was Karl who told me what he understood to be the truth, the first time he visited me after Ludwig's departure.

'He has gone to visit his mistress,' he explained.

I was flabbergasted. 'His mistress?!'

'The Marchesa Marianna Fiorenzi. An Italian lady. She has been the King's mistress for years.' And Ludwig had never once mentioned her name! 'The rumour going around Munich is that she has learned of, shall I say, your position in the King's affections, and has demanded an explanation.'

So he had gone rushing off like a lovesick schoolboy! 'Is this woman so very beautiful?' I asked, feeling like a bewildered schoolgirl myself.

'I have never seen her, but the King must have found her attractive once.'

'If what you have told me is true,' I said, 'he finds her attractive still. More attractive than anything else in his life.'

I was furious, less, I swear, with jealousy, than that I had, as usual, been surrounded by such duplicity, by a man to whom I had confessed my every secret – well, nearly every secret – and whose advice I had sought and always accepted (well, nearly always). 'What will you do?' Karl asked.

I stood up and held out my hand. 'Make love.'

In fact Karl, and everyone else, proved to be quite wrong. The King had left Munich, not on personal business, but on affairs of state. For the Battle of Navarino had borne fruit in the final acceptance of defeat by Turkey, with the result that Greece had been granted its independence in 1829 – a period of my life when I had been rather too preoccupied with my own affairs to take much notice of political events, certainly outside England. So, now the Greeks were free the question arose as to how they were to be governed. The Great Powers were not keen on the idea of a republic. Besides, although the various Greek warlords had found a necessary measure of unity in the struggle against their common enemy, once that enemy had been defeated their personal rivalries became too vehemently antagonistic to permit any one of them to be accepted by the others either as elected president or, much less, as king. It was thus necessary to find a king from outside, who could be acceptable to all parties. But this search necessarily precluded any member of the royal houses of Russia, France, Prussia or Great Britain, lest he use his position to swing Greece permanently into his own country's sphere of influence.

After much secret debate, of which the outside world knew nothing, the choice had fallen on Ludwig's younger son, Otto – an odd decision in view of the family history of mental instability. But Bavaria, while a prosperous and important kingdom, was one of the few countries not regarded by anyone as a potential threat. The negotiations having been completed, Ludwig had hurried off to seal the agreement. Not that he did not visit the Marchesa as well.

Unaware of all this – and no doubt reflecting that at last he had me all to himself, and was thus progressing towards his goal – Karl was as enthusiastic a lover as I remembered (while I wanted only to be loved) and we embarked on a virtual honeymoon. With the inevitable consequence. At the end of April I missed my period, and by the end of June there could be no doubt that I was pregnant. But the circumstances were very different to those I had previously encountered. I had wanted to tell Felix about my first pregnancy with him because I had hoped it would unite us, whereas I did not want to tell Karl about this pregnancy for the very reason that it might make him more insistent on uniting us. That meant that I could not have the baby in Munich.

But there were more compelling reasons for repeating the manoeuvre of 1829. I was not sure that Munich as a whole knew of my liaison with Karl, but it certainly knew of my liaison with the King. It therefore seemed entirely likely that it would be assumed that the child was of royal blood, despite the fact that if Ludwig were the father – even if the conception had taken place immediately before his departure – my pregnancy would have run to ten months rather than nine. But by the time I was delivered that mathematical conundrum would not matter much to the *hoi poloi*, and I had no intention of creating such an involved situation. The final reason was the most compelling of all. I simply had no idea what Ludwig's reaction would be to the news that I was once again going to be a mother – especially if he was not the father. So, not for the first time in my life, or the last, I had Emma pack our bags and we left.

This involved once again entering the world of subterfuge, half truths and downright lies. I could not inform Ludwig that I was planning to take a holiday, simply because I did not have an address for him. But even if I had been able to write to him, I presumed that he would not be very happy if, in the midst of explaining things to his beloved (as I supposed he was doing), he received a letter from the woman of whom she was jealous. Even less could I tell Karl either that I was leaving Munich for a while or about my reasons for doing so, as he would certainly have tried to prevent my departure. So I simply stole away at the crack of dawn, taking only Didi, Emma and Bonzo, the dachshund. We went first to Salzburg, where we stopped for a few days while I collected my thoughts. This was a mistake – because before I knew where I was, Karl was in our midst. My plans had been too simple. He had called at my house the very morning I had left, and then it was not difficult for him to discover which of the stage coaches had carried the so beautiful Lady Ellenborough (as most people still referred to me) out of the city, and where she was going.

We had a tearful reunion, and I explained to him that I needed to be alone to consider my situation, giving him to understand that it was the situation *vis-à-vis* him that continued to need consideration. This was not in the least untrue. When I told him that I would probably be back in Munich in a few weeks, he seemed reassured, and left. Then we took the stage road over the Alps – an unforgettably magnificent experience – to Milan, which was quite the reverse. The constant noise and frenetic activity reminded me of Paris, a city of which I did not have the fondest memories. And to crown everything, some lout attempted to steal Bonzo; as I was not yet inconvenienced by my condition, I saw him off with my parasol.

But the incident hastened my departure for Genoa, especially as I had heard from the Countess de Cetto that Ludwig was back in Munich. I wrote him a letter explaining that I had been upset by his departure – which was by no means untrue – and that I had simply needed to get away for a spell. I assured him of my undying affection for him, related our adventures so far, and took the opportunity to inquire, politely, as to his current relations with the Marchesa (I did not refer to her by name); finally, as I did not wish him sending after me, I told him that on medical advice I was taking a sea voyage. This I had in fact been advised to do by the British consul in Genoa, as he regarded travel by land through Italy to be a highly dangerous business, the north of the country being in a state of revolution against Austrian rule.

Thus for the first time I gazed upon that fabulous sea of which I had dreamed for so long. We had a restful voyage, the weather remaining calm throughout, and a few days later disembarked in Naples – to run straight into another crisis. Waiting for me on the quayside was Karl!

He had taken rooms for us at a hotel, and I was rather swept off my feet. 'A few weeks!' he declared as soon as we were alone – save for Bonzo, who seldom left my side and I had deposited on the bed. 'Or did you mean a few months?'

I sighed. There was no option but to tell the truth. I was now five months pregnant, and he would wish to have sex. Even if I had considered that appropriate, there was no way I could appear naked before him without revealing my condition. 'I am pregnant,' I confessed.

'You . . . you . . .'

'The child is yours, Charles.'

'Oh, my darling, darling girl!' He swept me from the floor in a glorious embrace.

'Who else did you suppose was the father?' I asked when he had set me down.

'Well . . .' he flushed. 'The King . . .'

'He left Munich before the end of March. I am not due until January.'

'You have made me the happiest man in the world. I shall arrange our wedding immediately.'

'I have never said I would marry you.'

'You cannot mean to bear an illegitimate child!'

'I have done so before.'

'But there is no necessity. Unlike Schwarzenberg, I am prepared to marry you. I *want* to marry you.'

'But I am not prepared to marry you, at this time.' He stared at me in disbelief. 'Anyway, it is not something that can be done on the spur of the moment.'

'The spur of the moment? I have been courting you for nine months!'

'There is your family, your mother, to consider; their assent to be obtained.'

'I have said . . .'

'That you would deal with that problem. But suppose they refuse to accept me? Will you really split your family to get your hands on something you already possess?'

'Do you think I am only after your body?'

'That is the reason I cannot marry you. I can only offer you my body.'

He regarded me for some minutes. Then he said, 'Where do you propose to have the child?'

'I thought of Sicily. Palermo. I have been told it is very liberal there.'

'Does the King know of it?'

'I would prefer him not to. I have told him I am travelling for my health. Well, that is not a lie.'

'Why do you not wish him to know? Are you saying that you intend to return to being his mistress?'

'Charles, I have never ceased being his mistress.'

He sighed. 'I will accompany you to Palermo. After all, it is my child.'

'And your family? Your estates? I have four months to go.'

'They will have to do without me for a while.'

'Oh, really Charles! What are you supposing? That I intend to run off to Palermo and jump into bed with the first man who approaches me? Contrary to what you think of me, I am *not* a whore.'

'I have apologized for that remark,' he said with dignity. 'I spoke in anger.'

'And I may say,' I went on, now quite angry myself, 'that I have no intention of sharing my bed with *any* man until after my confinement. And that includes you.'

'I will not have you alone in a strange country,' he insisted.

I was unused to such devotion. Certainly I had not experienced it before. So off we went to Palermo. As usual, I felt obliged to tell Ludwig what I was doing, and with whom, as I knew by now that his various agents would be reporting on my every movement; and I did not wish him to feel that I was concealing anything from him, even if I was concealing a great deal. I admitted that Karl was still asking me to marry him, but that I was steadfast in my refusal. Both of these were completely true. Obviously, I did not mention my condition.

In fact, the main reason I was going to Sicily was that I had been told that having a child adopted there was easier than almost anywhere else. Once again, I can hear the shrieks of 'heartless mother' from my detractors, but I could not possibly entertain any hope of a reconciliation with Felix if I confronted him with a child by another father. And having my babe adopted was surely far preferable to having it aborted; I intended to see that he, or she, lacked for nothing throughout his, or her, life. Accepting that plan, I still hoped to return to Munich in the new year, without anyone except Karl knowing I had ever been pregnant.

I found Palermo a most glamorous and exciting city. Only six hundred years ago, when the Emperor Frederick II (known to his contemporaries as Stupor Mundi, or 'Wonder of the World') made it his capital, it had been the most brilliant, cosmopolitan city in Europe – where Christians and Saracens, at the very height of the rivalry between the two religions, had rubbed shoulders in peace and security – to the consternation of the Papacy. Frederick's personal bodyguard had been composed entirely of Saracens, a measure of the trust he was prepared to place in men, rather than ideology. Since those great days, thanks to the pitiless enmity of the Popes – who, following the Emperor's premature death (at the age of fifty), had hunted down and exterminated every remaining male member of his family – the city had declined in political importance. But, even now, it remained a place of great churches and other splendid, sometimes fantastic, buildings, and was the home of everyone who wished to escape either the climate or the restrictions, whether social or political, of their own societies to bask in perpetual sunshine and liberal attitudes.

I loved Sicily; and Sicily loved me, or at least the men did. I doubt that the women cared any more for me than I cared for them, as they were collectively dark-complexioned and over-weight, with greasy hair and a generally unwashed appearance. But the men were exquisite, their appearance handsome, their manners flawless, though every movement, every gesture, every glance was redolent of amorous intent. I was now six months gone with my fourth child, and there could be no concealing the fact, yet they surrounded me wherever I went. I was welcomed at the theatre and the opera, as well as many soirées and recep-tions, my entrance invariably invoking a tumultuous round of applause. In his self-appointed role as my chaperone, Karl had his work cut out; and once it was established that he was not actu-ally my husband, he was unable to stem the tide. I was visited by poets, playwrights, travellers and, of course, painters – all, sadly, of the would-be rather than the established variety. One gentleman (I use the word loosely) was so intent upon gaining access to my person that, having been turned away, he came back the next day pretending to be a seller of goat's milk – and then, after this further failure, appeared a third time, in the guise of a piano tuner! All of these experiences enabled me to perfect my Italian. Karl informed me that all of these dashing fellows were almost certainly what were known as *mafiosi* – members of various secret societies, formed, in some cases five hundred years ago, to oppose the various foreign powers that had from time to time occupied the island. Under the guise of patriotism, they were actually, according to Karl, organized robbers, their only claim to virtue being that they shared their ill-gotten booty with the local people who supported them. However, they never attempted to rob me!

I should mention that another visitor to Palermo while I was there was the Countess Guiccioli. I did not meet her, but I saw her in the street. I knew that it was more than ten years since her tumultuous affair with Byron but I could not say she had aged well, although she could not have been much older than me; for one thing, she had put on too much weight. Well, so had I at that time, but mine was going to disappear in a couple of months; hers looked permanent. I was also intensely interested to learn of the political upheaval in England – a general election, as expected, having brought the Whigs to power on a platform of parliamentary reform. This they had immediately implemented. I had to suppose that Mama and Grandpa and Jane Harley were delighted – while, presumably, poor Edward was out of office!

But for me, the most important event of my Sicilian sojourn took place only two months before my delivery. I received another letter from Felix!

This nearly brought on a premature birth. I locked myself in my bedroom to read the letter. It contained the usual passionate affirmations of Felix's undying love, every one of which brought me out in goose pimples for all that I knew of him – I did not yet know enough – coupled with a reaffirmation of his desire, his determination, to end my long wait and arrange our marriage. All obstacles would be overcome, he assured me, if I would leave Italy and join him in Nice. Bringing his darling Didi, naturally. I did not of course show Karl the letter, or even mention it to him. Nor did I waste any time in wondering how Felix knew where I was and had ascertained my address. Presumably my presence was widely known through the gossip columns, and equally presumably my address was simple to obtain.

But travelling to Nice in my condition was out of the question; nor, as I have intimated, could I risk Felix discovering that I was on the verge of giving birth to another man's child. So I wrote him saying that my health would not permit me to travel at that time (which was true enough), but that I would come to him in the spring. Looking back, I have to admit that to reply to him at all was an act of utter madness. But his letter, couched in such endearing terms, was irresistible. I say again, he was the first man I had ever loved without reservation, and I was certain that he would remain the only man I could ever love without reservation. The thought that it might yet be possible to live my life in the bliss of being the Princess Schwarzenberg drove every other consideration from my mind.

Thus I waited in some trepidation for his reply. But I remained in a state of excited exhilaration, which was obvious to those around me. They related my mood to my approaching delivery. Felipo Antonio Herberto Venningen was born on 27 January 1833.

I was doubtful about having him so identified on his birth certificate, but Karl insisted. He was, not surprisingly, upset by my decision to put the child up for adoption, but finally agreed that it would be best to have him fostered until we had legitimized our union. So a nice Sicilian family was found, Karl settled on them a handsome income to care for the child, and I bade him a tearful farewell.

I was genuinely sorry not to be able to keep him at my side, just as I was genuinely sorry to deceive Karl – for the first time. Hitherto I had made it clear that my love for Felix would always take precedence over everything else in my life; and Karl had accepted this, confident that I would continue to be let down and thus that my love would eventually turn to hate. But he did not know of the letter, nor of the one that followed. Felix wrote most solicitously about my health, regretted that he could not remain in Nice for the minimum of two months I had speci-fied, but said that his sister was now resident in Rome, and that if I would visit her there as soon as I was able to travel, with Didi of course, he would join us as soon as he could and we would conclude our arrangements then. Once again I was in heaven. It seemed certain that things were moving in my direc-tion. I had to tell Karl that I intended to visit Rome on my way home to Munich and, also, who I was going to see, as obviously I did not wish him to insist on accompanying me. I did not tell him I was going to see Felix, only that I was visiting his sister to introduce her to her niece, who she had never met. Although Karl wasn't happy about it, he accepted that I intended only a brief visit and would be back in Munich within a month.

I had kept in touch with Ludwig as I always did, informing him of everything that had happened or that I had done – omitting only the fact that I had been pregnant and was now delivered. Equally, I did not tell him of Felix's letters. I felt they might upset him, and I was not yet married. Again I am prepared to be con-sidered a deceitful woman, but it was my life I was attempting to order – and did he not have his Marchesa? And so I departed on the most disastrous venture of my life, up to that point.

The Triumph

It would have been a disaster even if everything else had been equal. Princess Mathilde and I took one look at each other and decided that we did not like what we saw. I suspect that her opinion had been formed long before I got there, indeed long before the meeting was bruited. In fact, it had been formed the first time she had ever heard my name. I, on the other hand, approached her like an exuberant puppy, anxious to let bygones be bygones and become the best of friends with my future sister-in-law. But this was impossible to accomplish. Quite apart from the hostility that she emanated, she was tall, thin, hatchet-faced, her hair confined in a tight bun, her mouth small and her lips compressed . . . Anything less like a sister to so handsome a man as Felix was inconceivable! To make matters worse, she took an instant dislike to Bonzo, although I did gather that she was averse to any dog.

Still, she played her role well, did her best to make me feel comfortable when not actually speaking to me, and was clearly enchanted by Didi, who was now a fluent talker. Also, she took me exploring antiquities such as the Colosseum, which I found fascinating; and I reflected that I had only to endure her for a short time until Felix arrived. But as usual, he didn't. There were letters containing the inevitable excuses, coupled with the usual endearments. I was distraught, and to my surprise Mathilde appeared to be entirely on my side – with a two-facedness that would have done her great credit had she been acting a role on the stage. 'My dear,' she said. 'This is absolutely awful. I have no doubt that his reasons for not coming are genuine, but I know how you must feel.'

'What am I to do?'

She stroked her chin. 'I think your best course would be to return to Munich. Then Felix will know where to find you.'

'Will he wish to find me?' I asked dolefully.

'Of course he will. He adores you. And . . .' She paused. 'I have an idea!'

'Tell me.' I was willing to clutch at practically any idea!

'Well, why don't you leave little Didi with me for a few weeks? I shall be returning to Vienna, and she will come with me.'

'Can't I come with you?'

'That would be impossible. You are *persona non grata* in the Empire.'

I decided against reminding her that that was the doing of her family, and stuck to the point. 'I cannot consider being separated from Didi.'

'I know just how you feel. But I think it may be the solution to all your – our – problems. You see, I know that all these delays forced on Felix are a result of Prince Metternich's disapproval of the match. But I also happen to know that he has a soft spot for small children, especially if they are attractive. Please do not mis-understand me – there is nothing perverted in this, he just cannot be his usual stern self with them. If I were to have him meet Didi in our own home, well, I am sure he would fall for her. She is such a charmer. Believe me, I see this as our best oppor-tunity to clear up this whole business.'

'Should he not meet her mother as well? Perhaps he would also find me irresistible.'

'I am sure he would, but I have just explained that is not possible without a passport. But don't you see, my dear girl, that once the Prince goes for Didi, it will be a simple matter to have him revoke your ban. In any event, what have you got to lose? Vienna is only a day's journey from Munich. If it doesn't work out, Didi will be with you directly.'

So I agreed – because I so wanted to agree. But Vienna turned out to be as far away from Munich as was the moon.

Quite oblivious of the trap into which I had fallen, I returned to Munich in an optimistic mood. I entered the city as clandes-tinely as I had endeavoured to leave it, only with far more success. My servants were flabbergasted to discover me in their midst, and I warned them that anyone revealing my presence would be instantly dismissed. I knew there was very little chance of this not happening, but all I needed was a fortnight. This I spent in a state of exhilaration. But when two weeks had passed with no word from either Mathilde or Felix, I became agitated and wrote them a letter. When another week passed without a reply I became very disturbed, and in desperation turned to the only source of help I could envisage: I wrote to the King, begging for a meeting.

In view of my long absence, I had no certainty that he would reply. But to my surprise, and my gratification, he called the very next day, sweeping into my drawing room, handing Manfred his hat and stick and waving him away. He made no attempt to kiss me, but I could tell that he was in the grip of a strong emotion, and anticipated a difficult time.

'Welcome home,' he said.

'It is very good to be here, sire.'

'But you had a good holiday, I hope.'

I had to be careful, as I had no idea how much he knew of my activities. I needed to feel my way. 'I had an excellent holiday, sire.'

'And you found Rome congenial?'

A faint sigh of relief – he knew nothing of my babe. On the other hand . . .

'Lewis!' I held his hands and guided him to a settee. 'I am so miserable.'

'Tell me.'

I poured out my heart to him, and he listened, gravely, and without comment until I had finished and begged him to tell me what to do. Then he called, 'Manfred, pour her ladyship a large brandy. And I will have one as well.'

'Right away, Your Majesty.'

Ludwig took some papers from his coat pocket and unfolded them. 'These came in yesterday, in the diplomatic bag from Vienna. One is an extract from the court circular. It reads: *It is confirmed that Prince Felix von Schwarzenberg has been appointed to the Embassy in St Petersburg. The appointment will last for three years.*'

I stared at him with my mouth open. 'St Petersburg?'

'It's in Russia,' Ludwig said, unhelpfully.

'Three years!'

'That is the normal term of such appointments.'

Manfred had brought the brandy. I seized my goblet and drank half of it at a gulp.

'The second item,' Ludwig continued remorselessly, 'is an imperial proscription. It reads: *It has been learned that the notorious English adventuress, who masquerades under the name of Lady Ellenborough, may be seeking entry into Austria. The woman is an undesirable, and is to be arrested on sight, and deported to Bavaria, where she now resides.*'

I finished my brandy; Ludwig summoned another. The alcohol enabled me to speak. 'I don't understand.'

'I am afraid that you have been most cruelly and despicably duped.'

'But Didi! Why have they not sent her to me?'

'Ianthe, they are not going to do that.'

'But why?' I screamed. 'What harm can a three-year-old do to the Schwarzenbergs?'

'None at all, but she can do them a great deal of good. Don't you see, this whole charade was set up for one purpose only, to gain possession of Didi.'

I drank some more brandy.

'The point is,' he went on, 'that Princess Mathilde, as I am sure you observed when you met her, is a dedicated spinster, who I should say has never even been kissed, much less known a man. Her younger brother has entered the Church, and will never father a child. Now, Prince Felix will probably settle down and marry at some stage and become a father, on – if you will pardon me – the right side of the blanket. But life is an uncertain business, and until and unless he does do so, Didi is the last Schwarzenberg. She can easily be legitimized – and thus become the Schwarzenberg heiress, who, with the Schwarzenberg fortune, and the Schwarzenberg name, will be the greatest prize in Europe.'

'But she is *my* daughter!' I wailed.

'In these affairs you have no rights. Only the father matters.'

'Oh, my God, my God! Lewis . . .' I grasped his hands. 'You must help me.'

'I cannot help you, as regards Didi. It is the law, the only right you had was that of possession. On the other hand, as Didi grows up, and starts to think for herself, there may come a time . . .'

'Time?' I cried. 'Years, you mean. Years in which she will be taught that her mother was a monster!' I burst into tears. 'Without Didi, I have nothing left to live for.'

The King dried my cheeks and held my hands. 'You have

everything to live for, Ianthe. How old are you? Twenty-five? You are the most beautiful woman of her time. You are in perfect health. You have an independent income. The whole world lies in front of you.'

'The whole world?' I said bitterly. 'A world in which I am regarded as little better than a whore, in which I must confine myself to back stairs and surreptitious trysts, in which I am never entertained, nor able to entertain, never dance and be merry.'

'I would change that,' he said quietly. 'If you would permit me.'

I stared at him. 'You? How . . .'

'I adore you, Ianthe. I do not wish to live without you. I have only realized this over the past few months, when you have been away. Ianthe, I can give you the world. My world. The world of Bavaria.'

I was struck dumb, so he continued. 'Listen to me. I will make you the first lady in the land. You will be *maîtresse en titre*. No more clandestine meetings, no more whispered gossip behind your back. Every woman in Bavaria will have to bow to you.'

What a heady prospect for a fallen woman. But he had gone about it in such a cold-blooded, step by step, manner. I took refuge in matters of detail. 'And the Queen?'

'Will have to accept the situation. It is historically precedented. Think of Madame de Pompadour. Or Aspasia, in ancient Athens.'

Again, heady suggestions, but . . .

'You think Her Majesty will receive me at court?'

'I know she will. She will have to. She will accept you before the eyes of all Bavaria. Of all the world.'

My head was spinning.

'There is one caveat.'

I came back to earth with a bump.

'You must be married. You see, any child you may bear cannot be allowed to claim royal blood, and perhaps upset the tranquillity of the kingdom.'

I decided against telling him that such a child already existed, and again turned to detail. 'And who am I to marry?'

'Why, Venningen, of course. He adores you. He will make you the most perfect husband. And he understands the situation.'

'The situation has not yet arisen,' I pointed out.

'We both knew it would.'

'You . . . you mean this was planned from the beginning?'

'Well . . .' he had the grace to flush. 'He knew you were my mistress, and had to approach me for permission to become your escort.'

'And you granted him permission. You mean I have been duped there too!' I did not know whether to be furious or burst out laughing, at my own stupidity.

'By two men who love you, and wish only the best for you. Who knew that Schwarzenberg would let you down, and were prepared to wait for that to happen, irrevocably. Will you not now give us the chance to make you happy?'

It was simply too much. I had no idea what to do. As with my last major crisis, I wrote to Mama asking for a meeting.

We now seemed to be drifting further apart – geographically, at least. I would have liked Mama to come to Munich, but she felt that was too far, although I suspect that her reluctance was caused by the rumours which were now reaching England, carried by returning tourists, that I was the King's mistress. She would have liked me to go to England, but I had no wish to do that, for the same reason. So we settled on a halfway house, Paris, whither I went with Emma. To my great relief, Mama was not accompanied by Steely. In her absence, our two days together went off very well, even though Paris did not have happy memories for me. But Mama became more and more concerned as I related the events of my life since we had last met, now very nearly three years ago. She was, in any event, agitated by the growing no-toriety of my reputation. Like me, she had been placing her hopes on the complete restoration of my social standing that would have followed my marriage to Felix. Now her face grew longer by the moment. 'My dear girl,' she said, 'you must get Didi back immediately.'

'I'm afraid that will not be possible. They could not risk attempting to kidnap her, but once I was tricked into giving her up voluntarily . . .'

'My God! What are you going to do?'

'That is what I am hoping you will tell me. Lewis has offered me the most fabulous position.'

'As a king's mistress! And then this man Venningen . . . Is he a good man?'

'I would say he has to be one of the best men I have ever met.'

She sighed. 'Then marry him.'

'I do not love him, Mama.'

'But from what you have just said, you respect and trust him. Then you have all that you can reasonably expect from a husband.' She held my hand. 'Jane, you cannot have everything in life. You have enjoyed a tremendous romance. Now you must try to settle down and again become respectable. Baron von Venningen is offering you the opportunity to do this. You would be a fool not to take it.'

She was obviously not going to pursue the question of my position *vis-à-vis* the King, or the *ménage à trois* he proposed. There were so many things I would have liked to attempt to explain to Mama, but I knew it would be impossible to make her understand. But she had made up my mind for me. We parted, tearfully, and I went to Heilbrunn, where Karl had a house that he had placed at my disposal. I needed to think.

Although the decision was, of course, ultimately mine, I could argue to myself that I had very little choice. But I would be less than honest did I not admit that I was also moved by an unchristian desire to be avenged on all those who, over the past three years, had cast me into the gutter. In this group I included Grandpa and Anne, the Ansons, and all the great ladies of Almack's who sought to control the manners and morals of a nation. I knew they would still denigrate me as a whore, but if Ludwig kept his word I would rise above them all in wealth and station, and perhaps even power. After all, had not Madame de Pompadour become the most powerful woman in Europe?

The first thing to do was to write to Karl, requesting his presence urgently. Then I wrote to Ludwig, bringing him up to date; and sat back to await events, keeping my emotions as much under control as I could. I suppose situations like this play an important part in the moulding of one's character. It certainly affected mine.

Things now moved with startling rapidity. Karl arrived in a fury of anxiety, supposing something had happened to me. Which rapidly became a fury of anticipation when I told him I would marry him, and rapidly became fury pure and simple when I related how I had been treated. He promptly wrote to Felix, challenging him to a duel for defaming my name with reference to Jacques Tabourier. I presume his reasoning was that while everyone accepted that I had been Felix's mistress for two years, to suggest that I had slept with anyone else during that time would have made me a loose woman. How he reconciled this with the know-ledge that I had slept with both himself and the King while still considering myself betrothed to Felix I have no idea! Nor was I terribly interested. Men make up their own rules of conduct to which women are required to adhere, and most of us poor crea-tures do so blindly. Thus a man may have a dozen mistresses, one after another or all at the same time, and is still considered by his peers to be a very good fellow. Yet a woman in the highest eche-lons of society is permitted to have a lover, but more than one immediately brands her a whore. From my point of view, this hullabaloo as to who sleeps with whom and how often is utter nonsense: sex is an act of purely physical convenience and grati-fication. As for loving someone, that is a totally different matter; and has nothing to do with carnal desires, although the initial liking may result from physical attraction. But although I knew I could never *love* again, I was determined to *live* as I chose.

I must reiterate that I never tried, or wished, to hoodwink Karl in any way. He knew I did not love him as I had loved Felix. He was also very much aware of my relationship with the King and that I was, publicly, about to become the King's mistress. Yet he wished to make me his wife. Almost certainly he felt, with masculine arrogance, that he could provide all the love I could possibly wish; just as, again with masculine arrogance, he was certain that he could make me fall in love with him in the course of time.

Honour demanded that Felix respond to Karl's challenge. His carefully worded reply covered both angles. He assured Karl that he had never impugned my honour or accused me of infidelity – how his tongue must have been in his cheek when he wrote that, as he had to be aware of Munich gossip – and offered a complete apology for any hurt he might have caused me. At the same time, he slapped me across the face by wishing us both every happiness in our married life! And he did not mention Didi at all. So that was that. I had wasted three years of my life chasing a chimera – and lost my daughter.

But there was really no time for depression. As I have said, events now moved very rapidly, despite the still considerable obstacles that lay before us. To overcome the more obvious of these we enlisted the help of Ludwig – who could not have been more positive, writing personally to the Grand Duke of Hesse-Darmstadt, in whose domain Karl's family home was situated, requesting his assistance in overcoming the religious problem. This problem, I was assured, would cease to exist if the Church could be provided with proof that my previous marriage had never been. To my relief, no mention was made of my converting (although I had been prepared to do this in order to marry Felix, the idea no longer appealed to me). I wrote to Mama, and she replied that not only could the required document be produced, but that it would be brought to Germany personally by Papa. That he was to be the only member of my family attending my second wedding was clearly because I was still not considered socially acceptable by the rest of the family.

That this was all the most absurd mumbo-jumbo was obvious, but Papa duly arrived with the required document, which asserted that under English law my marriage was null and void, and thus need never have been. This was simply the English – and therefore Protestant – definition of the situation following a divorce, but it seemed to satisfy almost everybody, and certainly those who mattered. I was more concerned at the prospect of having Papa in my house after a separation of several years, especially in view of everything that had happened during those years. I would have been far happier had Mama felt able to accompany him – but his visit went off peacefully, even if, as usual, I could not escape the feeling that he could not actually believe that I was his daughter. There was a considerable stiffness at first, but it will be recalled that we had never been very close. He seemed to like Karl, was impressed by my new husband's wealth and social standing, and was clearly greatly relieved that I could, as it were, again emerge into the light of day.

Before my father's arrival I had had to undergo a far more severe ordeal, my first meeting with the Venningen family. This was every bit as disastrous an event as I had conceived a meeting with the assembled Schwarzenbergs would be – with the difference that there were many more Venningens. I faced a room that was absolutely packed; everyone present appeared to be at least a second cousin. Dominating the assembly were the Dowager Baroness and her eldest daughter, Mimi, who remained unmarried (she was rumoured to have an admirer, but apparently permitted him no liberties). This pair had undoubtedly heard all about me, and – like Mathilde Schwarzenberg – had not liked anything they heard. The sniffs were almost audible. However, there was a crucial difference between the Schwarzenbergs and the Venningens. In the case of Karl's family, there was no sour old man to preside over their decisions: these were made by the man who had elected to become my husband. Although, as I was to discover, Karl had no desire to push his mother too far, equally he had no intention of allowing her to interfere with his chosen course of action. Of the other members of the family, some were quite friendly; and I especially liked Karl's brother Phillip.

On 16 November 1833, Karl and I were married in a civil ceremony at Darmstadt; and the following week we were married again, in the cathedral at Sinshein, in a Catholic ceremony conducted by the Bishop of Rothenburg. Following which, I bade farewell to Papa; and after a brief honeymoon, Karl and I returned to Munich at the beginning of December.

I had, as always, kept Ludwig fully up to date regarding my activities, and was delighted at his response; he wrote to me, while I was still honeymooning, wishing to know the exact time of my arrival in his capital. My desire to renew my intimacy with the King may not have been the most correct attitude for a bride – but I had made it perfectly clear to Karl that while I was granting him the use of my body whenever he required it, I could offer him nothing more than that and also that I remained the King's possession.

This he understood and accepted. But there was an immediate bone of contention between us. I will freely admit that, because I had still been anticipating a reconciliation with Felix, I had not been as delighted as I should have been at the birth of Heribert (as he was always known in German). Now things were very different. I was married to Heribert's father, and I wanted my son back, certainly after having lost my daughter. To my surprise, and concern, Karl showed no enthusiasm for this. His reasons appeared specious, to me. He explained that the little boy was being brought up as a Sicilian peasant and would have to be extensively re-educated before he could take his place as a true Venningen. This of a child not yet a year old! His solution was for us to settle into our married life together and then reclaim our child. I was aghast, and the more so when I discovered the real reason for his procras-tination: his mother. The old lady had been unable to withstand her son's carnal lust for me; but she had absolutely refused to accept a bastard grandson, even though the question as to which side of the blanket he legally belonged on had been resolved.

At the time, I did not feel up to making an issue of it: I was too concerned with the resumption of my relations with Ludwig, and my return to society. I advised the King, as requested, of the precise time of my anticipated arrival in Munich, and found one of his enormous bouquets of violets awaiting me. He himself arrived only half an hour later. This was a situation Karl had not encountered before, and he had no idea of how to cope. He prudently left the house, and within moments of Ludwig's arrival we were in each other's arms. Oh, bliss! I had no complaints of Karl as a lover, but while his passion was unbounded and he was experienced enough to satisfy me as much as himself, I had never felt any true rapport between us. With Ludwig, hitherto I had always felt on the other side of the fence – that it was he whose mind was elsewhere. Today he was all mine, and I was all his.

So our reunion continued in the most uninhibited fashion for a couple of hours, until we were mutually exhausted, and lay side by side, head to head, shoulder to shoulder, thigh to thigh. 'Now you will take your rightful place in society,' he said. 'And will be the brightest star in our firmament.'

'If Her Majesty permits it,' I reminded him.

'She will,' he assured me.

It took a little time. But at the beginning of February the Baroness von Venningen received an invitation to visit the Nymphenburg Palace, from Queen Theresa.

I was now coming up to twenty-seven and considered myself,

with some justification, to be a woman of the world. But when I opened the envelope containing the priceless piece of cardboard I all but fainted. Because, for all Ludwig's confident assurance, I had begun to doubt that it would ever happen. Rumours as to the relationship between the King and I had now circulated for something like two years, but it was only after my return as the Baroness von Venningen that the flood burst the barriers, as it were. All that earlier speculation was confirmed, and I became public property. Within days, I overheard myself being described in the street as 'the King's Lady'; and when I sought to take tea at Tombosi's, such crowds gathered to stare at me that I had to abandon going there, just as I could not ride in the park unless Karl was with me. Not everyone approved, and I felt that even the Erskines were a little put out; but soon after our return to Munich they invited us to attend the wedding of their daughter Gabrielle to Count Paungarten. Needless to say, the gossips were divided into two camps: those who were relieved that I had finally emerged from the shadows, and those who felt that I had been too kindly dealt with by fate. And there was a further division – between those who believed that Karl and I were a genuine love match, and those who put it about that the King had commanded Karl to marry me so that he could make me his official mistress.

All of this was very trying for Karl (and even more for his family, as this last rumour was also circulating in Mannheim). For, although Karl knew that the King had not commanded him to marry me, Ludwig had certainly encouraged him; and he also knew that not only was I continuing as Ludwig's mistress but had now become the royal concubine in a way I had never previously been. But there were compensations. Now that I was the Baroness von Venningen, and no longer a fallen woman, I was acceptable in society; and by Christmas the invitations had begun to flow. I imagine a large number of these were prompted by curiosity, and I much preferred the company of those who had supported me from the beginning, such as the Erskines and the Countess de Cetto. But we went anyway, Karl being proud to enter a room with me on his arm. However, the ultimate accolade was the invitation to call on the Queen, whether or not that too was inspired by curiosity or by royal command.

★   ★   ★

In the event, I was overwhelmed. As custom dictated, I entered the great hall by myself, Karl being required to attend later. I wore a new pale-blue silk gown and, as had become my custom, my hair loose and undressed save for a couple of ringlets. And, of course, I wore a tiara.

Emma accompanied me as far as the antechamber for a last check.

'Will I do?' I asked.

'You would do for an emperor,' she assured me. 'So why not for a king and queen?'

At the door a major-domo used his staff to silence the throng, and announced in stentorian tones 'The Baroness von Venningen!'

As on my first night at Almack's, I was the cynosure of all eyes. But this was not a mere Wednesday-night dance. The room was packed. Never had I beheld such a panorama of naked shoulders, sparkling jewels, and brilliant uniforms. I felt quite unsteady on my feet, and drew a deep breath as I slowly walked up the centre aisle, amidst endless whispers.

I kept my eyes fixed on Queen Theresa (a faded but still commanding beauty), reached the step before her chair, and sank into a deep curtsy. 'Your Majesty.'

I was aware that Ludwig was seated beside her, but for this moment his was a secondary role. The Queen stood up, came down the step, and held my hands to raise me up. 'Charming,' she said, in a strong, clear voice, intended to be heard in every corner of the room. 'Quite charming. Your presence, Baroness, will enhance the beauty of our court. Now, come and sit beside me.'

I could not believe my ears. Nor, it seemed, could anyone else. The room was completely hushed. Then as Theresa, her hand still resting on my glove, escorted me up the step to the chair next to hers, there was an explosion of round after round of tumultuous applause. As I seated myself and smiled at them, I realized that I had reached the pinnacle of my existence.

But had I? Did I now not seek more worlds to conquer? Or rather, would Fate, having tossed me around like a doll, virtually since the age of eight, now stand back and leave me to pursue my life in my own way? Perhaps fortunately, the future is hidden from us. But even as I sat there basking in the glory of my new position, I suddenly found myself thinking of La Normande. She had said that I would be loved by three royal princes. And thus far, I had known only one.

Withdrawn

**Indianapolis
Marion County
Public Library**

Renew by Phone
269-5222

Renew on the Web
www.imcpl.org

For General Library Information
please call 269-1700